ALTERED

JENNIFER RUSH

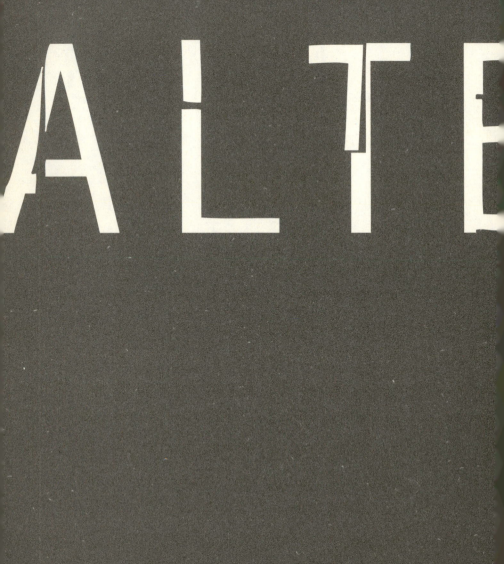

RED

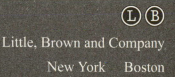

Little, Brown and Company

New York   Boston

Copyright © 2013 by Jennifer Rush
Excerpt from *Erased* copyright © 2013 by Jennifer Rush

Little, Brown and Company

Hachette Book Group
237 Park Avenue, New York, NY 10017
Visit our website at lb-teens.com

Little, Brown and Company is a division of Hachette Book Group, Inc.
The Little, Brown name and logo are trademarks of Hachette Book Group, Inc.

The publisher is not responsible for websites (or their content)
that are not owned by the publisher.

First Paperback Edition: December 2013
First published in hardcover in January 2013 by Little, Brown and Company

Library of Congress Cataloging-in-Publication Data

Rush, Jennifer.
   Altered / by Jennifer Rush. — 1st ed.
      p. cm.
   Summary: Seventeen-year-old Anna finds herself on the run from her father's enigmatic Branch, along with the four teen boys the Branch had been experimenting on, as they try to make sense of erased memories, secret identities, and genetic alteration.
   ISBN 978-0-316-19708-3 (hc) — ISBN 978-0-316-19709-0 (pb)
   [1. Runaways—Fiction.   2. Genetic engineering—Fiction.
3. Memory—Fiction.   4. Identity—Fiction.   5. Fathers and daughters—Fiction.
6. Science fiction.]   I. Title.
   PZ7.R89535Alt 2013
   [Fic]—dc23
                                                                                          2012007545

10 9 8 7 6 5 4 3

RRD-C

Printed in the United States of America

To JV, for believing in me

and for letting me sleep in

1

FOR MOST OF THE LAST FOUR YEARS, I wasn't allowed in the lab. But that didn't stop me from sneaking down there. And while I no longer needed to wake at midnight in order to visit the boys, my internal clock was still fully tuned to the schedule.

I sat on the edge of my bed, rubbing the sleep from my eyes, bare feet rooted to the hardwood floor. Moonlight crept through the window, the shadows from the maple trees sliding this way and that.

Dad had asked for my help in the lab eight months earlier, so I could go downstairs anytime I wanted now. But seeing the boys with permission wasn't the same—wasn't as thrilling—as sneaking down there in the dark.

I'd long ago mapped the creaky floorboards in the hallway, and I skipped over them now, pushing through the living room and the kitchen, taking the stairs down to the basement two at a time.

The stairs ended in a small annex, where a keypad had been installed in the wall, the buttons glowing in the dark. For someone who worked for a clandestine company, Dad had never been cautious with his codes. Four years ago, when I first broke into the lab, it took me only a week to figure out the right combination. It hadn't been changed since.

I punched in the required six digits, the buttons beeping in response. The door hissed as it slid open, and I was greeted by the stale scent of filtered air. My breath quickened. Every nerve in my body buzzed with anticipation.

I went down the short hallway and the lab opened before me. The space felt small and cozy, but the lab was actually much bigger than the footprint of the house. Dad told me the lab had been built first, and then the farmhouse was built on top of it. The Branch had gone to great lengths to make the program, and the boys, disappear in the middle of New York's farmland.

To the right sat Dad's desk, and next to it, mine. To the left was the refrigerator, followed by a tower of filing cabinets, and a hutch stuffed with supplies. Directly across from the mouth of the hallway were the boys' rooms: four of them lined up in a row, each separated by a brick wall and exposed by a sheet of thick Plexiglas in the front.

Trev's, Cas's, and Nick's rooms were dark, but a faint light spilled from Sam's, the second room from the right. He rose from his desk chair as soon as he saw me. My eyes traced the etched lines of his bare stomach, the arch of his hips. He wore the gray cotton pajama pants all the boys had, but that was it.

"Hey," he said, his voice reduced to the sound the tiny vent holes allowed through the glass.

Heat crept from my neck to my cheeks and I tried to look calm—*normal*—as I approached. The whole time I'd known the boys, they had suffered from amnesia, an unplanned side effect of the alterations. Despite that, I felt like the others had shown me parts of who they were, deep down. All of them but Sam. Sam gave only what he thought was necessary. The things that truly defined him were still a secret.

"Hi," I whispered. I didn't want to wake the others if they were asleep, so I kept my steps light. I was suddenly more aware of the sharp edges of my elbows, the knobs that were my knees, the loud thumping of my feet. Sam had been genetically altered, made into something more than human, and it showed in every efficient curve of muscle in his body. It was hard to compete with that.

Even his scars were perfect. A small one marred the left side of his chest, the skin puckered white, the jagged lines of the scar branching off in a shape that seemed more deliberate than accidental. I'd always thought it looked like an *R*.

"It's after midnight," he said. "Something tells me you didn't come down here to watch infomercials with me."

My laugh sounded nervous even to me. "No. I don't really need a Chop-O-Matic."

"No, I don't suppose you do." He shifted, pressing his arm against the glass above his head so he could hunch closer. Closer to me. "What are you doing down here?"

I tried out a dozen possible answers in my mind. I wanted to say something clever, something witty, something interesting. If it had been Trev, I would have had to say only, "Entertain me?" and he would have shared a handful of memorized quotes from his favorite historical figures. Or, if it had been Cas, I'd have split a set of markers and we'd have drawn ridiculous pictures on the glass. And Nick... well, he rarely acknowledged my existence, so I would never have come down here for him in the first place.

But this was Sam, so I just shrugged and suggested the same thing I always suggested: "I couldn't sleep, and I wondered if you wanted to play a game of chess."

I clasped my hands awkwardly in front of me as I waited for him to answer.

"Get the board," he finally said, and I smiled as I turned away.

I grabbed what we needed and pulled my desk chair over. He did the same on his side. I set up the small folding table and the board, putting the black pieces on Sam's side, the white on mine.

"Ready?" I asked and he nodded. I moved my knight to F3.

He examined the board, elbows on his knees. "Rook. D-five." I moved his piece to the correct square. We ran through a few more plays, focused only on the game, until Sam asked, "What was the weather like today?"

"Cold. Biting." I moved my next piece. When he didn't immediately counter, I looked up and met his eyes.

An unremarkable green, like river water, his eyes were nothing to look at, but they were something else to be watched with. Sam's gaze, at quiet moments like this, made my insides shudder.

"What?" I said.

"The sky—what color would you use to draw it?"

"Azure. The kind of blue you can almost taste."

For some reason, everything I said and did around Sam felt weightier. As if merely his presence could shake my soul, make me *feel*. He savored every detail I gave him, as if I was his last link to the outside word. I guess in some ways I was.

"Sometimes," he said, "I wonder what the sun used to feel like."

"You'll feel it again. Someday."

"Maybe."

I wanted to say, *You will, I promise you will, even if I have to break you out myself.* I tried to imagine what it would be like to punch in the codes and let them all go. I could do it. Maybe even get away with it. There were no cameras down here, no recording devices.

"Anna?" Sam said.

I blinked, stared at the chessboard in front of me. Had he told me his next play? "Sorry, I was—"

"Somewhere else."

"Yeah."

"It's late. Let's finish tomorrow?"

I started to protest, but a yawn snuck up on me before I could hide it. "All right. It will give me more time to work on my strategy."

He made a sound that fell somewhere between a laugh and a snort. "You do that."

I moved the table to the far corner and took a step toward the hallway. "I'll see you in the morning."

The light shining from his bathroom caught his dark, close-cropped hair, turning it silver for a second before he drew back. "Good night, Anna."

"G'night." I waved as the lab door slid shut behind me and that empty feeling settled back in.

I didn't belong in the boys' world. Not that I belonged in the real world, either. I was too afraid that if I let someone in, they'd figure out my secrets about the lab and the boys. I didn't want to be the reason the Branch moved the program. Mostly, I didn't want to risk losing Sam. Because even though our relationship was based solely on testing and the lab and my sketches and midnight chess games, I couldn't picture my life without him.

EVERY WEDNESDAY MORNING, MY DAD made a pitcher of lemonade—fresh-squeezed, lots of sugar—and I made cookies. It was our tradition, and we had always been short on traditions.

The ice clinked against the glass as Dad handed it to me. "Thanks," I said, taking a sip. "Perfect."

He slid the pitcher into the refrigerator. "Good. Good."

I shifted at the kitchen table, looking out the window to the forest beyond the backyard, struggling to think of something else to say. Something to keep Dad here just a minute longer. Dad and I weren't good with small talk. Lately, the only thing that seemed to connect us was the lab.

"Did you see the paper this morning?" I asked, even though I knew he had. "Mr. Hirsch bought the drugstore."

"Yeah, I saw that." Dad set the measuring cup in the sink before running a hand over the back of his head, smoothing his quickly graying hair. He did that a lot when he was worried.

I sat forward. "What is it?"

The wrinkles around his eyes deepened as he put his hands on the edge of the farmhouse sink. I thought he might reveal whatever it was that was bothering him, but he just shook his head and said, "Nothing. I have a lot of stuff to get through today, so I think I'll go downstairs. You'll come down later? Nick's blood sample should be drawn."

Dad wasn't the type to talk about how bad his day was, so even though I wanted to push him, I didn't. "Sure. I'll be down in a little bit."

"All right." He nodded before disappearing from the kitchen, his footsteps audible on the basement stairs. And just like that, my time was up. Dad was endlessly consumed by his work, and I'd accepted that a long time ago. I'd never get used to it, though.

I grabbed my mother's journal from the counter, where I'd left it earlier that morning. In it she had written her most beloved recipes, along with her thoughts and anything she found inspiring. There was a special section in the back devoted to cookie recipes. It was the only possession of hers I owned, and I treasured it more than anything else.

A few months earlier I'd started adding my own notes and

sketches to the blank pages in the back. I'd always been afraid of ruining the book, as if my additions would somehow dilute what was already there. But I had aspirations and ideas, too, and I didn't think there was any other place I'd rather record them.

I ran my fingers over the old food stains on the pages, reading and rereading her tiny cursive handwriting.

I decided on Cas's favorite cookie, pumpkin chocolate chip, since he had aced the previous day's mental evaluation—and because they were my favorite, too.

After gathering the ingredients, I got to work. I pretty much knew the recipe by heart, but I still followed Mom's instructions, and the notes she'd made in the margins.

Do not use imitation vanilla.
Stock up on pumpkin puree close to holidays—
stores tend not to stock it in spring and summer.
It can't hurt to add extra chocolate—ever.

Dad said Mom ate chocolate like some people eat bread.

She died when I was one, so I didn't really know her. Dad didn't talk about her a lot, either, but every now and then a story would shake free from his memory and I would listen intently, not making a sound, worried that any noise on my part would break the spell.

I poured the bag of chocolate chips into the mixing bowl, the little bits plopping into the layer of rolled oats. Outside, the bleak sky hid the sun, and the wind had picked up since I'd crawled out of bed. Winter was on its way. If this wasn't a day for cookies, I didn't know what was.

Once the dough was mixed, I filled two cookie sheets and slid them into the oven, setting the timer so they'd finish somewhere between baked and doughy. Cas liked them that way.

With the timer ticking in the background, I sat at the table, my science book open in front of me. I had reached the end of the chapter on fault lines and was supposed to write an essay about it. I'd been homeschooled my whole life, and my dad was my teacher. Recently, though, he'd left me on my own. He probably wouldn't even have noticed if I'd skipped the assignment, but I couldn't stand the thought of giving up so easily.

By the time the cookies were done, I'd made zero progress and my back was stiff. I'd pulled a muscle during Saturday night's combat lesson—Dad's idea of an extracurricular activity—and I was still paying for it.

Leaving the cookies to cool, I headed upstairs to my room. At my dresser, I pushed aside a pile of old sketches and travel magazines, spying my bottle of ibuprofen tucked behind them.

After swallowing two pills down with a gulp of water, I tossed my hair up in a messy ponytail, leaving a few wispy blond strands hanging in my face. I peered at myself in the mirror and curled my upper lip. Making things beautiful on paper with a pencil in my hand was easy for me. Making things beautiful in real life wasn't.

It was just past noon when I loaded the cooled cookies onto a plate. On my way down to the lab, I grabbed the new tube of tennis balls I'd bought for Cas. I swore that boy had ADD, though his unwavering attention when food was present indicated he had *some* focus skills.

When I entered, my gaze went to Sam's room first. He sat at his desk, the full bow of his mouth pressed tightly in a line of concentration. He didn't even bother to look up from the book in front of him. Sometimes, the Sam I spent time with at night was completely different from the careful and serious Sam I saw when other people were present. Did I act differently depending on who was around? I doubted Sam would even care if I did.

Dad was at his computer, typing away. He gave a half wave without taking his eyes off the screen. Cas, his blond hair sticking up in messy tufts, moved to the front of his room when I approached. He pressed his face against the glass and puffed out his cheeks like a blowfish. When he pulled back and smirked, his cheeks dimpled in that innocent-but-mischievous way that only five-year-olds can pull off. Well, five-year-olds and Cas.

Despite their altered rate of aging, caused by the treatments, Cas looked the youngest. With his dimples and round cheeks, he had a classic baby face. And he knew exactly how to use it to his advantage.

"Pumpkin?" He nodded at the cookies.

"Of course."

"Anna Banana, I love you."

I laughed and unlocked the hatch—a small opening in the brick wall between his room and Trev's—and slid in four cookies, along with the tennis balls. I hit the button so he could open the hatch on his side.

"Oh, sweet Jesus," he said, then inhaled an entire cookie.

"You are the black hole of food."

"I need my protein." He patted his hard stomach. The gesture made a solid *thwack*, *thwack* sound. Despite all the food he crammed down his throat, he never gained an ounce.

"I don't think two eggs in a batch of cookies counts as protein."

He flicked the lid off the tube of tennis balls, unfazed. "It totally counts."

"Did you finish that model car I brought you last week?" I looked past him to his desk, which I could hardly make out beneath the pile of half-finished projects and junk. I spied one lone wheel on top of a sports magazine. "Should I take that mess as a no?"

He screwed up his face and made a *pfffffftt* sound. "I have plenty of time."

I went to Trev's room next. He'd been doing yoga when I first came in, but now stood at the wall, waiting for me. My gaze met his eyes and I smiled. His were a unique shade of brown, like firelight, warm and liquid and inviting. When I drew him, I used colors I rarely used on anyone else. Which was maybe why I drew him the most. While I felt like I knew Trev the best, his heritage was the hardest to pinpoint. Through the sheen of yoga-induced sweat, his earthy olive complexion hinted at a background different from those of the others. I'd been unable to find anything concrete in his files, but I thought he might be Native American, and maybe Italian, too.

"You want some?" I asked, showing him the plate.

He slicked back his dark hair with a quick swipe of his hand. "You know I live for Wednesdays."

I gave him four cookies, and in return he slipped something into the hatch for me. When I reached inside I felt the soft spine of a paperback. *Letters from the Earth*, by Mark Twain. It was a library book I'd checked out the week before. My membership was used more for Trev's reading habits than it was for mine. I bought him his own copies when I could, all of which were lined up on the shelves above his desk. Alphabetized, of course.

Inside the front cover, I found a note.

> Did you come down last night?
> What did you say to Sam?

I looked behind me to see if Dad had noticed. He hadn't. I'd divulged a lot of secrets to Trev. If I had a best friend here, he was it. He was the only one who knew how I felt about Sam.

I quickly grabbed a pen from my desk and scribbled a response.

Yes. why? Did he say something?

I pressed the note to the glass and Trev read. He wrote down an answer and held it up for me.

He's been acting strange. He snapped at Nick early this morning, after Nick said something about you and cookies. And he's been sleeping less and less lately. Something's going on with him.

My next note read,

I don't know. I'll keep an eye on him.

"I'm sure you will," Trev said with a knowing smile.

Smirking, I crumpled the paper and ignored the comment. "Any requests for the next book?"

"Something on Abraham Lincoln?"

"I'll see what I can do."

I started for Sam's room. He tended to eat pretty well, so cookies were never his thing, but I slowed my pace just the same. He still sat at his desk, back hunched, reading his book. *Technology in the Twenty-First Century.* I'd ordered that one special for him.

There were a few books on the shelves above him, mostly reference manuals. Sam's room was neat, tidy, and bare.

He looked up as I passed. "Hey," he said.

I smiled. "Hey."

And that was it.

Nick's room was last. He and I had never gotten along. As a matter of fact, he once told me he couldn't stand the sight of my face. As far as I knew, I hadn't done anything to offend him, and if I had, Nick wasn't the kind of person to hold back.

I slid a couple of cookies into the hatch. "Do you have any requests? I'll probably go to the store later this week. A new *Car & Driver*? How are you on shampoo?" He liked this special stuff that was made from avocados and shea butter. I had to order it from a website that sold only organic goods, using my own money. Not that he cared.

When he didn't answer, I muttered, "Maybe a stone to sharpen your horns?"

He called out as I headed back to my desk. "How about a fifth of vodka?"

Ignoring him, I dropped into the desk chair, munching on a cookie with a high chocolate content. Like my mother, I wouldn't turn down extra sweets. At least that's one thing I had in common with her. That, and our hazel eyes, according to Dad. With my free hand, I held the previous day's physical chart in front of me and snuck glances at the boys. Cookies in hand, Nick kicked back in his bed, watching a TV show about wolves. Sam was still reading. Trev stood at the front of his room, chatting with Cas about the difference between regular chocolate and white chocolate, their conversation not at all hindered by the wall between them.

Dad wouldn't tell me what the program tested for, despite my repeated questioning. When I'd first found the lab, it was all I could think about. What were four boys doing in our basement? Where were their parents? How long had they been down there? Dad knew exactly how much information to give to feed my curiosity and keep me quiet. I knew about the Branch, of course. But even though I knew who ran the program, I still didn't know *why*.

Dad said I should trust him, that he knew what he was doing, and so did the Branch. It was for the greater good.

It was our job to observe, record data, and make necessary changes to the treatments. Dad may have been a little neglectful in the parenting department, but he was a good man, and if he trusted the Branch and our role in the program, then so did I.

I thought the Branch was most likely funded by the government. Dad was obsessed with wars and foreign conflicts, so it made sense. My latest theory was that the boys were being made into super-soldiers. The world could use more heroes.

As Nick finished his cookies, I prepared my tray for the blood draw. I double-checked each supply. Three vials. One new needle. Rubber strap. Band-Aids. Alcohol swabs. Everything was there.

I only had to go into Nick's room every other Wednesday, but each time it left me rattled. I'd rather draw blood from a mountain lion. If Nick was being made into a hero, the program had taken a wrong turn with him.

I tried to shake the feeling off as I went to his room. "You ready?"

"Does it matter if I am or not?"

I was tempted to say something equally snotty in response, but I held back. I just wanted to get this over with.

Dad had three rules about the lab that were to be followed without question. Rule number one: Do not go into the boys' rooms when they are awake. Rule number two: Turn on the sleeping gas only once the subject is safely lying down. Rule number three: Wait four minutes for the gas to kick in.

The boys knew the rules, too.

But Nick hated rules.

"Will you lie down, please?" I asked. He sneered at me. "*Lie down*, Nick." The sneer turned into a snarl, but he finally did as I asked.

Behind me, Dad's cell phone rang. "I need to take this. You'll be okay if I head upstairs?"

I refused to tell Dad I was scared of Nick; I didn't want him to think I couldn't hack it in the lab. So I nodded and said, "Sure."

Phone at his ear, Dad hurried out.

With Nick finally in place on his bed, I scooped up my supply tray. "Here it comes," I warned, right before I hit the Cell #4 button on the control panel. The twin vents in Nick's ceiling scraped open and white smoke hissed out.

He managed to say "This shit gives me a headache" before the gas hit him and his eyes slipped closed. The ever-present tension in his long, sinewy body eased away.

I looked at the stopwatch hanging from a lanyard around my neck. Four minutes was too long for most people to hold their breath. Dad said he was ninety percent sure the boys were stable at this point, and that they probably wouldn't pose any sort of danger to me, but ten percent was too much of a risk for him.

When four minutes had passed, I hit the button to reverse the vents, and the gas was sucked back out. I punched in the entrance code to Nick's room and half of the wall pushed forward and slid aside. The acrid scent of the gas still lingered as I placed my tray on the floor and took a seat next to Nick on the bed.

It was odd seeing him so relaxed. It almost made him look vulnerable. The dark scowl was gone, softening the sharp angles of his face. His black hair curled around his ears. If he hadn't been so infuriating when he was awake, I might have even thought he was handsome.

It didn't take me long to fill the required three vials once I'd located a good vein in the crook of his elbow. I was about to leave when something caught my eye below the hem of his shirt, where a sliver of bare skin was exposed.

I checked my stopwatch. One minute, thirty seconds remained before the effects of the gas would start to wear off. I set the tray back down and lifted the corner of his shirt.

A scar discolored his skin, the wound old and white now. But the shape of it made me pause. It almost looked like an *E*. I thought of Sam's scar, the *R* on his chest. How could I not have noticed Nick's?

Because you weren't ever looking at him.

"You're running out of time," Trev called from two cells over.

Nick's eyes fluttered. His fingers flexed at his sides.

My heart lurched. I snatched up the tray and started for the door as Nick reached for me. His fingers grazed my forearm, but he was still sluggish from the gas and missed. I slammed the control button and the wall slid back into place as he rushed forward. His blue eyes met mine and the scowl returned. I tried to act unafraid, even though I was anything but. Nick had the bluest eyes I'd ever seen, the color of the sky where night meets day. A blue that made him seem more mature, more dangerous, more *everything*.

"Next time," he said, "just do your job and don't fucking touch me unless you have to."

"Nicholas, stop," Sam barked. I locked eyes with Sam as he pressed his hands against the glass, like he meant to pound his way through if it came to that. "Are you all right?"

"I'm sorry," I managed to choke out, still breathless. "I just..." I wanted to mention the scar, wanted to know if it was connected to Sam's, but the strained look on Sam's face said now was not the time.

"I'm sorry," I said again before turning away and carrying my tray over to the counter so I could bury my head in my work.

———

Dad shuffled back into the lab a good hour after he'd disappeared to answer the phone.

"Nick's sample is ready," I said.

A half-chewed straw hung between Dad's index and middle fingers. He'd quit smoking three years earlier, and the straws had taken the place of cigarettes.

"Did it go okay?" He popped the straw in his mouth and sat down in front of his computer.

"Fine," I lied. I spun around in my desk chair so that I faced the boys. Cas was bouncing a tennis ball off the ceiling of his cell. Trev had disappeared into his bathroom. Nick was still watching TV.

Sam, though... Sam just lay on his back, eyes closed.

"How was your phone call?" I asked Dad. "Was it Connor?"

"It was. And it was fine."

Connor called from the Branch to check in a lot, but he only showed up every couple of months to look the boys over, and to ask Dad if he thought "the units" were ready. Dad said no every time. And when I asked him what the boys had to be ready for, he gave me his default answer: *That's classified.*

Sam shifted to a sitting position, the muscle in his forearm dancing. Every day, at exactly two PM, he worked out. Watching him was like watching a tightly choreographed routine—every move counted.

I glanced at the digital clock hanging on the wall: 1:55 PM.

Sam tore off his white T-shirt and turned around, giving me a view of the tattoo on his back. Four birch trees covered the majority of his skin, the branches twining across his shoulders and partway down his arms.

Bending over, legs straight, he started a series of stretches before dropping into push-up position. I'd counted his push-ups once while pretending to read some charts. He did a hundred in a matter of minutes and never slowed. Dad said strength was a trait he and his team had manipulated, and Sam was proof that the genetic alterations had worked.

After the push-ups, Sam moved to sit-ups, the muscles in his stomach bunching on the rise. Two cells over, Cas was doing his own version of the workout, which was half karate moves collected from TV, half hip-hop dance.

At 2:51, Sam slowed to cooldown mode and ran through more stretches. When he finished, he grabbed a towel from his desk, wiped the sweat from his forehead, and looked over at me.

I blushed and turned away, pretending to find something extremely interesting in the control panel as he disappeared into his bathroom. He came out a second later and tapped on the glass.

I raised my eyes.

"Can I have some ice water?"

"And a beer for me, please!" Cas said, then added, "But water would be fine, too."

If I had been alone, I would have gotten up, filled two glasses, and handed them over without question. But with Dad there, I deferred to him, because he was the boss, even if I was his daughter.

"That's fine," Dad muttered, squinting through the lenses of his glasses as he read over a file.

"A straw, too?" Sam called, gesturing toward the canister on the counter.

"Sure," Dad said, barely glancing up.

I gave Cas his water first, then went to Sam's room. He pulled his cup out of the hatch a second later. "Thanks." He was still shirtless, and I couldn't help but examine the scar on his chest. I thought of Nick.

Were there other scars? And if so, why? Did Trev or Cas have scars?

When I dragged my eyes up a second later, I found Sam still staring down at me with an intensity that warmed my skin. "Anything else?" I asked.

"No."

"All right then," I said. "I should get back to work. Lots of data to input. Files to . . . file."

I wheeled around to find my dad looking at me strangely. Did he know how I felt? Could he tell? But he just picked up his straw and returned to his work. I inhaled, trying to shake off the uneasiness. Sam had the ability to reduce me to the thirteen-year-old girl I was when we first met.

I spent the next hour pretending to organize test charts.

WHEN I FIRST DISCOVERED THE BOYS

in the lab, Nick immediately scared the crap out of me. Thirteen-year-old me had stared at his hands, tightened at his sides, tracing the swell of veins threading up and around his arms. It was like he'd known he hated me right from the start.

I might never have gone back down there if it hadn't been for Sam.

The sight of him there, the inquisitive tilt of his head, as if he were reading me from the inside out, was enough to ensnare me even then. I'd never felt so interesting, so special, as I did at that moment.

"What's your name?" he'd asked, ignoring Nick.

"Anna. Anna Mason."

"Anna, I'm Sam."

In the next room over, Nick growled. I could sense the others on my periphery. Trev paced in his cell. Cas leaned into the glass, the pads of his fingers turning white.

And then Nick slammed a fist into the wall and I flinched.

"Nicholas," Sam said, his voice razor-edged.

I didn't see how that would help any, but within seconds Nick retreated. He disappeared into the bathroom at the back of his room, slamming the door shut behind him.

The boys didn't look much older than sixteen. I didn't find out until later that their alterations slowed the rate at which they aged. They were closer to eighteen at the time, and over the course of the following years, they would age very little.

I wanted to know what they were doing down there, how long they'd been in those rooms. I wanted to know who they were, and if they were okay, because they weren't acting okay. But those thoughts tangled in my head, and not one rational question made it past my lips.

"You should go, Anna," Sam said. "Nick isn't well."

"Cookies make me feel better when I'm sick."

It was such a stupid thing to say, but it was the only thing I managed to get out.

The cookies would give me an excuse, later, to return. Not even Nick could have kept me from Sam, the boy who looked at me as more than just a little girl. And he'd tried. Nick had been the one to tell Dad I'd broken into the lab that first time, the whole reason I'd been grounded after, the whole reason it took me a few months to sneak back in without getting caught.

Nick never told on me again, though, and part of me had wondered if Sam had been the one to keep him quiet. And if he had, did that mean Sam *wanted* me to visit?

Every morning—and almost every night—it was that hope that propelled me from my bed and pushed me down the stairs.

———

The next morning, while Dad took care of some phone calls upstairs, I started on my to-do list. Lots of filing. Some paper-shredding. Running Sam through his mental tests. I decided to do the latter first; everything else could wait.

"So what is it this week?" Sam asked as I grabbed his folder from my desk.

I looked over at him. I always fought for his attention, but when I got it, I found it hard to concentrate beneath his gaze.

I opened the folder. "Foreign language."

Sam pulled his desk chair up to the front of his room, and I did the same. I set the folder on my lap and opened it to a fresh chart. Next to the Branch's logo—two interlocking circles with a double helix inside—I wrote Sam's name. Then: *October 11, 11:26 AM.*

This week's packet was a series of flash cards with Italian phrases on one side, the English translations on the other. Since the boys suffered from amnesia, the Branch wanted to know what they were capable of, and what skills from their old lives they still possessed.

Apparently, Sam had been a languages genius before entering the program. When it came to skills, I was only good at sketching and solving sudoku puzzles.

I held up the first card and Sam's eyes moved over the words. *"I am searching for the train station."*

Correct.

I held up the next card.

"What time is it?"

We went over fifty cards total. I marked Sam's responses on the log. He scored a hundred percent, as usual.

Casually, after sliding my materials into the folder, I said, "Do you remember anything about that scar? The one on your chest?"

He didn't allow a second's worth of hesitation before answering. "No. But then, I have a lot of scars."

"None of them look as purposeful as the one on your chest."

He went still. I'd caught him in a secret; I could see it on his face. The scars meant something. "Does Cas have a scar like that?"

"Anna." My name came out a warning, but it served as fuel.

"What do they mean?"

He turned away from me. His back was hunched, the blades of his shoulders rising beneath his shirt. I could see the sharp points of the tattooed tree branches peeking out from his sleeves.

Tell me, Sam.

I sensed the boys shifting, moving toward us.

"Not now," Sam muttered.

"Excuse me?"

The others slunk away, and the edginess I'd felt slipped away with them.

"I think we're done, Anna," Sam said.

I put his folder away with a petty slam of the filing cabinet drawer, because he'd dismissed me and I didn't want to leave.

At the lab door, I punched in the code with short jabs, making a promise to myself that I wouldn't sneak into the lab later. That I would hold out for as long as I could, let him see how boring the lab could be without our chess games, without our nightly conversations about the outside world.

But it was more of a punishment for me than for him. And I knew I wouldn't stick with it.

4

THAT NIGHT AT DINNER, I PICKED AT
my bowl of chili, running the spoon through it in a figure-eight pattern. Dad sat across from me at the dining room table, his spoon
clinking against the side of his bowl. Behind us, a football game
played on TV. Every now and then, Dad looked up and checked the
score. He never got overly excited about the games, though—not like
guys on TV. A good play and they'd leap from their chairs, their arms
held victoriously above their heads.

I couldn't see Dad ever doing something like that—not for football, or for science, or even if he won the lottery. Dad was even-keeled,
subdued about everything. I thought his lack of emotion stemmed
from losing my mother.

Mom had liked sports. At least that's what Dad said. So maybe he watched for her.

"Dad?"

"Hmm?" He dipped a cracker in the chili.

"Were the boys ever branded?"

He sniffed. "Of course not."

"Have you noticed Nick's and Sam's scars? The ones that look like letters?"

"They have a lot of scars." An announcer on the TV said something about the second down, but I missed what came next. Dad set the spoon in his bowl and looked up at me. "By the way, I've been meaning to tell you. . . . Let's hold back on the number of things we give Cas, all right? Why not bring him a book, like you do for the others? He never finishes any of his projects, and his room is a mess. . . ."

"Cas isn't really a book kind of person."

"Well . . ." Dad ran his hand over the back of his head and sighed. "Just try to give him something he'll actually stick with." The burst of wrinkles around his eyes furrowed.

"Is this really about Cas, or is there something else?"

The TV crowd cheered behind us.

"No. It's nothing."

"Is Connor coming for a visit?" I asked. He wrestled with the sleeve of crackers, avoiding looking at me. "Dad?"

"Yes. Tomorrow. Him and Riley."

Connor was head of the Branch, and Riley was his second-in-command. Together they oversaw Dad and the program.

"They want to inspect the group," Dad went on. "See how they're progressing."

"Are they taking the boys this time?"

Though I wanted the boys to be released, the lab, the logs, and the tests had all become my life as much as theirs. Now I didn't know how I felt about them leaving.

Dad shrugged. "I won't be privy to that until it's time."

"Where would they go?"

"I don't know that, either."

I couldn't picture Sam in the real world, buying a doughnut at a coffee shop, reading a newspaper on a park bench. The others, maybe. Cas was like any other party boy trolling for girls. Nick was the epitome of an asshole jock, with the cockiness and pretty face to match. And Trev once told me that if he ever got out, he'd want to go to school to study English literature.

But Sam...

"Will they ever be released?"

Dad removed his glasses and rubbed the bridge of his nose. "I don't know, Anna. Really. I don't know."

I sensed the demise of the conversation and shut up. We finished eating. I did the dishes and wiped down the table, while Dad passed out in the living room. I threw some laundry in the washer.

By that time, it was after eight and dark outside. Upstairs in my room, I flipped through the TV channels and found nothing worth watching. I didn't have any new books to read. Since most of the chores were done, I decided to sketch something new in my mother's journal.

I lay on my stomach on the bed and opened to the last sketch I'd done. It was of a girl in the woods, boughs of maple trees hanging heavy with snow. Her silhouette was blurry, fading, curling, like ribbons of smoke. Like she was disappearing with each new gust of wind. Being lost or broken had been a running theme in my sketches for about a year, ever since I'd taken a weekend art class at the community college.

But it wasn't the class that opened up the new vein of inspiration. It was the conversation I'd had with Trev afterward.

My final review from the instructor said that I possessed raw talent, but that I hadn't yet tapped into my full potential, that my art was lacking inspiration. I'd gone down to the lab to vent, and Trev, as always, had talked me off the ledge.

"I don't get it," I'd said to him, leaning against the brick wall between his room and Cas's. "Lacking inspiration?" I sighed. "What does that even mean?"

Trev came to the glass and mirrored my slouch so that we stood side by side. "It means you're only drawing what you see, not what you feel."

I folded my arms over my chest as I looked at him. "The sketches of my mother have lots of emotion."

His amber eyes softened. "But you don't know your mother. You only know what you've heard, and that you miss her. What about what you want? Your hopes? Your dreams? What are you passionate about?" He swiveled to face me full-on. "Your instructor was telling you to dig deeper."

The look on his face transitioned from open understanding to something guarded, as if he was silently prodding me. As if he was holding back what he wanted to say because a frank answer would make it too easy.

I rested my head against the wall and stared at the ceiling, at the pockmarks in the tiles. Trev liked wrapping his advice in complex philosophies. Nothing was ever simple with him.

The problem was, I didn't know what I wanted out of my life. What was I passionate about? The boys. The lab. Dad. Baking. But sketching a pumpkin pie sounded pretty darn boring.

Maybe Trev read the confusion on my face, because he added, "Start with your frustrations. How about that? It's easier to tap into anger or annoyance."

When I returned to my room that night, I'd opened my sketchbook and stared at the blank page. What frustrated me? My mother being dead, yes, but I needed something fresh.

And then it came to me: Nick. Nick frustrated me.

Soon, my pencil began to slide across the paper at an alarming pace. As I sketched, I felt it: a fire in my arm, a tingling sensation in my fingertips, like I was bleeding that passion onto the page.

When I was finished, I had one of the best drawings I'd ever done. In it, Nick stood in the middle of a deserted street, bottles broken around him, liquid spilling everywhere while he peered out from the page, a prickly expression on his face. I was so proud of the sketch that I almost considered showing him, but then I realized that he'd probably take offense, or automatically hate it.

I did show Trev, though, the next night. He looked from the sketch to me and nodded his approval. "There you go," he said in a hushed tone so the others wouldn't hear, so we could keep the sketch between us. "Continue to draw like that and you'll turn into the next Vanessa Bell."

I scoffed, but inside I was beaming. Vanessa Bell was a brilliant painter, one of my favorite artists. She was also the older sister of Virginia Woolf, Trev's favorite writer. That was the best compliment he could give me.

My sketches changed after that. For the better.

Now I turned to a fresh page and stared and stared and stared. Sometimes it was easy to begin drawing; other times I needed a jump start. I couldn't always count on Trev to spur me. I grabbed an issue of *Traveler* magazine from my dresser and flipped through the glossy pages. I stopped on a spread of a quiet Italian village.

I started sketching the buildings, the blush of light from the old street lamps. I added a traditional Italian café with tiny two-seater tables, window boxes dripping with flowers, bikes with baskets, and scalloped awnings.

Before I knew it, I'd sketched myself walking the cobblestone street, Sam next to me. I ran my finger over the lines and the graphite smeared.

I often found myself sketching fantasies like this one, where Sam was no longer locked in the lab and I was no longer tethered to it because of him. With my pencil, I could set us both free.

But I couldn't help wondering what Sam would want if he could choose his own life. Had he chosen this? Had he wanted to be some kind of perfect soldier, to serve his country?

What did he want now that he couldn't remember his reasons for being here?

I grabbed the magazine and went downstairs. I tiptoed through the living room and down to the basement so I wouldn't wake Dad. The lab door slid open when I punched in the code.

It was nearly ten, and the lights in the boys' rooms were off. I hesitated just past the opening of the hallway. The magazine suddenly felt cumbersome in my hand. I started to turn away.

A light flicked on behind me. I stopped, turned back.

Sam stood at the glass wall, barefoot, shirtless, in his usual loose gray pants. "Hey, Anna," he said, but the words came out unsure, heavy. His shoulders hung crooked. When I took a step closer, he scratched his jaw, and looked down.

Was Sam . . . uneasy?

"Hi."

"Listen. I'm sorry about earlier. I didn't mean to snap at you."

I folded my arms and the magazine crinkled. "It's no big deal."

He nodded, then gestured at the magazine. "What is that?"

I held it out, suddenly unsure of my reasons for coming down here. "It's just . . . You don't have any pictures on your wall."

A frown pulled at the center of his brow. "You came down here to ask about my bare walls?"

"Yes." I ran my teeth over my bottom lip, glancing at the other rooms, waiting for the boys to stir, at the same time hoping they wouldn't. "Why haven't you hung anything?"

"I don't know. Didn't seem like there was any point."

I inched forward. "If you could go anywhere in the world, where would you go?"

His eyes moved from the magazine in my hand up to my face. "What's this about?"

"Just answer the question."

I wanted to know everything about Sam. I wanted him to trust me with his secrets. And since he couldn't remember most of his life before the lab, asking him this was as close as I would get.

"I think I like water."

"The ocean?"

"It doesn't matter what kind."

I held up the magazine. The cover was of a tropical island getaway. "Maybe this?" I flipped through it until I landed on a two-page spread of the ocean. I tore the pages out and put them in the hatch. "Take them."

"Why?"

I shrugged. "To hope."

He held the pictures up and studied them. After an excruciatingly long moment, he asked, "Do you have tape?"

I fished around in my desk and pulled out a roll of packing tape. I slid it through the hatch.

"Where would you go if you could go anywhere?" he asked.

I knew I wanted to do things, see things, but what and where, I didn't know. I stuck a hand in my jeans pocket. I thought of the Italian village I'd sketched. "Probably somewhere in Europe."

"Where *are* we, exactly?"

"You mean…you don't know?" We never talked about it. I just thought he knew. "Treger Creek, New York. It's small. An everyone-knows-everyone kind of place."

"Does it say in my files where I was before here? What state I used to live in?"

I tried to look anywhere but at the bareness of his torso. He had easily seven inches on me, so it was difficult to look him in the eye. "Not in the files I've read, but there are others upstairs."

"Could you look? I think it might help with the memory loss if I knew some details of my life before here."

I'd tried breaking into the upstairs filing cabinets the previous winter, but Dad had caught me. I'd never seen him as mad as he was then, not even when I broke into the lab. I hadn't dared try again.

But things were different now. For one, I had permission to be in the lab, which gave me permission to read the files, right? And two... well, Sam was asking me to look.

"Yeah." I nodded. "I can do that."

"Thanks." He leveled his shoulders. Any trace of the earlier discomfort had vanished.

I pushed a strand of hair behind my ear. "Well...I should probably go. We'll have to finish that chess game later. Tomorrow, maybe?"

"Sure. Good night, Anna."

"'Night."

I looked back and saw him taping the magazine pages above his desk. I thought of the awkward way he fidgeted when he apologized, and I couldn't help smiling.

"Oh, by the way," I said, before I punched in the code to leave, "Connor is coming tomorrow...so...I just thought you should know."

His expression darkened. "Thanks for the warning. I hate his surprise visits."

"Me, too."

———

The code to get into the lab was 17-25-10. Seventeen was Mom's birthday; twenty-five was the date of Mom and Dad's anniversary;

and ten was for October, the month they got married. Dad, being predictably predictable, set the code to the filing cabinet in the study as 10-17-25. It took me only four tries to get it right.

When the drawer popped open, the tracks squeaked and I froze, listening. The rest of the house was silent save for the ticking of the clock above Dad's fireplace.

I found Sam's files in the second drawer. There were five green legal-sized folders, each of which held smaller manila folders. I pulled out the two farthest back and sat down with them on the leather couch.

Seeing nothing worthwhile in the first folder—just basic logs and charts—I moved on to the second. That's where I found tiny bits of information about Sam's life at the start of the program.

There were notes on plain paper in a barely legible handwriting I didn't recognize:

> Sam shows extreme signs of aggression and defiance to anyone within the program.

And later:

> Sam slipped seamlessly into the leader role. The others allowed him in without hesitation. Must continue to isolate this characteristic to replicate in future groups.

I skimmed a few more pages, stopping when something caught my eye.

Sam has escaped us again. Alerts sent to all the proper channels. Possible aliases—Samuel Eastlock. Samuel Cavar. Samuel Bentley.

Sam had escaped? Why would he have had to? And more than once?

Apparently his relationship with the Branch stretched further back than I'd thought. Sensing that I was closer to the information Sam wanted, I scanned through the stack of papers, looking for the name of a town, something concrete I could tell him about his life before all this.

Sam and team found at Port. Wiped. OP ALPHA will soon commence.

Port—Sam had said he liked water. But what was OP ALPHA?

I kept reading, but an hour later, I had made it through two files and really had nothing to show for it except more questions. I'd just gotten up to grab another folder when I heard the couch in the living room creak.

Dad.

I scrambled, straightening the files. I went to the cabinet to replace them, but accidentally opened the third drawer down. An empty file caught my eye, an old label still attached to the outside.

O'BRIEN, it read.

Dad coughed.

I stuffed Sam's file in the correct drawer and made sure it locked as I closed it. Tiptoeing up the stairs, I made it to the second floor without a sound and finally let out the breath I'd been holding.

Dad never checked on me at night, but still I hurried into my pajamas and climbed into bed. The sheets felt cool to the touch. I lay awake for a while, staring at the ceiling. I couldn't stop thinking about Sam's file.

Why had he needed me to look in the first place? Why hadn't Dad filled in the blanks for Sam a long time ago?

Unless the Branch wanted to keep something about Sam's past from him. And if that was the case, I was violating protocol by sharing the details.

I didn't like going against Dad, but Sam deserved to know about his past, didn't he?

5

I SET MY ALARM CLOCK FOR SIX THE next morning, thinking I'd sneak into the lab before Dad got up. I must have turned it off without realizing it, though, because I didn't get up until after eight. By the time I headed downstairs, Dad was already in the lab. I was kind of relieved; I still wasn't sure how much to tell Sam.

Stomach grumbling, I threw a couple of slices of bread in the toaster. I popped a few ibuprofen and massaged the healing muscle in my back. My lack of sleep the night before hadn't done me any favors, and my next combat class was just a couple of days away. I'd been in the course for several years, and the instructor was not the type of guy to go easy on me.

Not that I was complaining. I always left the studio feeling strong, agile, and powerful. Sometimes I wished the boys could see me in class—I wanted them to know I was capable of more than just making cookies and filing charts.

As I waited for my toast to finish, I stood at the sink, watching the tree branches sway in the wind. In the distance, a trail of dust billowed behind a line of black Suburbans traveling down our dirt road.

I straightened. *Connor.* I'd forgotten he was coming today.

I ran back upstairs, threw off my pajamas, and dressed quickly in jeans and a henley. I slipped into a pair of tennis shoes as the trucks pulled into the driveway and parked wherever they could find room. Riley was the first to climb out of his vehicle; behind him came Connor, followed by several agents.

The men shadowed Connor to the side of the house. He didn't bother knocking before opening the door into the mudroom, and I met him and Riley at the few steps up to the kitchen.

"Morning," Connor said, flashing me a smile of unnaturally white teeth. Tall and gorgeous, he was charismatic on every level, and often plied me with compliments I knew weren't true.

I tried to avoid him whenever he came for a check-in because he made my skin crawl, but this visit was different. They'd never shown up with an entourage before. And certainly not dressed like this.

The agents wore black jackets with armored quilting at the shoulders and elbows. The necks of the jackets were high and close-fitting, made tighter by a fastened strap.

Over the jackets they wore thick black vests. Handguns hung from the waists of their black pants, and their hands were hidden in black gloves with plates of rubber on the fingers.

They clustered in the doorway between the kitchen and dining room, waiting for further direction. In addition to Connor and Riley, I counted a total of seven men and one woman. Two agents per boy.

None of them made eye contact with me, even when I stared. Were those bulletproof vests? I was suddenly on full alert.

"Come with me." Connor led his team to the basement. I followed silently at the back, afraid of being caught and sent away.

Riley punched in the entrance code at the lab and the door rushed open. Dad's voice carried out as he greeted Connor, then Riley.

"Arthur." Connor clasped Dad by the shoulder. "We got word this morning from OB that we're ending the project. We're taking the units."

Dad said nothing. The agents broke into pairs in front of each cell. Connor and Riley murmured to Dad while Sam stared down the men at his room, fists clenched. I caught Trev's eyes and saw panic.

"No." The word was out before I could stop it. Everyone turned to me, standing at the mouth of the hallway.

The boys shifted in their rooms. Shifted closer, as if they would group together if not for the walls between them. Sam's eyes were on me.

"Excuse me?" Riley snapped. He was far older than Connor, impatient, no-nonsense.

I warmed beneath the attention and the glow of the fluorescent lights. "You can't...yet...I mean...they're not ready. We can still—"

Sam shook his head and I went quiet.

"She's right," Dad added. "They aren't ready."

Connor gave Dad the kind of smile you give someone when you're tired of their excuses, when you think you know better than they do. "Every time I talk to you, they aren't ready. I'm beginning to think you've grown too attached."

Dad started to object, but I beat him to it. "We still need to run a few more tests."

Connor slid toward me, wound an arm around my shoulders. "I know you've put in a lot of effort down here with Arthur these last few months, and that won't go unrewarded. How much longer do you have before you finish school?"

I had only about six months to finish homeschooling and told Connor so, though I had no idea why it mattered.

"Come see me when you're done. We'll find a spot for you. I'll keep you close to me. Sound good?"

Sam shook his head again, but Connor missed it. Cas stood at the front of his room, arms crossed over his chest. Nick rolled his head back and forth, the bones in his neck cracking. Trev curled his hands into loose fists.

Connor dug his fingers into my shoulder as he turned us both toward the rooms. "I think you would make a wonderful addition to the Branch," he continued, keeping his eyes on the boys. "Would you like that?"

My limbs felt weak and airy. "Um..." I was overwhelmed by the smell of his cologne, sweet and musky all at once.

There were things I wanted outside of this lab. I wanted to travel, to visit the places in my magazines. But I'd never pictured my life without Sam and the others in it. If I worked for the Branch, would I work close to Sam? Did it even matter? If he left today, would he forget about me?

"You don't have to find a place for me."

"Nonsense. I *want* you there. It's my pleasure." Connor ran a hand over his blond, perfectly coiffed hair, as if checking its placement. "Clearly the boys respect you. Look at them."

Riley, Dad, and the other agents turned to the boys.

"Where will you take them?" I asked.

"That's classified," Riley said.

"Headquarters," Connor said, and Riley looked chagrined. I wondered if Riley hated that someone younger than him was his boss.

Dad cleared his throat. "Will I be reassigned?"

Connor moved away from me. "ALPHA is ongoing. You can manage that."

Alpha? That was in Sam's files. OP ALPHA.

"That program is connected to the boys," Dad replied. "There is no program without them."

"Arthur," Riley said, putting heavy emphasis on Dad's name, "this is something that will be discussed later."

Dad's shoulders sagged.

I tried to catch his eyes, to send him a silent message: *Fight for the boys. Don't let Connor take them!* But he avoided looking at me, avoided looking at anyone.

"So," Connor said, "shall we get started?" Though it was phrased as a question, no one waited to answer. The agents squared their shoulders, and Connor looked over at Dad and said, "I trust you'll cooperate?"

Dad nodded. "Of course."

The lights overhead felt blinding. I looked at all the files piled on Dad's desk, at the desk I'd claimed as my own next to it. This was *our* place, *our* job.

Say something, Dad, I thought. The boys had been here for years. The lab was their home. Wasn't here better than some Branch building?

"How would you like to proceed?" Dad asked.

"Gas them all at once," Connor said. "My men will move in from there." He clapped his hands together, and Dad hurried to the control panel.

I stood unmoving near the mouth of the hallway, staring at Sam, lips parted, unsaid words stuck behind my teeth. His gaze flicked to the chessboard in the back corner of the lab and something like regret flashed across his face.

"Miss?" the female agent said. I blinked. "Perhaps you should wait upstairs."

"I'm staying." I pursed my lips and moved out of the way.

"I don't know if that's such a good idea—"

"Anna has as much right to be here as any of us," Connor said with a wink. While I was grateful that he didn't kick me out, I wasn't sure why he was sticking up for me.

I turned and caught Dad's eyes, and his expression made me pause. It was a look that said a million *sorry*s, none of which I would ever hear: *Sorry for bringing you into this mess. Sorry that you even have an excuse for being here. Sorry. Sorry. Sorry.*

I wanted to say, *Who cares about me? Don't let them take the boys.*

But Dad didn't say anything. Not one word.

6

CONNOR HIT THE CONTROL BUTTONS

and the rooms' vents opened, expelling the gas. Riley stood in the center of the lab, hand poised over the butt of his gun. The boys dropped where they stood. We waited the required four minutes. No one moved.

I clenched and unclenched my fists. Connor had broken Dad's second rule. I didn't understand why they couldn't just escort the boys out.

As the four minutes stretched thin, like a rubber band ready to snap, I focused on Sam. He'd fallen on the other side of his bed, so I could see only his legs from where I stood. When he woke up, he'd probably already be gone, on his way to headquarters. Wherever that was.

Would he think of me when he woke? If I had known the night before would be our final night together, I would have spent more time with him.

I would have told him how much he meant to me, that not a second went by when I didn't think about him. Every muscle in my body tensed with anxiety as I realized I would wake up in the morning and there'd be no one here. I could already feel the emptiness settling in.

"Time," Dad said.

The vents scraped shut, and the doors to the rooms slid open. The men moved in as the lab filled with the acrid scent of dissipating gas. I pushed away from the wall, closer to Sam's room. Next week was supposed to be his week for blood work. The fact that I wouldn't be able to see him up close, in person, to touch him, tugged at cords I didn't know I had.

One man stood at the front of Sam's room like a guard, while his partner crouched down at the foot of the bed. The second man secured Sam's wrists behind his back with a zip tie before pulling a syringe from an inside jacket pocket. He picked off the orange cap. Then he froze.

"What the hell?" He stepped over Sam's legs. "Shit." He whipped his gun from its holster as Sam rocked back, jamming his foot up and between the man's legs.

I sucked in a breath. The man fell to his knees. The one on guard fumbled for his gun. Sam leapt in the air, swinging his tied-off wrists beneath his feet, putting his hands in front of him in one quick motion.

"Cell three! Cell three!" Riley shouted.

Sam tore the gun away from the first agent and cupped it in both hands. He didn't waver. He pointed. Shot. Blood splattered across the wall. The man slumped over. I tasted the gas, bitter in the back of my throat. I jammed myself in beside the row of filing cabinets.

Sam shot again. The man on guard collapsed. Someone yelled. Dad ducked toward the control panel. The men in Cas's room came barreling out into the lab, guns ready. The woman guarding Trev's room hunkered down at the partition wall. Sam aimed for the light fixtures in the ceiling and took out three rows as one of the agents in Nick's room tried a countering shot.

The bullet missed Sam. The room plunged into a murky half darkness.

Riley took a shot, the gun sparking to my left. Concrete pebbled from the wall. I could just make out Sam at the front corner of his room, gun up. *Thwap. Thwap.* Two bodies hit the floor. The sound rooted me in place.

"Turn the gas back on!" Connor shouted, and Dad fumbled at the controls.

The woman sprang from her hiding spot, and Sam killed her with one pull of the trigger. Another agent rushed in, landing a punch to Sam's jaw. As Sam stumbled back, he brought the gun up and put a bullet in the man's forehead.

Riley ran to the exit as Sam eliminated the last two guards.

I was next. Sam was going to shoot me. On purpose or by accident, I didn't know.

Hands gripped me, wrestling me to my feet, an arm closing around my neck. I thought it was Dad, trying to save me, but the barrel of the gun rammed against my skull said otherwise. Connor's cologne filled my nose.

"Sam!" Connor yelled.

Sam went rigid. Though I could see nothing else, I could see that—the sharp line of him in the dark. My head swam.

"Put the gun down." Connor tugged me toward the door. He was crazy if he thought Sam would quit, just like that. Maybe I'd spent the last several years of my life trying to make Sam's a little bit better, but he wouldn't trade his freedom for me.

Dad hovered near the controls. Sam, hands still tied together, eased the gun toward the floor. His jaw tensed, like his brain didn't agree with what his hands were doing.

He was throwing away his freedom for my life. The realization left me both cold and hot all over. I couldn't stand to watch the unfairness of it register on his face. I didn't know what any of this meant, or what Sam intended to do once he broke free of the lab, but if I had to pick sides, I had to pick Sam's.

This was my chance. And I'd always known my answer.

I swung an elbow back, catching Connor in the stomach. He doubled over, sending his gun skittering across the floor. Sam shot.

The first bullet clipped Connor in the shoulder. I ducked as a second bullet hit him in the side. He dropped. Riley fired a shot from the hallway and Sam flattened himself against the floor.

"Get me out of here!" Connor ordered as Riley popped off another round.

The lab door swished open. Sam rose to a crouching position. He aimed. I pressed myself harder into the wall.

Riley hooked his arms beneath Connor and dragged him out. Sam pulled the trigger again, but the chamber answered back with a hollow *click*.

"Go! Go!" Connor yelled.

The door closed behind them, sealing with a definitive *whump*. The keypad beeped from the other side and the bolts slid into place.

I shakily rose to my feet. My stomach swirled with nausea. I looked to Dad in the far corner. *What now?* I thought. But Dad just stood there, his fingers twitching like he needed a straw to hold.

Sam put the gun down and sprang into action. He stole a pocket-knife from one of the dead men and flipped it open, then used it to split the zip ties on his wrists. He went to Cas's room and shook him until he woke. Cas sat up, dazed. Sam went down the line, waking the others. I remained at the mouth of the hallway, unsure of what to do with myself.

I swallowed hard against the uneasiness sitting at the back of my tongue, like I might vomit at the slightest encouragement.

"We need to move," Sam said to Cas. "I doubt we have much time—"

"Wait." Dad stepped forward. The boys tensed. "I'm not going to stop you"—Dad held up his hands—"but you have to think about what you're doing. Do you have a plan?"

Sam plucked another gun from the floor. "My plan starts with getting out of here."

"I can help you." Dad held up a set of keys. "Take my car. It doesn't have a tracking device on it, but you'll want to switch vehicles soon. If Connor is badly injured, you have a half hour, tops. There's a safe house not too far from here. I'm sure that's where Riley took him."

Sam took the offered keys. "Cas, gather the guns. Trev and Nick, check out front."

"The door is locked—" I started.

"Five-zero-five-nine-seven-three," Sam interrupted.

That wasn't the code I used to get in and out of the lab. Not that I thought Riley or Connor had locked us in using the normal one.

Nick slid a daggered look my way as he passed and I mashed myself even closer to the wall. Trev punched in the numbers and the lab door hissed open.

"H-how—" I sputtered.

Sam released the gun's clip. Finding it empty, he tossed it aside and dug out a fresh one from a dead man's vest. He slammed it in place with a *snick, clack*. "The keypad beeps when you punch in the numbers. You just have to know which tone comes from which number."

I stared at him. He'd figured out the combination by listening? While he was being shot at?

"So now what?" Cas said. He and Sam glanced at Dad.

The line of Dad's Adam's apple sank as he swallowed, and I wondered if he felt like throwing up, too. "Go ahead," he said.

I took a step. "Go ahead with—"

Sam pointed the gun at Dad and shot.

A gasp fluttered at the back of my throat and anger set me in motion. I wanted the gun gone before Sam hurt someone else, even though there was no one left but me.

Sam saw me coming, and tossed the gun to Cas, who snatched it easily from the air. I threw a punch, connecting first with Sam's jaw, then his shoulder, before he grabbed me by the wrists and swung me around. He shoved me into the wall between his room and Nick's, the bullet-riddled brick piercing my back.

"It won't be fatal!" he shouted. "He'll be fine."

I fought for air but came up short, like I was drowning, like the panic had filled my mouth, my nose. I gulped. Sam tipped my head back and air trickled into my lungs. This was not happening. Those men were not dead. And Dad was not shot. And I was not so close to Sam that I could feel his breath on my face.

I squeezed my eyes closed and inhaled in the controlled way my instructor had taught me. I never thought I'd need to use the lessons, not like this. Slowly, the hysteria ebbed. Sam righted me, put his hands on either side of my face, and forced me to look at him. I blinked, the edges of my vision fuzzy and smattered with black, but I could see the green flint of his eyes and it reminded me of so many nights spent down here with him.

I thought I could trust him. I thought he was my friend.

"Why did you shoot him?" I choked out. "He never did anything to hurt you."

"When Connor realizes we escaped, he'll think your father was harmed in the crossfire. This way he isn't an accomplice."

I harnessed what little courage I had left and clenched my teeth. "Then will you shoot me, too?"

He cocked his head and sighed, exasperated. "No," he answered. Short and sweet. No explanation. I wasn't sure what that meant, or if I even cared.

He and Cas searched the men lying on the floor, swiping anything else that might be useful. I hurried over to my dad, sidestepping the trail of smeared blood left in his wake. From what I could tell, he'd been hit in the right leg, just above the knee.

I took his hand in mine. "Are you okay?"

He tried to straighten but winced. "Of course."

"Should I put pressure on it? Or tie something around it?"

"I'm fine. Really."

I sniffed back a sob. My hands were still shaking. "You're not fine. None of this is fine."

The lab door slid open again and Trev and Nick appeared. "Three men out front," Trev said. "Armed. Looks like they're waiting for us."

"So we need to move," Nick added.

Dad pushed me. "You need to go with them."

"What?" The word came out a squeak.

Dad called to Sam over my shoulder. "Take her with you. Please. I won't ask for anything else."

"I'm not leaving you," I said.

"Anna. Listen to me." Dad pulled himself up straighter. "Stay with Sam. Don't come back here. *Ever*. Do you understand me?"

"I'm not leaving you," I repeated.

"You can't be here when Connor comes back. You have to stay away from him."

"But—"

"Go." He pushed me and I stumbled. Trev caught me and put a reassuring arm around my shoulders. Nick made a grumbling noise.

"Samuel?" Dad motioned to him and Sam crouched by his side. "Go to 4344 West Holicer Lane, Elk Hill, Pennsylvania. It's a safe location. Someone will be there to help you."

Sam nodded and rose to his feet. "Thank you," he said before ushering us toward the door.

I wrenched myself away from Trev and wrapped my arms around Dad's neck.

"I'll find you later," he said. "I promise. In the meantime, don't call. It won't be safe."

I stood up, trying to obey but paralyzed by the fear of leaving him here like this, of disappearing with someone who had just killed eight people in front of me.

The lab door slid open and clean air filtered out the smell of death and stale gas. I looked back at Dad as we left the lab, until the hallway blocked him from my sight.

7

"GIVE ME THE LAYOUT," SAM SAID ONCE we reached the top of the stairs.

Trev stuck a gun in the waistband of his pants and pointed at the front of the house. "Picture window in the living room. There's a man stationed there." He gestured toward the kitchen. "Man hiding in the garden. Clear shot from the window above the sink. The third is out by the garage."

I didn't know Connor had more agents than the ones he'd brought into the lab. Either that, or he'd called for backup. And if they were already here, how long before more arrived?

"Cas, out front," Sam said. Cas nodded and disappeared down the hallway. I watched him go. The sight of him inhabiting the space that had been only mine and my dad's was unsettling. "Nick, take the garage?"

Nick disappeared into the small half bath across the hall.

"I'll go with Cas," Trev said, and then waited for Sam's consent before leaving.

Sam and I went to the kitchen. My stack of schoolbooks sat in the middle of the kitchen table. My unread *Artist's* magazine lay near the bread box. Dad's empty coffee cup remained in the sink, unwashed. It all felt surreal.

Planting his hands on the edge of the counter, Sam lithely hoisted himself up. He shoved aside the flour canister and a box of tea, slinking closer to the window above the sink. "Open the back door and call out. Say you need help."

"But—" He silenced me with a look. And the gun in his hands ended any thought of further protest. I moved to the sliding door, flipped up the latch, and hauled it open. "Help! Please! Someone!"

The man in the garden straightened, placing his eyes firmly on me. The window slid open, the gun slid out, and Sam pulled the trigger. The man's head bounced back from the impact of the bullet and a new heat spread through me.

Two more shots followed Sam's. A few seconds later, the boys regrouped in the kitchen. "Clear," Trev said, and my stomach see-sawed. More dead. All of them dead. And I'd helped.

"Where are the files?"

Someone shook me.

"What?"

"Where are the files?" Sam said. "Where did Arthur keep them?"

"Down the hall." I pointed. "In the study." I rattled off the code to the filing cabinet, and the boys left me.

I leaned against the sliding door. The man from the Branch lay facedown in the grass. Not breathing. Not moving. *What if he had kids? A wife?* He must have crawled out of bed that morning thinking he'd return home that night to the life he lived. But he wouldn't. Not now. Because of me.

I felt the guilt of that decision right down to my core.

"Anna," Sam said from behind me.

"Yeah?"

"We're leaving."

I turned to face him. "Did you get the files?"

"They're gone. Riley must have taken them."

Numbly, I followed Sam into the hallway. Nick scowled as he pushed past me. Trev and Cas hurried after him, their excitement so thick I could almost feel it. They bounded outside. Sam and I watched them through the screen door of the mudroom.

Cas ran three circles around the garage before dropping to his knees and fake-kissing the cement. Trev looked out over the yard, the woods, the field, taking it in, his hands on his hips.

I stayed where I was, wondering if I could get back downstairs to

Dad before Sam could stop me. Would he stop me? Would Dad be angry?

"We need to go," Sam said.

I looked toward the basement door.

"Anna," he repeated, the command stronger the second time.

I put on a jacket and went outside. Trev rummaged around inside one of the Suburbans and came out with a wrapped package for each boy. "Looks like there's some clothes and a pair of shoes in there."

Cas tore into his package and the shoes spilled out. "Sweet Jesus, I have real shoes! No more prison loafers!"

Nick snorted, a look of disdain hardening his eyes. "Just throw them on so we can go. Is no one else worried that we've been here too long?"

"Calm down," Trev said. "We're fine on time."

"And you know that how?" Nick countered.

Cas donned a white long-sleeved shirt, then shoved his feet into the tennis shoes. The others followed suit, though Sam had found one of my dad's old flannel shirts hanging in the mudroom and slipped into it without my noticing. It was navy blue with red and white stripes and pearl snaps. It hid the gun at his back.

I hovered between the house and the garage, trying to stay small and inconspicuous, because I wasn't sure what the plan was or if my having been witness to this escape would become a liability. If it came to that, would Trev stick up for me? Would Cas?

Trev gestured to Dad's car. "Is that what we're taking?"

"Who's driving?" Nick said.

"I'm driving." Sam pulled the keys from his pocket. He slung a glance my way. "Anna?"

I swallowed. "Who *are* you? How did you know how to use a gun like that? How..." What else had he hidden from me? "Do you really have amnesia?"

The keys clanged together as he let his arm drop to his side. "Yes, but I am not having this discussion with you right now. We need to go."

Nick grumbled. "Leave her."

"Hey now," Cas said. "Disarm the torpedoes, soldier."

Nick narrowed his eyes.

"I'm coming," I said. "Just...give me a second. Please?"

Sam sighed. "One minute."

In my bedroom, I grabbed my mother's journal from my dresser. I didn't know where I was going, or even *why* I was going, but if I was leaving with a promise to Dad that I would never return, I wanted to take this book with me. It was the only thing I cherished more than my sketches, and I couldn't stand the thought of leaving it behind. If anything, it would serve as a link to home.

Back outside, Sam already had the car turned around and facing the road. Never mind the fact that I wasn't sure if he even had a license. I climbed into the empty front seat and dutifully clipped my seat belt in place, tucking the journal safely in my lap.

Sam eyed it before ripping into drive and stepping on the gas.

When we reached the end of our long gravel driveway, he slammed on the brake. "Which way to town?"

"Right."

He turned and stomped on the gas again, kicking up dust. I clutched the book, the feel of the worn cover a comfort in my hands. There was a reason the boys had remained in those rooms all those years, but I no longer knew what it was. I'd thought the Branch wanted to make the perfect soldier. If that was the case, then we'd failed. Perfect soldiers don't kill their commanders.

An ache bloomed behind my eyes as I tried to make sense of it all. If Sam's treatment had somehow backfired, then why had Dad pushed me to leave? And why had he insisted I get as far away from Connor as possible?

Dad knew something I didn't. And Sam…a part of me wanted to trust him. He hadn't killed me. He hadn't killed Dad, even though he *had* shot him.

"So what's the master plan?" Cas said, drawing me from my thoughts.

Sam eyed Cas in the rearview mirror. "Ditch the car. Find something new."

"Are we splitting up?" Trev asked.

"Do you want to split up?"

Trev shrugged and scratched at the back of his head. "It's harder to track down parts of a whole. But mostly, I'm just glad to be free. So whatever we decide, I'm okay with it."

"We need to stay together," Nick muttered.

"Dude." Cas put his hands on the back of my seat and leaned forward. "When I saw Connor show up with all his lackeys, I thought for sure your plan was toast."

I swiveled around. "You were *planning* to escape?"

Sam didn't say anything. Didn't even look at me. I stared at him, mouth agape. I'd told him about Connor's visit. I'd prepared him for the escape. What if I hadn't said anything? If I could, would I change it?

Only a foot of space separated Sam and me. Being with him in the outside world was what I'd always wanted, but not like this. A flash of the lab, the blood, and the dead agents came back to me and my stomach clenched.

"When were you planning to escape?"

"Next week," Cas said. "During Sam's blood draw."

My eyes widened. Would I have been the one on the wrong side of a bullet? "What about the gas?"

"Straws," Cas said.

I frowned.

"He taped several together," Cas explained. "Ran them through the vents between the room and the bathroom. You might have noticed his bathroom door was shut? That's because he sealed it off. Gas goes on, Sammy goes down and pretends to be out, but really he's using the straws like a snorkel."

"You really did that?" He didn't answer, but it didn't matter. It all made sense now. It was why he'd been asking for straws, and why he'd asked for a roll of tape last night. I hadn't bothered to get it back from him.

I'd supplied him with the tools for escape and intervened when Connor tried to stop him. I was as much a fugitive now as they were. Maybe that's why Dad sent me away—to escape certain punishment.

God. I was such an idiot. I'd thrown everything away for Sam. For a boy. I'd thought I was on his side. And hadn't I considered breaking him out a few nights ago, during our chess match? Somehow it didn't feel as good as I thought it would. It wasn't supposed to happen like this.

"Brilliant, huh?" Cas said and patted Sam's shoulder. "I knew there was a reason I kept you around."

"As if you had other options?" Sam asked.

Cas shrugged a shoulder before dropping back into his seat. "I'm just saying."

Nick snorted. "Would you quit blowing smoke up his ass? He'll get a big head."

The drive into town seemed to take twice as long as it normally did. Sam ditched Dad's car in the back lot behind Emery's Pizzeria. Trev was ordered to stay with me on Main Street while Sam and the others scouted for another vehicle.

The chill October air stole through the thin material of my jacket. I cast a glance at Trev. He still looked like the same friend I had shared secrets with, the one who loved reading biographies and who had a vast memorized cache of famous quotes. But something about him seemed off now. Maybe it was the gun I knew was hidden at his back.

"Anna," he started. "I'm sorry you had—"

"Do I have time to use the bathroom?" I cut him off and motioned to the drugstore across the street.

He looked crestfallen, but he nodded. "Yeah. I think that'd be okay."

Inside, with the door locked behind me, I took a huge, gulping breath and tried to cool the burning in my eyes. I washed my hands, scanned my reflection in the mirror. I hadn't showered that morning, and my blond hair looked dull, like dried, cracked wheat. My eyes were heavy. I looked tired but, shockingly, not disturbed, like I hadn't just watched Sam kill all those people. I still looked like Anna.

But I didn't feel like her at all.

I met Trev in the pet food aisle. We started for the front of the store.

"You know, you don't have to be afraid of me," he said. "I'm still the same guy."

I frowned. "I'm not afraid of you."

He tipped his head my way. "The distance between us says maybe you are."

Mentally I calculated the feet separating us. Five. Maybe six.

"It wasn't anything on purpose."

Overgrown black hair hung in Trev's face, hiding a clear view of his soft, amber eyes. I'd always trusted him. In another life, he could have easily been the boy every girl had a crush on because he was clever and good-looking and kind.

I still trusted him. Didn't I?

Outside, Sam met us at the corner. "Go find Cas and Nick in the parking lot out back," he told Trev. Trev glanced my way before heading off at a jog.

The tangy smell of rising yeast in the bakery next door made my stomach growl—a reminder that I hadn't had a chance to eat my toast before Connor showed up. A reminder that nothing was as it should be.

"Are you really going to steal a car?" I asked as I followed Sam in the opposite direction from Trev.

"Yes. Unless you have one we can take."

"No," I said. "I just…I don't know if I'm comfortable with all this."

He gave me a look. "Now is not the time for your morality to make an appearance."

I stopped walking. "What's that supposed to mean? My morality was never gone." When he didn't respond, I plowed on. "You know, I'm starting to wonder if you were ever the guy I knew. Because I don't see the morality on *your* face. I can't see you at all. What happened to the Sam who was my friend?"

He got in close, lowered his voice. "We were never friends, Anna. I was a prisoner in your basement for five years. Before that, I suspect I was with the Branch for several more." A vein in the middle of his forehead swelled. "I wanted out, so I did what I needed to do to win your trust. If you had been in my position, you would have done the same thing."

His words stung. "No, I wouldn't have. You could have asked me." I spread my arms out. "All you had to do was ask for help."

He started to say something and then clamped his mouth shut. The surprised look on his face told me that it had never crossed his mind to come to me. My chest felt hollow, like all the good things I'd experienced with Sam in the last few years had been carved out and mashed to pulp. My life in that lab was a lie.

Tears blurred my vision. I was an idiot to ever think he cared. An idiot to think there was anything special about me. Because there wasn't. I was just another tool he'd used to break free of that lab.

"We should go," he said, his jaw tight as he looked everywhere but at me.

I considered running back to the drugstore and begging for help. Dad needed me. Dad would *want* me around. To Sam, I was nothing more than a burden.

I could escape this, whatever it was. I would leave Sam for good.

"Anna?" He cocked his head to the side, narrowed his eyes. I wondered if he saw the indecision freezing me in place. He didn't push, didn't pull. He gave me the opportunity to escape right then and there.

But I didn't.

I couldn't.

And what did that make me? Pathetic. Sad. Desperate. Dad had made me promise not to come back to the farmhouse. I really had nowhere else to go.

"Lead the way," I said.

So he did.

SAM HAD SEVERAL CRITERIA A VEHI-

cle had to meet before he'd steal it. The vehicle had to be large enough for all of us, it had to have a big engine, and it had to be discreet. Cas was the one who picked the navy blue SUV.

I sat in the passenger seat, slumped down, wondering if anyone would notice us stealing this big vehicle, if someone would call the cops. But we made it to the highway without incident and Treger Creek faded in the rearview mirror.

There really was no going back now. The farther we pulled away from home, the tighter the knot in my chest grew. I ran my fingers down the cracked spine of my mother's journal, glad I'd grabbed it.

"What is that?" Sam asked, gesturing at the book.

I tugged it closer. "It was my mother's."

"Sura," Sam said, and I nodded. It was odd, hearing someone else speak her name. Dad hardly ever did.

Sam headed south, driving at an even sixty miles an hour. The surroundings flashed by in a blur of color. To keep my mind on something other than what was happening, I tried to think of the colored pencils I'd use if I were drawing the landscape. Burnt umber. Cadmium green. Scarlet for the leaves that were starting to change.

"So," Cas said, "any idea where Arthur sent us?"

I felt the weight of Sam's gaze. "Did that address sound familiar to you?"

I shook my head. "I don't know anyone in Pennsylvania. And there was no mention of it in your files."

"It's probably a trap," Nick said. "Arthur is part of the program. I don't know why we're trusting him."

Irritation flooded me and I turned to face Nick. "My dad never wanted to hurt any of you."

The dark scowl returned. "Doesn't mean it isn't a trap."

"Would you rather stay here?" Sam looked up at the rearview mirror, making eye contact with Nick. "I can stop the vehicle so you can bail."

"Yeah," Cas added, "you can hitchhike your way across the country. Just flash your abs. I bet someone would stop."

Nick snorted. "Shut the hell up."

"Damn," Cas said. "You're cranky. We're free! You should be doing the Hokey-frickin'-Pokey!"

"I would rather light myself on fire."

"Awesome." Cas rubbed his hands together. "Anyone have some marshmallows?"

Sam ignored them and punched the address my dad had given him into the portable navigation system on the dashboard. A cool female voice told us where to go. It took us nearly three hours to reach the Pennsylvania border. While Cas and Trev discussed all the things they wanted to eat now that they were free, Sam focused on the road. Nick slept in the back.

I leaned closer to the passenger-side window. I'd never been to Pennsylvania before, but it looked exactly like I thought it would, the land undulating like the sea. I marked pencil strokes in my head to keep myself busy.

No one said it, but I think we all felt like we were being watched. Like Connor was waiting for us to screw up to make his next move. I just wanted to find the safe house Dad had told Sam about.

A freeway sign overhead read EXIT 28. We drove past it and continued southwest for another half hour before the navigation system steered us to an on-ramp. Sam exited, veering sharply to the right, the force of the turn pushing me in his direction. I swept a gaze over his arm, draped on the center compartment, the sleeve of his shirt rolled back to the elbow. Less than forty-eight hours earlier I'd been in the lab, studying him through the glass, studying his scar.

"What are the letters? The scars," I clarified. The others went quiet in the back.

"Uh-uh," Nick muttered. Apparently, he wasn't sleeping after all.

"She read some of our files," Sam said. "Something might stand out if she knew what the letters were."

Cas tapped his fingers on the back of Sam's seat. "Yeah. What'll it hurt if she knows?"

"We're forgetting that she spent the last five years on the other side of the wall," Nick said. "You want my opinion? Tell her nothing and ditch her at the next town."

"I didn't ask for your opinion," Sam warned.

"I'm sitting right here, you know."

"No one's ditching you," Trev said. "He doesn't make the decisions."

Nick draped an arm over the back bench seat. "Oh? And you do?"

"Stop." Sam's voice cut through the argument and the boys went silent. "You've seen the *R* on my chest," he said to me, keeping his attention on the road. "There are more. Another *R*, an *O*, and a *D*."

"I have an *L* on my hip and a *V* on my knee," Cas said.

"I have two *R*s and two *E*s," Trev said.

When I glanced at Nick, he sent a withering glare my way and I shifted back around.

"Don't mind him," Cas said. "He doesn't know how to spell."

Trev suppressed a snicker.

"Nick has an *I* and an *E*," Sam said. He flicked on the blinker as he switched lanes and sped past a semitruck.

I ran over the scar letters in my head, counting them. Twelve total. Four boys. That was three letters per boy, if they'd divided them up evenly. But they hadn't. Trev and Sam had four; Cas and Nick had two. I wished I had a pen to write the letters out. Though I suppose Sam must have already done that a thousand times.

"Could they be a code?"

He shook his head. "Not one I'm familiar with."

We drove for a while longer before Cas's complaints of hunger became too much to bear. Sam pulled off at the next freeway exit, following the signs that directed us to the closest gas station. He parked at a gas pump, with the brightly lit store in front of us. The clock in the vehicle's dashboard said it was ten after seven. The sun had set a good hour before, leaving the sky a drained shade of blue.

Cas was the first one out of the vehicle. He bounded inside.

"Here," Sam said, handing Trev two twenty-dollar bills. I didn't want to know where he'd gotten the money. "Put some gas in the truck. Use the rest on food."

Nick climbed out the back to fill the tank. Trev crammed the money in his pocket and said to me, "Need anything?"

"A bottle of water? Maybe some crackers or something."

Trev glanced at Sam and Sam nodded.

I unsnapped the seat belt and arched my back, stretching my sore muscles. When I settled back in, the silence settled in next to me. The car's engine ticked as it cooled. Sam didn't move an inch. The uneasy quiet slithered along my skin, making me restless, until I couldn't take it anymore.

"When the boys ask for your permission," I said, "does it have to do with the gene manipulation?"

"I think so." The store lights illuminated his profile. This close to him, I could see a tiny bump in the bridge of his nose, like it'd been broken before.

"Are you the leader or something?" I asked, remembering the term *alpha* from his file.

"In a sense."

"What exactly did the alterations do? Do you even know?"

He looked away, toward the far edge of the parking lot, and a sigh escaped his lips. "It made me something more than human, but I can't know how, exactly, until I know who I was before."

"And you think the address my dad gave you is a start to finding your past?"

"Yes."

Through the store windows, I watched Cas and Trev approach the counter and drop armfuls of junk in front of the register. Cas threw in some jerky for good measure before turning his attention to us, in the car. I could also feel Nick watching us from the gas pump. They could tell Sam was uncomfortable.

"You're all connected," I said, realizing it only then. "It's like you know what the others are feeling without actually saying anything."

It reminded me of when Sam and I first started playing chess. He'd fed me tips every now and then because I knew absolutely nothing. He was a genius when it came to strategy.

"It isn't just about the game," he'd said to me one night in the dead of December. That was long before I had permission to be down there, and every breath I took felt amplified in the lab, as if the sound of it would travel through the vents and wake my dad.

"The pieces are only a small part," Sam went on. "You have to know your opponent, too. Study them when they're calculating their next move. Sometimes you can tell where they're going before even they know."

I smirked. "That's not true."

He draped an arm over the back of his chair. "Then try me."

"I always lose. It's hard to prove you're right when we have nothing to compare it to."

A sliver of a laugh had escaped him. "All right. I suppose you have me there."

I looked at him now, his eyes hooded in shadow. He'd always been good at reading me. Better than I was at reading him. But now I wondered if it had more to do with the alterations than with reading facial expressions. Or knowing me in a way that was important, a way that made us friends.

I wanted to ask if he could sense what I was feeling, especially now, but deep down I didn't want to know. I didn't want to suffer the embarrassment.

"What is it like? The connection. How does it work?"

He propped an elbow on the arm rest of the door. "It seems to be based on instinct, and it is hardest to ignore when one of us is uneasy or in trouble. I usually felt something when you drew blood from the others, like I needed to be there to protect them, whether I liked it or not. It's hard focusing on what I want to do when I have to think about everyone else. Ultimately, the decisions I make have to be what's best for the group."

He'd used me all those years, knowing that eventually my trust would aid him in their escape. As much as it hurt to know this, I could see the logic. I could see how far down his need to protect the others reached. And it was because of the alterations that had been programmed into him. He had no choice.

"And now?" I said. "Who are you thinking about now?"

He parted his lips and I stilled, wanting to hear his answer more than anything. I wanted to know if I was under his protection. Though if I was, I wasn't sure what that meant for me, or even how it would make me feel.

Mostly I wanted to know if he thought of me at all.

Just then Cas bounded up to the SUV. "Sweet Baby Jesus, look what I found!" He slammed into my door with a gigantic grin on his face and held up a package of Twinkies. "See?"

I laughed. "I see." I turned back to Sam as he started the car. "What were you going to say?"

"Nothing."

The boys climbed in back. The radio cut in, playing the pop music Cas loved, and I could see Sam shutting down again.

Maybe he wouldn't have answered, anyway.

———

As we traveled farther south, I flipped through my mother's journal, trying to pass the time, even though I had memorized the entries a long time ago.

I drew my fingers over the slant of her writing, the pen's indentation a leftover piece of her.

> Went to the lake today. It was nice getting away from work.
> Lately, I feel less connected to what I'm doing.
> What would they do if I left?

Dad had told me that she used to work for a medical company.

I flipped to the last page she wrote on, a few dozen pages from the back.

> I am quitting. For good. I have to believe in what my heart is telling me, and it's telling me to go. I am both scared and happy.
> I am liberated.

"Turn right," the navigation system intoned. "In. One. Point. Two. Miles."

Sam turned as instructed.

There weren't many houses on Holicer Lane. As we drove the road climbed higher, winding back and forth like a snake. Trees hung over the street, creating a tunnel that darkened the night. The vehicle's headlights caught reflective tape on the next house's mailbox, and it shone metallic yellow as we passed.

I read the address: 4332.

"Turn left," the navigation said a few minutes later. "You have reached your destination."

Sam stopped in the middle of the street. The house we were looking for was dead and black. Not a single light blazed in the windows. The driveway was empty, the garage door shut tight. An old Jeep sat beside the garage, but the grass around the tires was tall, like the Jeep hadn't been moved in a while.

Our vehicle idled, the engine the only sound between the five of us.

"Now what?" Trev said.

Sam pulled into the stub of a driveway and left the car running. Just in case. He didn't have to say it for me to know the line of his thoughts. Maybe this wasn't a safe house after all. Maybe my dad had set him up.

"Stay in the car," he said.

"It's empty," I said. "The house."

He leaned out the open door and threw a look over his shoulder at me. "How do you know?"

I didn't. I didn't even know why I'd said anything. But instinct told me it was empty. "I'm not sitting in the car."

As if my stubbornness gave him an excuse, Cas bounded out of the vehicle. "Yeah, dude. We've been driving for an eternity. Time to stretch the gluteus."

Sam shut the SUV off and started for the house.

The boys and I followed.

The house was a plain two-story with little character and even less paint. The shadows deepened beneath the flakes still clinging to the old wood siding. A rickety screen door had been propped open by a rusty milk can, the screen torn in one corner.

Sam tried the inside door, and it popped open without complaint. We filed into a laundry room. The scent of soap hung in the air. Sam slid his gun out from beneath his flannel shirt.

Farther in, a dining room chair lay on its back. A cupboard door stood open, like someone had rummaged through it and hadn't the time to slam it shut. The hair at the nape of my neck bristled. The floor creaked beneath our feet. A faucet dripped in the kitchen and an old grandfather clock ticked in the hall.

I rounded a corner into the living room. Sam went down a hallway. Cas shadowed me, while Nick disappeared with Trev to the back of the house.

"What do you think happened here?" I asked.

A half-full cup of tea sat on an end table next to an easy chair. A stack of magazines had been knocked over and fanned out like cards across the coffee table. A folded newspaper lay on the floor. I checked the date: yesterday.

"I don't know," Cas said. "If this was a safe house, it isn't anymore."

A sticky note had been stuck to an end table right next to a cordless phone. I ripped it from the glass top and instantly went numb.

The writing. A tight, cursive slant. I knew that writing.

Check in with P @ 6PM

I returned the note to its spot on the table and inhaled deeply. It couldn't be. It wasn't.

I started for the kitchen but froze when I passed a collection of art on the wall above the couch. My skin prickled. The framed piece at the far right was a watercolor painting of the birch trees tattooed on Sam's back.

"What is it?" Cas asked.

"That's Sam's tattoo," I said, realizing Cas probably hadn't seen the real thing, since the boys had never been allowed out of their rooms.

I snatched the frame from the wall and inspected the back. It was sealed on all sides.

Cas gestured at the end table. "Smash it."

"But…" I wasn't sure what stopped me. There was no one here, and this was clearly a clue. But breaking something that wasn't mine seemed wrong.

"Fine." Cas grabbed the painting. "I'll do it."

With one swift move, he whacked the frame against the edge of the table and the glass shattered. The picture slid out, and with it a note. The crisp half sheet of paper fluttered toward the floor and I plucked it from the air as the others clustered behind us.

"What happened?" Trev asked. "We shouldn't touch anything, just in case."

"Anna found something." Cas nudged me, like we were teammates who'd scored a goal together. "So, what's it say?"

I ran my eyes over the note and gasped.

A FEW HOURS EARLIER, I'D RUN MY
fingers over the familiar words written by my mother in her journal.
Here, now, were new words, foreign words that I hadn't memorized
but were eerily similar. It looked like her handwriting.

"Anna?" The look Sam gave me—pinched brow, pursed lips—
said he knew something was wrong. So I started reading aloud,
purposefully dodging the questions before he had a chance to ask
them.

"'Sam, if you're reading this, it means I'm not there to give you the
message myself. And if I'm not there, that must mean I'm either dead or I
had to leave in a hurry.

"'Since I am not there, I will give you the key you gave me. You'll
need a UV light. There's one in the kitchen. First drawer on the right.'"

I met Sam's eyes. "That's it."

As he reached for the note, a car turned into the driveway, the glare of its headlights shining through the front window curtains, illuminating us. There was a split second when no one moved. And then everyone moved but me.

A car door shut. "Mrs. Tucker?" someone called. "You home?"

I hurried after Sam, keeping my steps light, silent.

A knock sounded on the door. "Mrs. Tucker? Chancy said you didn't show for tonight's potluck."

I poked my head into the kitchen. Sam hid inside the laundry room doorway, the overturned chair now in his hands, hoisted over his shoulder. Blood rushed through my ears as the back door creaked open.

I caught movement inside the bathroom. Nick, crouching, ready to strike. My mouth went dry.

"Mrs. Tucker? You in here?" the man said, his voice now on edge. He made slow progress through the laundry room, up the one step to the kitchen, and then: "Hands up!"

Sam swung the chair. It exploded when it hit the man, slivers plinking against the floor. A gun smacked against the countertop, then dropped to the floor. It wasn't Sam's. It was the man's gun—the *cop's* gun.

The cop sank to his knees. Blood ran from the split flesh on his forehead. He scrambled for the gun, now lying four feet behind him, as Nick stepped out of the bathroom brandishing a metal wastebasket. He positioned it low to the ground, cocked back like a golf club, aiming for the cop's head.

"Stop!"

Nick froze mid-stride and frowned at me.

"He's a cop," I blurted. Like that somehow explained it.

"So?"

The man spat blood onto the floor, then wiped the excess from the corner of his mouth.

"He's innocent."

"We don't know that," Nick countered.

Cas popped up behind me. "Clear outside," he said, and Sam gave a definitive nod. Where was Trev?

"Trust no one," Nick argued, still holding the wastebasket like a weapon. A lock of hair fell across his forehead.

Sam grabbed the cop by the collar of his jacket and hauled the man to his feet. He slammed him into the fridge, pinning him in place. The man grimaced.

"What are you doing here?" Sam bit the words out.

"I came to check on Mrs. Tucker."

"Why?"

"She didn't show up to the town potluck." The man looked from Sam to me, and then back to Sam. "Never misses one without letting someone know."

If Mrs. Tucker was the woman Dad had sent us to, and she was gone, had Connor gotten to her? Was she somehow connected to the Branch?

Trev came through a side door. "I didn't see anything down the street. No stakeouts." Sweat glistened on his forehead.

Nick tossed the wastebasket into the bathroom. "Let's get the hell out of here."

"I don't usually side with Ol' Crotchety Pants," Cas said, "but I'm on board with that."

Sam's grip on the cop loosened. "Someone grab the UV light. And see if one of you can find a set of keys for the Jeep by the garage."

Cas went to the row of keys hanging from separate hooks near the door. Trev squeezed past me and tugged open the first drawer in search of the light. He pulled out a small box and checked its contents. "Got it."

Cas shook a set of keys. "I'll see if I can get the Jeep started." He disappeared outside.

The cop slumped against the fridge. He wasn't very old. Mid-twenties, maybe. Buzz-cut hair, like Sam's, except the cop was blond, tan, and slight in build, whereas Sam was tall and broad-shouldered.

"We don't know Mrs. Tucker," Sam said, "and we didn't come here intending to hurt anyone. We're going to walk out of here, and you're not going to follow."

The cop acknowledged the order with a slow nod, and Sam let him go. Trev and Nick made their way to the door. Sam motioned me forward. I sidestepped the pile of splinters, skirting around the cop. As I passed he reached for me, but Sam was quicker.

Sam snatched the man's wrist, threw a punch. The cop crashed to the floor with a howl.

"Go," Sam said, pushing me through the laundry room. Out the door. Down the driveway. "Get your mother's journal."

I grabbed it from the SUV while Cas wheeled the Jeep around.

Sam popped the hood of the cop car and yanked at the hoses; something hissed in return. Nick tore out the computer, smashed the radio.

Trev slid into the Jeep as Cas abandoned the driver's seat for Sam. I climbed into the passenger side.

Five seconds later, Sam was behind the Jeep's wheel. He tore through the yard, kicking up clumps of grass with the spin of the tires. When we were out of the hills, far away from the house, he slammed on the brakes.

I braced myself with a hand on the dash. Trev hit the backside of my seat with an *umph*. A cloud of dust swirled past us, dancing in the glare of the headlights.

"What the hell?" Nick said.

Sam twisted sideways. He leaned toward me and I took a shuddering breath. "What aren't you telling me about the note?"

My mouth went dry. "Nothing."

"Don't play dumb."

I couldn't tell him what I thought I saw, that the writing was similar to my mother's. I was too tired, too stressed. I was seeing things.

"I'm not *playing* anything."

I wiped any shred of emotion from my face as Sam analyzed me. Before I knew what he was doing, he had my mother's journal open in his lap, the note spread out over its pages. I scrambled for it, but he pushed me away.

Now he would see how crazy I was. He would know I saw my mother where she couldn't possibly be. It was wishful thinking.

When he met my eyes a moment later, I shrank away.

"It's your mother's handwriting."

"Holy shit," Cas said.

Trev leaned forward to see for himself.

"Great," Nick muttered.

I shook my head. My mother was dead. DEAD. My father wouldn't lie about something as big as that. Furthermore, Mrs. Tucker, or whoever she was, knew Sam. My mother couldn't possibly know him.

"It's just a coincidence," I said meekly.

Trev cleared his throat. "Things are rarely coincidental. It's a lazy excuse."

I scowled at him. Wasn't he supposed to be on my side? "I'm not trying to make excuses." He, out of all the boys, knew how badly I wanted my mother in my life. I didn't want to hope—because it would hurt worse when I found out it wasn't true. "My mother is dead. That's a fact, not an excuse."

The boys stared at me in the murky dark.

I didn't have the energy or the confidence to argue with them. Doubt filled my head. It *did* look like her writing. And I should know; I'd spent almost every day for the last five years reading her journal cover to cover time and again.

If she was alive . . .

I struggled to picture that house again. The kitchen. The color of the walls. The smell of the living room. I tried to see the things "Mrs. Tucker" had surrounded herself with, trying to decide if I saw my mother.

But it was no use. I hadn't paid close enough attention until I found the sticky note, and by then it was too late.

"We should go," I said. "The cop has probably called for backup by now." When no one moved, I shouted, "Sam! Go!"

Sam pulled onto the road and pointed us toward the freeway.

10

A FEW MONTHS EARLIER, TREV AND I
had had a conversation about mothers, and families in general.

"Families are important," he'd said. "Families define who we become."

I'd thought of my dad. If he defined who I became, I'd be a work-aholic with no life outside the lab. Sometimes that didn't seem so bad, though, if Sam and the others were there.

"Do you miss your mother?" Trev had asked.

I leaned a hip against the glass wall. "I miss the idea of her."

"You and I are the sum of a void left by the absence of someone we love."

"I don't even know what that means."

He smirked. "It means I understand your pain."

If I'd thought I didn't have anything in common with the boys, that conversation with Trev had proved otherwise.

"Have you ever thought about what you'd say or do if you finally met your mother?" I'd asked.

Trev had answered without hesitation. "I would memorize everything about her—how she looked, how she smelled—so that if I lost her again, I would always have her."

There were so many things I didn't know about my mother. She was as much a mystery to me as Sam was. Even though I had her journal, it wasn't the same as having her.

I wanted it to be true. I wanted her to be alive. I wanted to have a second chance, to see her for myself. Sketch her in my mind and memorize her.

"We should probably stop for the night, don't you think?" Trev said as he and Cas divided a leftover Twinkie.

"We need to put more distance between us and the cops," Sam said. "We'll get a room soon."

"Then how about we talk food?" Cas said. "Particularly something that starts with *ice* and ends with *cream*."

A car passed on the opposite side of the road, its headlights illuminating Sam's face. An overhead freeway sign said we were on course for Brethington.

I leaned between the seats to look at Cas. "Do you ever stop eating?"

He shrugged. "No. Why?"

"'To keep the body in good health is a duty....'" Trev said, pulling out one of his quotes. "'Otherwise we shall not be able to keep our mind strong and clear.'"

Cas snorted. "Who said that? The Dalai frickin' Lama?"

"Buddha."

"Yeah, well, wasn't it George Washington who said, 'Be careful about reading health books. You may die of a misprint'?"

"Oh, good one," I said.

Trev sighed. "Mark Twain said that."

"Close enough." Cas crossed his arms.

I poked him in the knee. "What would we do without you?"

"Die of boredom."

"Or prosper in the silence," Trev added as he looked out the window.

———————

After nine, Sam pulled off the freeway and into a small town. We stopped at the first hotel we saw, a basic national chain that stood behind a strip mall. Trev and I did the checking-in part, and lied about our personal information. It seemed to work especially well once we handed the clerk a few extra twenties.

We met the others at the hotel's side entrance. "Rooms 220 and 222." Trev held up the cards. "How are we splitting up?"

Sam snatched a key for himself. "Anna and Cas with me."

Trev met my eyes. "Is that all right with you?"

"Um..."

"Anna is with me," Sam repeated.

Trev held up his hands. "All right. Calm down."

The others went inside. I hurried ahead of Sam, stopping him at the door. "What was that for? Trev was just being gracious enough to ask my opinion. Which you seem to have a hard time doing."

He bent closer and lowered his voice. "I promised your father I would keep you safe. I can't do that if you're not even in the same room as me."

I frowned. "I don't think that's what my dad meant."

"Then what did he mean?"

Had Dad meant for Sam to protect me from *everything*? Even the other boys? "Never mind," I said. I was too tired to argue what my dad's intentions were. Besides, I wasn't sure I'd ever know what he meant to accomplish by sending me away in the first place.

A tiny voice in my head said maybe he'd wanted me to meet my mother. Maybe he knew exactly who he was sending us to, and what it would mean. But why lie all those years? What purpose would keeping her from me serve?

I shook the tangle of questions out of my thoughts and tugged the door open. Maroon carpet quieted our footsteps up the stairs. Nick and Trev were already inside their room by the time Sam and I joined Cas at our door.

Sam let me go in first. I held my journal in one hand and fumbled for the light switch with the other. There were two double beds directly in front of me. A table and chairs. A TV. The maroon carpet followed us in from the hall, ending at the doorway to the small bathroom, where dingy white tile took over.

Cas moved past me and dropped down on the bed, the frame squeaking in response. "Sweet Jesus, I'm frickin' exhausted."

"Actually, I think that's a sugar crash," I said.

He fluffed the pillows. "Well, if it is, it was worth it."

Sam sat at the table in the corner and opened the package containing the UV light. I fell into the chair across from him. "Any ideas on that yet?"

"No." He flicked on the light and the bulb glowed purple.

Behind us, Cas rifled through the drawer in the end table. "One Bible, two phone books, and a take-out menu. Awesome." He slammed the drawer shut.

Sam unscrewed the top of the UV light and the plastic cap plinked against the table as he set it down. "Are you ready to talk about what we found at that house?"

I rubbed the corners of my eyes. "There's nothing to talk about."

He popped out the light's batteries. "That's not true and you know it."

"Anna takes being naïve to a whole new level," Cas interjected. "Remember that time we convinced her we'd developed our own language?" He let out a roar of laughter. "*Pavaloo dunkin roop*, which means—"

"'May I have some Amazonian swine,'" I recited. "I remember.

But it was mostly you doing the convincing, and I rarely believe a word you say, anyway."

"A wise choice," Sam said.

"Hey now." Cas bounced off the edge of the bed to his feet. "In medieval times I would have been worshipped for my stories. They would have named a castle after me."

"I doubt that."

He shook his head as he made his way to the bathroom. "I need some peace and quiet. Maybe I'll take a long, hot bath. With bubbles." He shut the door but failed to lock it. Not that he was ever concerned with modesty.

Water rushed through the pipes when Cas turned on the faucet. It was the only sound in the room. I held my mother's journal closer.

"So?" Sam said.

I slouched. "All right, fine. I admit that the handwriting is similar to my mother's, but it doesn't mean—"

"The slant of the *E*s is identical on both samples." He inspected the bulb of the UV light while he talked. "The *L*s and *D*s are exaggerated. The *S*s curl back and loop. They're the same."

He held the bulb overhead, letting the ceiling light shine through the glass.

"My dad would never lie about something as unforgivable as that. Besides, didn't you say you trusted him?"

"Yes, but that doesn't mean he's always been truthful. Like our memories, or lack of. I don't buy for one second that it's a 'side effect' of the treatments."

"Then how—" I stopped myself when I picked up his line of thought. "You think your memories were deliberately tampered with?" I scoffed. "No way. First of all, how is that even possible? And second of all . . . no. Dad wouldn't do that."

Sam set the bulb on the table and met my eyes. I could see the dull green striations in his irises. I'd spent so long looking at him through a wall of glass that it was stunning seeing him with nothing but air between us. I imagined what it would be like to draw him now, in full, vivid color. The lines it would take to create the strong sweep of his jaw, the arrowhead shape of his nose. The bow of his lips.

"Why were we locked away for so long?" he asked, his voice measured, steady. "Did you ever wonder about that?"

I tugged at the sleeves of my henley. "You were being made into soldiers."

He snapped the bulb into the light's frame, taking his eyes off me for only a second. "If you're trying to make the ultimate weapon, you don't lock it in a basement for five years. You put it on the field and test and alter it until it's perfect."

"Maybe that's what they were doing. You received treatments all the time. And the logs . . . we were tracking your progress. . . ."

He clicked one final piece into place. "The four of us—our first memories are exactly the same. If the amnesia was a side effect of the treatments, there's no way it would have cleaned us of everything up until the exact same moment in time."

Wiped. I'd read the term in Sam's file the previous night. I didn't want to believe it, but more and more, it made sense.

"What does any of this have to do with me and my mother?"

He flipped the black light on again and it glowed between us. "I don't know, but if your mother was connected to the Branch, then you are, too, and we need to figure out why."

I sighed and rubbed at my eyes with the heels of my hands. I couldn't take any more. I muttered something about being tired and crawled into bed. I just wanted to be alone to sort through my thoughts. Not that it would help. Sam raised a lot of good questions that I was too afraid to face. And it all hinged on the simple fact that the handwriting on the note left for him looked awfully similar to my mother's. Maybe it really was a coincidence. Maybe we were blowing the connection way out of proportion.

I needed rest. Things would be clearer in the morning.

But I didn't make it that far. Sam nudged me awake two hours later. "Hey," he said. "Get up. I found something."

11

I PROPPED MYSELF UP ON AN ELBOW.
"What is it?"

A shred of moonlight shone across the foot of my bed. It was the only light in the room. I could barely make out Sam's face as he stood over me.

"Come to the bathroom."

I slid out from beneath the blanket, set my feet on the floor. It was just Sam and me in the room. "Where's Cas?"

"He's getting the others."

I shuffled after Sam, and once we were inside the bathroom, he shut the door. The total darkness disoriented me. I didn't like dark, small, enclosed spaces, and the bathroom was the size of a closet. I stumbled backward, ramming into the towel rack. "What is going on?"

The black light flicked on, weakly illuminating the strong edges of Sam's face. "I'm not going to hurt you," he said, sounding almost offended. He shoved the light into my hand, then tore off his T-shirt and tossed it onto the counter. "Put the light to the small of my back."

I stood there motionless for far too long, looking from the light in my hand to Sam's shirtless back, convinced that I was stuck in some sort of dream world.

I'd never been this close to Sam's tattoo before. From the tops of the trees to the grass at the bottom, the tattoo covered a good portion of his back and arms. Whoever had done the work had shaded everything perfectly, catching the fine details and curling peels of the birch bark. There was only one mistake I could find: The trees' shadows were all wrong. Their sizes and shapes didn't match the trees they were attached to, and the two shadows at the left blended together, but the corresponding trees didn't overlap.

I moved the light back and forth over the tattoo as Sam had instructed. "What exactly am I looking for?"

"Look in the grass."

I bent down. "I don't think I see—" Something shone in the hazy light and I sucked in a breath. The writing was tiny and faded, but it glowed like one of those neon necklaces every kid wears at a Fourth of July parade.

"How is that possible?" I said.

"It's UV ink, tattooed into the skin on top of the visible tattoo. Read it," Sam said. "Please."

Over time, the lines had lost their clarity and the letters had blurred together, but I was able to make out the first word. "*Rose. Rose* something."

I heard the room door open and the others' voices rumbling outside the bathroom door. "Where is he?" Trev asked.

"Must be in the bathroom with Anna," Cas answered.

A knock sounded on the door. "Anna? Sam?" Trev said. "You okay?"

"Give us a minute," Sam replied. To me he said, "What else?"

"There are two more words." I got in closer, readjusting the halo of light. "How did you even know to look for this?"

"The letter scars made me think of it. I would have known my body was the only thing I could take with me if the Branch wiped my memories. When I took the UV light to my back, I saw something, but couldn't make it out."

"Why didn't you ask Cas to help you?"

He didn't answer for a long time, and the stillness made me anxious. I felt like the walls were closing in on me. But I was here, with Sam. So close I could feel the heat of his body. As much as I wanted to escape the confined space, I didn't want it to end, either.

Finally he said, "I'm not in the mood for Cas's sarcasm right now." He exhaled loudly. "Besides, I had to send him for the others."

"I think the last word is *Ohio*," I said, wishing the tingling crawling up my spine would dissipate. "The middle one..." I tried to assemble the word letter by letter, hoping to put as much of it together as I could, like a crossword puzzle. "*C. E. M* or *N*, maybe. *A*? *T. E. K*...no, *R. Y*." I ran the letters over in my head, mouthing them as I scanned the word again. *CEMATERY*.

"The *A* is an *E*," Sam said.

"*Cemetery*. Rose Cemetery, Ohio."

Sam snatched up his T-shirt, bumping into me as he did. His eyes met mine in the weak light. "Sorry."

I pushed the hair from my face. "It's fine. I'm fine."

"Thank you. For doing this." He took the black light from my hands and clicked it off, plunging us back into darkness.

"You can always come to me for help." As soon as the words left my lips, I grimaced. It sounded so lame and pathetic. *Please need me, Sam.*

When he answered, his voice came out husky. "What I said yesterday, outside the drugstore—"

"You don't have to explain."

"I know, but I need you—"

"Sam?" Trev cut him off and Sam shifted away. He tore open the door, meeting Trev face-to-face. Someone had turned on the desk lamp and its light spilled into the bathroom, washing away the dark and the intimacy it had created.

"Did you find something?" Trev asked, his eyes locking on mine. A blush spread across my cheeks.

Sam tugged his T-shirt over his head. "Yes. Pack up. We're leaving."

"Where the hell are we going now?" Nick snapped. "And why in the middle of the night?"

Sam put the flannel back on and unrolled the sleeves. "I'm not going to sit here until dawn so you can sleep. I've been waiting too long for this. Now get your stuff and let's go."

Sam met us at the Jeep after checking out. He handed Cas two beat-up flashlights.

Cas pressed the button on one of them and a circle of light shone on the dashboard. "What are these for?"

"We're going to a cemetery." Sam pulled out of the parking lot.

"And where is this cemetery?" Cas asked.

"Rose Cemetery in Lancaster, Ohio. I had the hotel clerk look it up."

For the next three hours we traveled in total silence. I leaned my head against the window, closed my eyes, and fell asleep. When the car stopped again, I grumbled at the soreness in my neck. In addition to the scant two hours of sleep in the hotel, I had been cramped in a vehicle for almost a full day.

"What exactly are we looking for?" Trev asked from behind me.

I looked out the Jeep's window at the darkened cemetery, muddled silhouettes rising here and there.

"I don't know." Sam rested his forearms at the top of the steering wheel. "Let's start by checking the headstones."

"Dude," Cas said, "that's going to take forever."

"If we split up, it'll only take an hour or two."

The others sounded doubtful, but at that point, we didn't really have a choice. Years before, when Sam had planted the UV tattoo clue, it would have been something he knew he'd be able to figure out. So if the answer was here, we'd find it.

We climbed from the vehicle, following the gravel road into the cemetery. Though I knew it was only my mind playing tricks on me, the cemetery felt creepier than the world outside it and I couldn't shake the goose bumps rising along my skin.

"Nick, head to the far back," Sam said. "Trev opposite him. Cas to the right. I'll take the left. And Anna..."

"I'll stick here to the middle, if you want."

"Cas, give Anna one of the flashlights."

I gladly took the offering.

The others dispersed and silently I cursed myself for wanting to appear strong and useful. Now I was stuck alone in the middle of a cemetery at four AM.

I went to the end of a row of gravesites. Marble statues rose up from the jagged line of headstones, their pale forms seeming to glow against the darkness. I passed an angel with a cascade of marble hair falling over her shoulders. Her eyes were two blank orbs, but it still felt like she watched me.

A shiver raced down my back and I folded my arms around myself, stifling it. I read the names on the headstones as I passed, and the sentiments printed beneath.

BEVERLY BROKLE. 1934–1994. BELOVED WIFE AND MOTHER.

STUART CHIMMER. 1962–1999. YOU WILL BE MISSED.

Dad had promised for the last few years that we'd visit my mother's grave in Indiana as soon as he was able to take a break from the lab. I'd never really counted on the vacation; I knew it wouldn't happen. But now I wondered if the grave even existed.

If my mother was alive, why did she leave me? Did she not want me? I wished I could call my dad and confront him. I wanted answers.

Once I'd reached the end of the first row, I started down the second, running my flashlight over everything, looking for something that didn't quite fit. I read a few odd engravings. Like Michael Tenner, whose headstone read, I KILLED THE CAT. SORRY, LOVE. And Laura Basker's headstone, which read, DON'T CRY FOR ME. THERE IS NO LAUNDRY IN HEAVEN!

I didn't think Sam's planted clue would be about laundry, but I made a mental note of the odd headstones anyway. By the time I'd reached the back part of my section, I hadn't found anything that stood out, and I'd counted a total of eight gravesites with the name Samuel on the headstones.

I caught sight of Cas off to the right, his shoulders hunched as he inspected a big monument with a cross rising from the top. I shut off the flashlight and stuck it in my pocket, sauntering over to meet him.

"Did you find anything?"

"Zilch." He stepped back from the monument and ran his hands through his blond hair, leaving it in unkempt spikes. "This seems pretty useless, doesn't it? Don't tell Sammy, but I think this is a dead end. Pun intended."

I smirked. "Yeah, but it took a while to figure out the UV-light clue. We've only been at this for an hour or so."

Cas raised his eyebrows. "And you want to hang out in a cemetery for eight hours? I don't. I want a damn pizza."

"Aren't you mildly curious to see what this all means?"

He picked up a twig tangled in the weeds and twirled it around. "I don't know. Who cares who I was before? Maybe I was a country club snob with one of these"—he held up the stick—"shoved up his ass."

I snorted. "I doubt that. Sam seems to think this is important."

"Maybe." Cas looked up as footsteps scuffed through the leaves behind us.

"You find anything?" Nick said.

"I found a twig."

"No, dumbass, did you find anything *important*?"

A short, shrill whistle sounded through the cemetery.

Trev.

We ran to the back corner. I ducked beneath the arm of a Celtic cross and fell in behind the boys at the gravesite. Overhead, the bare branches of an old tree creaked in the wind. My hair flew in my face and I turned, facing the wind, facing Sam.

"What is it?" he asked, the moonlight catching the beads of sweat on his forehead.

Trev gestured at a small headstone made of granite, the front face smooth and shiny. "There are no dates."

I read the engraving—SAMUEL CAVAR—and gasped. "Samuel Cavar was an alias you used," I said to Sam. "I read about it in your file."

"*Cavar* is Spanish," he said. "It means 'to dig.'"

Cas pushed up his sleeves. "Well, then, *amigos*, I guess we *cavar* the shit out of this grave."

12

SAM HAD BROKEN INTO A MAINTENANCE
garage toward the back of the cemetery, where he found two shovels.
Cas, Trev, and Nick took turns digging alongside Sam. Sam hadn't
rotated out yet. Sweat covered the front of his T-shirt. His pants were
caked with dirt. If he'd buried something here years ago, he'd buried it deep. Only his head and shoulders were visible over the
mouth of the hole.

"You don't think you're digging up a body, do you?" I said, click-
ing off the flashlight. The sky had brightened to a chill shade of gray
and the sun threatened to peek over the horizon.

"I doubt it." He hefted more dirt onto the pile, then struck down
again. A sound rang out as the metal point of the shovel hit something metal in the ground. Cas tossed his shovel aside and got down

on his hands and knees. He and Sam cleared away the wet soil, revealing a box.

I peered inside the hole.

"What is it?" Trev asked, shifting his weight from one foot to the other.

Sam put his hands to the edge of the hole and hoisted himself out, biceps bulging. "Hand it up," he said to Cas.

Cas lifted the box and passed it off. I crouched next to Sam as, with some effort, he popped open the lid. The hinges were rusty and packed with mud, but once he got them moving, they gave way easily enough. Inside the box lay a key and a tri-folded stack of paper tied tight with twine. Sam slid the twine off and unfurled the document, leaving smudged fingerprints behind.

The paper was old and brittle, but the writing was still legible. I couldn't help reading over his shoulder, adrenaline spiking like a jolt through my veins. This was it. This was what we'd been searching for since yesterday.

From what I could tell, it was the deed to a house, which would explain the key. I scanned the pertinent information. The address: Whittier, Michigan. The person named as owner was Samuel Marshall. Another alias, most likely. Which made me wonder: What *was* his true name?

"Is any of this familiar?" I asked him.

"No."

"But it's something, right? I mean…it's a step."

He gave a barely perceptible nod.

Behind us, the boys filled the hole in a fraction of the time it had taken to dig it. Cas and Trev patted down the disturbed earth. Nick sauntered over to Sam's side. "So, what did you find?"

Sam held up the deed. "It might be a safe house."

"Yeah, like the last one?"

"No one's making you stay, Nick. You got somewhere else to be, you can leave whenever you want."

Nick leaned against the trunk of a nearby tree and crossed his arms over his chest.

As Trev attended to the hole, replacing the scalped sod, Cas said, "I gotta take a piss," and disappeared. Sam returned the shovels to the maintenance shed, leaving me to awkwardly stand by as Nick sulked.

"I think he's doing his best." The statement was punctuated with a white cloud of my breath.

Nick shoved his hands into his pants pockets. He must have been freezing without a jacket. "Self-preservation is more important than figuring out these clues, like it's some shitty board game."

"It's hard to protect yourself when you don't even know who you are or why you were part of the program to begin with."

Nick pushed off the tree with one foot and set his steely blue eyes on me. "I might not remember who I was before all this, but I can bet it wasn't all sunshine and fucking roses."

The hard edges of his scowl softened, but just barely. Seeing an opening, I said, "Your parents might be out there somewhere, looking for you."

"Or maybe not. Maybe they never cared to begin with." He stalked off before the others returned, leaving me to wonder: Was he right? Were the answers to the questions worse than not knowing?

13

AFTER WE LEFT LANCASTER, DREARY clouds blotted out the sun, spitting rain against the windshield. Back at home, Dad had watched the weather report every morning. If I got up early enough, I'd make some coffee and join him in the living room. But I always knew what the weather was supposed to be like whether I watched or not. Dad warned me about the forecast if he thought it important.

It bothered me that I hadn't prepared for this weather, never mind the fact that we weren't in New York. I was so used to knowing everything. The weather. My school schedule for the day. My to-do list for the lab. I didn't know anything anymore. I didn't even know where my next meal would come from.

Using the map Sam had bought at a gas station, we drove through

Whittier—a small town with country charm fit for a nostalgic post-card. A big banner strung up over the main road said the town's Pumpkin Palooza was scheduled for the following weekend. Scare-crows stood like sentries in front of the little shops.

The downtown strip faded behind us as we headed farther and farther north. When we started down the road indicated on the deed, Sam reached over and turned off the pop song playing on the radio. Silence inflated like a life raft, filling the spaces around us. I wrung my hands. What would we do if this house was a dead end?

We drove up and down the long dirt road, checking mailboxes. None of the addresses matched the one on the house deed, but maybe that was deliberate. Finally, we spotted an overgrown track leading back into the woods, the drive located where our address should be, between 2156 and 2223.

As Sam pulled into the driveway, Nick racked a bullet in the chamber of one of the guns. Cas and Trev followed suit, all of them working in perfect synchronization.

About a mile from the road, the trees thinned out, giving way to a clearing. A cabin sat in the middle. Even in the shade of the storm clouds and in its state of disrepair, the cabin still managed to look homey. The shake-shingle exterior was weathered and faded to the perfect shade of red. A few rusty lawn chairs sat on a crooked porch, an empty flowerpot forgotten between them. A dead tree branch hung off the porch as if it had fallen there in a storm and had never been moved.

The windows were dark and covered in a thin sheet of dust and dirt. The only car in the driveway was ours. The place looked empty, but despite that, it *felt* empty, the loneliness hanging in the air like old tobacco smoke, waiting for someone to blow it away.

"What now?" I said. Rain continued to plink against the windshield, the drops becoming fatter and more frequent.

"Nick and Cas around back," Sam said. "I'll take the front door. Trev, stay here with Anna."

I didn't want to sit idly in the vehicle, but I didn't want to search the house, either. I was afraid of what I'd do if I found more evidence of my mother.

The boys exited the vehicle with the sort of silent agility that contradicted their size. Nick and Cas ran around back, guns at their sides. Sam went right, to the tiny garage that sat detached from the house. He checked the lone window there before leaping onto the house's front porch and sliding along the wall.

At the front door, he pulled out the key he'd found in the cemetery and tried the lock. The key worked, the door opened, and he disappeared inside.

"What do you think?" I whispered.

Trev propped an elbow on his knee. "It seems safe."

"More so than the one in Pennsylvania."

"Agreed." I felt him watching me. "There's nothing wrong with hoping."

I turned around. "For what?"

"Your mother."

I didn't know what to say to that. Hearing someone else talk about my mother made it more real, like it was possible she was inside that cabin, waiting for me.

"What if she isn't alive?" I slumped against the seat. "What if all this wishing is for nothing?"

"'In all things it is better to hope than to despair.'"

"Whose quote is that?"

Trev smirked, folding his hands together. He loved it when I asked him for more information, when I gave him the opportunity to show off. "Johann Wolfgang von Goethe."

"What's the Aristotle one? The one about hope?"

His eyes lost focus as he dug for the quote I wanted. I could see the moment when he remembered it, the glimmer returning to his amber eyes. I'd never met anyone with a real lightbulb expression like Trev's.

"'Hope is a waking dream.'"

I let the words echo in my head. The quote reminded me of that feeling you get when you start to wake from a dream you don't want to leave. That crushing sensation in the center of your chest, like you are losing an important piece of yourself you won't ever get back.

That's what hope was. Clinging to something you weren't sure would ever be yours. But you had to hold on anyway, because without it, what was the point?

That fit my life perfectly, in so many ways. Even more so now.

Sam reappeared on the front porch and waved for us, which I thought revealed enough of what he'd found. If my mother had been inside, he would have come out to warn me himself. So she wasn't waiting. And even though I'd told myself I wouldn't believe she'd be there, I had. The eagerness burned out and crackled.

We entered into a living room, where a few armchairs faced a brick fireplace. A couch rested against the far wall. Cobwebs hung like Spanish moss from a brass lamp.

A large kitchen took up the back corner of the other side of the house. A long, rectangular table filled the space to the right of the front door. Directly in front of me, stairs led up to the second floor.

Thunder followed a flash of lightning, the low rumble reverberating through the bare wood floors. Rain continued to patter against the windows, washing away the dirt. I pulled my jacket closed as the wind kicked up and crept through the cabin's cracks.

"Is it safe?" I asked as Sam walked by.

"As far as I can tell."

My shoulders relaxed. We'd just left the lab the day before, but it felt like we'd been on the run forever. Being in an actual house, tucked in the middle of nowhere, drained some of the pent-up anxiety from my bones.

I dropped onto the couch and was greeted with a cloud of dust. I coughed, clearing the air with a wave of my hand. This place needed a good scrubbing. My fingers itched to do something. I'd been in charge of the cleaning at home, and I worried about it now that I was gone. I couldn't imagine the house surviving on its own without me there to look after it. Or maybe what I really meant was that I couldn't imagine my dad surviving without me to take care of him.

Was he worried about me like I was worried about him?

I jumped from the couch, restless, and joined Cas in the kitchen. A cobweb stretched over his hair. I nabbed it, holding it in front of him so he could see. "Sometimes I think you're hopeless."

He put an arm around me. "That's why I have you. You're good at keeping us in line."

"And by *us* you mean you."

"Sure. Whatever." He left my side and tried the burners on the stovetop. Nothing happened. "Damn it. I'm frickin' starving."

"You are perpetually starving."

"I'm used to having three square meals a day."

"If the house has been untouched for years—and it looks like it has been—I doubt anything is usable." I moved around the L-shaped kitchen counter to the window that looked out on the garage. "Have you been out there yet?"

"No. But I'm game for an adventure. What do ya say?"

I grinned. "Game."

The others were in the living room, inspecting the fireplace and the chimney. Cas let Sam know where we were headed before we eased out the back door. We ran from the porch to the door at the side of the garage. A kiss of rain hit my face and I shielded my eyes with one hand. Cas rammed his shoulder against the door and it swung open, scraping against the concrete floor. Poor light stole through the two small windows, but it was enough to see what we were dealing with.

"Look." I hurried to the far left corner. "A grill. We could barbecue."

Cas's expression was nothing short of ecstasy as he caressed the black steel dome that made up the grill's hood. "Do you have any idea how long it's been since I had a grilled steak? Or a barbecued chicken leg?"

I raised my eyebrows. "Um…a long time?"

He ignored me. "All those damn barbecue commercials on TV. Dangling it right in front of my face like a frickin' carrot in front of a donkey."

"How do you even know what barbecue sauce tastes like? You never had it in the lab."

"A man never forgets the taste of barbecue. I probably had it *before* the lab." He hoisted the grill hood and took a whiff. "Oh, God—it still smells like charcoal and sizzling meat."

"It's amazing you don't weigh three hundred pounds."

He pushed up the sleeve of his sweaty, muddy shirt and flexed his biceps. "All that food gave me this svelte figure, I'll have you know."

I eyed the bulkiness of his arm, the broadness of his shoulders. "*Svelte* means 'slender.'"

"But it also means to have clean lines. Which obviously I do."

I couldn't argue with that.

I left him to drool over the grill while I surveyed what else might be useful. Some yard tools had been organized on rubber-coated hooks on the far wall. Different-sized boards were stacked up below the tools. Directly across from that, I spotted a power box and a bulky contraption on the floor beneath it. "What is that?"

"That's a generator."

I looked over my shoulder to find Cas rummaging around a loft area built beneath the peak of the roof.

"How did you get up there?"

He nodded at the stack of boards. "I jumped."

"You are such a monkey. Now come look at this."

He hung over the edge of the loft headfirst, flipped and then dangled there for a second in a backhanded pull-up, the threads of muscle tightening in his forearms before he let go. "Whoa. Am I badass or what? I didn't even know I could do that."

I stood there, mouth hanging open. "Then why did you? You could have been hurt!"

"Because I felt like it." He nudged the boxy generator with his foot. "Looks like it's been wired into the power box. Good to know." He twisted off the gas cap. "Not much juice, though, and considering we're broke..."

"We'll have to get by without it," I guessed.

He nodded, but shot the grill another meaningful look. "At least we have that beauty."

"Do you want me to help cart it out? We could put it on the back porch."

"Are you kidding me? I got this." He positioned his hands on the underside of the grill and picked it up without much effort. More evidence that he was stronger than any boy his age and size should be.

We spent the next hour scrubbing the grill with an old wire brush we found in the kitchen. Sam built a fire in the fireplace. Nick and Trev gathered wood in the surrounding forest. No one mentioned how long we planned to stay, but judging by the firewood now stacked along the back porch, we could survive at least a week without having to worry about warmth. Food was an issue, though. We had no money, no provisions.

We gathered in the living room to discuss strategy after dusk.

Sam stood near the fireplace, arms crossed tightly in front of himself. He was still covered in dirt from the cemetery. As far as I could tell, we had no running water to clean up with.

Cas sat on the arm of one of the easy chairs, a foot propped where his butt should have been. "You didn't happen to find any money lying around here, did you?"

Sam shook his head. "If I left anything, it wouldn't be easy to find. It might take some time."

"I'd stand on the street corner to score a steak," Cas said.

I couldn't help laughing. "You know, you might be flooded with business."

His mouth stretched into a lecherous grin. "If you come with me, we could be rich by morning."

"Very funny."

"Cas and I will head into town," Trev said. "We'll see what we can come up with."

"And what am I supposed to do, boss?" Instead of joining us, Nick leaned in the doorway between the living room and dining room.

"You're on watch."

While Sam ran Cas and Trev through the specifics—which sounded an awful lot like "Steal whatever you can get your hands on without getting caught," but not in those words—I went to inspect the kitchen.

Sam had mentioned earlier that there was a pantry, but half the food had expired. I wanted to see for myself what was inside. It wasn't like I had anything else to do.

The pantry was a large walk-in tucked beneath the staircase. Enough light spilled in from the kitchen windows that I didn't need a flashlight to start taking inventory. Gallons of water lined the baseboards. The lower shelves were stocked full of medical and emergency supplies, like batteries, matches, and rubbing alcohol.

The other shelves held hard grains, beans, and pasta. There were vacuum-sealed bags of salt, sugar, and freeze-dried food. Boxes of powdered milk, dried soup mixes, and cereal.

I started checking expiration dates. The cereal and beans had gone bad a while ago, but I thought we might be able to get away with eating the pasta and soup mixes.

It was just like Sam to be prepared for anything. He could probably survive an apocalypse.

The doorway darkened behind me. "Find anything useful?" Sam asked.

I turned around and pressed my back against the shelves. "Yeah."

He stepped inside with me, and suddenly the pantry didn't seem as big as it had before. He reached for a bag of rolled oats, grazing my arm as he did. Heat rippled out from where he'd touched me, even though it wasn't on purpose and there were layers of clothing between us.

I slid aside, but it took every ounce of self-control I had to do it. "Anything come back to you yet?" I asked. "The house seem familiar?"

He set the oats down. "I'm having a hard time deciphering what's real and what's merely a sense of déjà vu."

"Trev would say there's no such thing, that it's the mind recalling something from the past."

"Trev thinks there's a deeper meaning to everything."

"True." I clasped my hands behind me. "What was it that triggered the déjà vu?"

I could make out only one side of his face in the filtered daylight as he looked over at me. "There's a dent in the wall on the other side of the refrigerator, like something smashed into it." Worry lines ran across his forehead. "I thought I could remember doing it myself."

I took a step toward him. "Do you remember anything else?"

The worry disappeared, replaced by some other emotion. A moment of discomfort, or misgiving, or maybe both. "No. That was it." He pushed away from the corner. "I'll be upstairs if you need me," he said and escaped before I could ask anything more.

I might not have the ability to read Sam as well as he did me, but I knew enough to know there'd been a secret there, one he wasn't willing to part with yet. And I wanted to find out what it was.

14

I DIDN'T TALK TO SAM MUCH FOR THE next few days. He was too preoccupied with turning the house inside out looking for clues. I played a lot of Connect Four with Cas after he found the game stuffed in a kitchen cabinet. Shockingly, even though I was not genetically altered for greatness, I won almost every round. It probably had more to do with the fact that Cas couldn't focus on a game long enough to strategize, but I figured I'd take what I could get.

Trev and I inventoried a few of the closets downstairs and found a cache of dusty novels and moth-eaten blankets. I didn't see a lot of Nick. When he wasn't tending to the fire or collecting kindling, he was helping Sam. While those two didn't always agree, they worked well together because they didn't waste time with idle chat.

On our third afternoon at the cabin, in one of the rooms upstairs, I lay on my stomach listening to Trev read passages from *The Duke's Plight*. He was propped up against the headboard, the book open in his left hand. The cover showed a girl in a big flowy dress, wrapped in the arms of a long-haired, brooding duke.

Trev let out a sound that was somewhere between a breath and a laugh. "You'll like this one."

"Let's hear it."

He licked his lips. "'He tried desperately to look at Margaret with an expression of hard contempt, but she appeared so vulnerable, so sad before him, that he went to her immediately. They embraced, her bosom heaving against him.'"

I rolled onto my back and laughed. "Oh, God, I can't take any more."

The book thumped closed. A second later, Trev eased down next to me. We both stared at the wide plank ceiling. Downstairs, the fire crackled and snapped as someone poked at it. Cas, probably. Nick and Sam were in the garage rummaging through the loft as far as I knew.

"Did you ever imagine you'd escape the lab?" I asked.

Trev clasped his hands together over his stomach. "Not the way it happened. Sometimes I thought it'd be you who would let us out. I never could decide if that would be a good or bad thing. Bad for you, maybe."

Citrine sunlight blazed through the window and shone across

his face. His eyes seemed to glow when I turned to him. "I wanted to, if that's any consolation. I thought about it all the time."

"I know you did."

I leaned on my elbow. "Really?"

"Sam was working his way into your subconscious. Whether you knew it or not. Whether he meant to or not. If he hadn't planned to escape, eventually you would have done it yourself. For him."

Long threads of my hair tickled my arm as I hung my head back. "For you, too. For all of you."

He smiled when he looked at me, but it didn't reach his eyes. "Thanks, but I think you're lying."

"I am not." I picked at a loose thread in the blanket. "So when this is all over, whatever this is, what do you think you'll do?"

"If I have a choice, you mean?"

"Yeah. If you could do anything."

He considered the question. "Well, I guess I'd like to go to New York City. I want to study lit somewhere, though I suppose having no identification or school records might pose a problem."

I'd been so focused on Sam and what my life would be like without him that I hadn't taken the time to consider what it'd feel like to lose Trev, too. The sorrow was immediate, and pressing. "I'll miss you, if you go."

He waved the idea away. "I'm not going anywhere. No matter how much I want to."

"Come on. Someday, you'll be free. Just promise me you won't leave me for good."

There was a long pause, and I thought maybe he wouldn't answer. His eyes were glossy, like some far-off thought had summoned forgotten emotions. He blinked before I could ask, though, and whatever had been there disappeared. "I promise."

I collapsed onto my back again. "I guess this is what it'd feel like if we were normal, if we'd gone to school together and were about to go to separate colleges."

"I guess."

"You don't have a quote for that?"

He sighed and closed his eyes. "No, but I wish I did."

———

On our fourth morning at the cabin, Sam called me outside and handed me one of the Glocks he'd stolen from a Branch agent. He wanted me to learn how to use it in case we were ever separated.

I hadn't thought about that, and I didn't *want* to think about it. If Connor got to me and pushed for information, I'd probably cave easily. Knowing how to operate a gun was a good thing, but would I ever have enough courage to use it? As much as I disliked Connor, I didn't think I could kill him. I didn't think I could kill anyone, for that matter. I still felt guilty for helping Sam kill that man in the garden behind the farmhouse.

"Have you ever shot a gun before?" Sam asked. He was wearing an old coat he'd found in one of the closets the day before. It was the color of cut wood and fit him perfectly. The longer we were out of the lab, the more he looked like a real person and not some experiment. He was also standing incredibly close—close enough that the back of my neck tingled with his every breath.

"I've never even held a gun before this," I answered. It wasn't as heavy as I'd thought it'd be.

"Here." He took the gun back and pointed to a button on the side. "Press this to drop out the magazine." He demonstrated, and the clip slipped from the frame. "This is the slide," he went on, gesturing to the top of the gun. "Pull it back to make sure the gun is empty, or to initially rack a bullet in the chamber. It's a semiautomatic, though, so you only have to do that once. Got it?"

No. But I wasn't going to tell him that.

Sunshine poured over the treetops, and I squinted in the light. I readjusted my weight as I took the gun and a fully loaded magazine.

"Load the clip," Sam instructed.

I pushed the magazine in, heard it click. I fumbled with the slide at first, but finally managed it without looking too awkward, and a bullet slid into the chamber.

"Now shoot." His words hung between us in a cloud of dense air.

I held the gun out in front of me and pulled the trigger without hesitating. I didn't want Sam to think I was scared. The recoil bounced up my arms, startling me. I squared my shoulders and steeled myself before squeezing off another round, then another. I didn't hit anything, but that was okay. I wasn't aiming. Not yet.

I tore through several more bullets, emptying the clip.

"That's good." Sam gestured for the gun. I wanted to keep going, to perfect my aim, but our supply of ammunition wasn't endless. I handed it over.

"How do you even know how to use a gun?" I asked, repeating the question he'd failed to answer a few days earlier.

He pulled a handful of bullets out of his coat pocket. "There are things I can remember doing, physical things. Shooting a gun is one of them. Driving is another." He replaced the bullets I'd used. Fully loaded. Always ready. "Foreign languages, complicated equations, marking exits, reading people."

I followed him up the steps to the back porch. He held the door open for me and, once inside, I exhaled in relief at coming in from the cold. Nick had stoked the fire that morning and the cabin was comfortably cozy.

"So what else can you do?" I asked.

Sam set the gun on the countertop, next to the bag of Oreos that Cas had nabbed a few nights before when he and Trev had gone to town.

Trev sat at the table reading a western he'd found tucked next to

The Duke's Plight. The pages were barely holding on to the spine. He was either searching for clues or extremely bored. When we came in, he looked up.

"Are you telling her about the tests?" he asked.

I sat next to him, rubbing my hands together to get rid of the numbness. "What tests?"

Sam leaned against the counter that separated the kitchen from the dining area. "In the lab, we ran tests to see what we could do. Trev was in charge of data."

"But...my dad inspected your rooms every couple of months. Wouldn't he have found the notes?"

Trev smirked. "Come on, Anna. Look at who you're talking to."

I frowned, at first unsure of what he meant—then I realized. "You memorized the data." He nodded. I knew Trev was good at filing away quotes and poems, but to memorize research results? That was much more impressive.

"So what did you find?"

A log snapped as it burned in the fireplace. The poker dragged against the hearth. Nick. Most likely listening in.

A barely noticeable look passed between Sam and Trev before Trev answered. "Sam is the strongest out of all of us. Cas has the best motor skills, but the worst recall. Nick's got good endurance, but is nowhere near as fast as Sam—"

The fire poker clattered into its holder. Nick was definitely listening. I wondered where Cas was, and then remembered that he'd gone out to the garage to snoop.

"I seem to have a photographic memory," Trev went on. "A good memory all around, actually. We all recall driving, shooting, using some technology. Sometimes we have flashes of other memories, but nothing substantial."

I watched Sam for a reaction. He'd had a flash the other day. Was that not the first? Other than his comment about liking water, he'd never mentioned memories at all. None of them had.

"Sam's are the worst," Trev said. "The flashbacks. It's why he doesn't sleep very well."

"You never told me...." I straightened in my seat. All those nights I'd snuck down to the lab, Sam was always awake. "Why didn't you say something?"

He lifted one shoulder in a shrug. "What was I going to say?"

"If you were recalling things, maybe it meant your memories were coming back. I could have helped you, or my dad could have—"

"Unless our memories were deliberately wiped," he cut in, repeating the same theory he'd shared earlier. "Then mentioning it would have posed a risk to the program, and they would have fixed the problem."

And by "problem," he meant him.

"How bad are they? What do you remember? What do the others remember?"

Nick appeared in the doorway. All the boys had found clothes in the closets and changed into whatever fit them. While everything worked on Sam, the blue button-down Nick had on was a tad too small. He was broader in the shoulders than Sam, and maybe an inch or two taller. The shirt was open, revealing a white T-shirt underneath.

Some silent conversation passed between them. Sam ran a hand over the dark stubble covering his face before turning away. "I'm going for a run."

I lurched to my feet. "Right now? But..."

"I'll be back later," he said.

The door shut behind him and his footsteps pounded down the steps. I whirled on Nick. "Why did you do that?"

He cracked a knuckle. "You think you have any right to my memories? To my life before this? You don't."

Trev rose behind me. "Anna. Stop."

"Why do you make me look like the bad guy? Like I can't keep your secrets or something."

Nick tsked. His expression turned coarse. "Because what if you can't? You're the *daughter* of the *enemy*. We never should have brought you in the first place."

I started for him, not that I even knew what I planned to do. Punch him? Gouge out his eyes? *A hard dig of the thumbs, don't give in, even if it makes you squirm.* That's what my instructor used to say.

Thankfully, it didn't come to that. Trev stepped between us. *Don't*, the look on his face said. *You're being ridiculous.*

I huffed in resignation as Nick cracked another knuckle. The tension felt thick enough to braid. If it weren't for Trev, I was almost certain Nick would have fought me.

And that was a fight I would never win.

THAT NIGHT AFTER DINNER, I ESCAPED

into one of the bedrooms with a pencil I'd dredged up from the back of a drawer. The east-facing room had a window seat with a dusty old plaid cushion and one lone pillow. It was enough.

I curled up there, spreading a wool blanket over my lap. The upstairs was warmer than the downstairs, but next to the window there was a faint chill. I opened my mother's journal to the next blank page.

Spending all that time in the lab back at home, I'd often wondered what the outside world looked like, what it would feel like to draw it. Using a torn-out magazine page for inspiration wasn't the same as seeing something with my own eyes. Each place has a special energy. Landscapes breathe. Trees whisper.

In the lab, I'd allowed myself to fantasize about leaving my small town one day, but it usually ended abruptly, reality pulling me back—back to Sam. It wouldn't be the same without him. Outside the farmhouse, I felt like something was missing. Like there were pieces of myself left within those basement walls, tied to Sam and the others.

Now that I was out in the world, with a pencil in my hand, I wanted to immortalize what it felt like. I set out to draw some of the gorgeous Michigan scenery, but a few minutes in, I realized my hand had other ideas. The sketch began to take the shape of my mother. I had only one picture of her, and I'd had to steal it from my dad's study, but I'd recycled the image in tons of drawings.

In the photograph, she sat at the shore of a lake, a fleece blanket spread out beneath her. A deep purple scarf was wrapped around her neck, and her hair had been tied back in a bun.

I'd analyzed that picture so many times I had it memorized, right down to the angle of the leaves hanging off the trees and the slant of the shadows. In one of my favorite sketches, I'd copied the photo exactly, but had drawn myself in beside her.

I hadn't thought to grab that sketch before we left. I wished I had.

Now I drew her in the field behind the farmhouse, her dark hair caught in the wind, the grass parting around her. She was running away. Leaving me.

Why did she leave me?

"Anna?"

I started at the sound of Sam's voice. I hadn't even heard him come in. Sometimes sketching turned off every other sense I had. It was like my hand drew of its own free will.

"Hey." I readjusted in the window seat, tucking my legs beneath me. "What's up?"

In the time I'd been drawing, the sun had set, painting the woods beyond the cabin in various shades of gray. The temperature had dropped, too, and my hands were stiff, my fingertips numb from the cold stealing through the glass.

Sam sat at the other end of the window seat, facing the room, the heels of his hands on the edge of the bench. He didn't say anything at first, and I thought I could deduce where he was headed.

"I'm sorry about the Nick thing this morning," I said. "I didn't mean to yell at him—"

"I didn't come up here to talk about Nick."

I ran my thumb over the pencil's eraser. "You didn't? Then what?"

"Do you know the names of the drugs your father gave us? Components of the treatments? Dosages?"

I shook my head. "I was never allowed access to that part of the program. I only worked with the tests and logs. Why?"

He sighed and rubbed his eyes. "It's nothing. Just something I've been meaning to ask."

He rose from the bench. I dropped my mother's journal to hurry after him, cornering him in the doorway. "Tell me, Sam. Please."

Once I got a good look at him, I saw the dark shadows beneath his eyes, the faint sheen of sweat on his forehead. "You're going through withdrawal, aren't you?" I reached out to touch him, telling myself I wanted to see if he was feverish, but it was because I *wanted* to touch him, because I could.

He tensed. I froze.

Just because I could didn't mean I should. I pulled back.

"And the others?" I asked.

"Headaches. Minor memory flashes. I suspect they're not as bad as mine. Yet."

"Are their flashes important? About the Branch? Or what happened before the lab?"

"No. Nothing like that."

I wanted to say, *Then what are they about?* But Nick's earlier warning, that I had no right to the information, kept the question firmly lodged in place. It was none of my business, and if the others wanted me to know, they'd share when they were ready.

I put my hands on my hips as I thought. "If your withdrawal symptoms are worse, it could mean any number of things. It could be that your treatments were different, or your dosages higher. Or that you've been receiving treatments longer than the others."

He nodded. "It would help if I knew what the treatments were for in the first place. I don't think they were altering us for better performance—strength, or healing, or improving senses. We tested ourselves every day. Whatever extra skills we had, we had them from the start, and they never changed."

Something clattered in the kitchen. A second later Cas said, "I'm all right! Everything's fine!"

"You think the *physical* alterations were a onetime deal," I said. "So they were treating you for something else?"

He'd said as much our first night out of the lab: *If you're trying to make the ultimate weapon, you don't lock it in a basement for five years.*

Another crash. Nick called out, "What the hell?"

Sam stepped past me onto the landing. "I should go check on that."

"Will you let me know if you find anything else? Or if there are more symptoms?"

"Sure," he said as he hurried down the stairs.

I curled up in the window seat again, wishing I'd dug for more information at home. If I'd looked into the treatments, I'd have something to give him now. I should have read every file I could get my hands on.

Maybe we wouldn't even be in this mess if I had.

16

noise. I hoisted myself up to a sitting position and caught sight of Sam on the other side of the room, rummaging inside one of the built-in cabinets. I had no idea what time it was, but judging by the darkness outside, it was still early.

"What are you doing?"

Sam tensed. I'd startled him. That wasn't easy to do; Sam was always on alert.

"I woke up and..." He trailed off, hands resting on the edge of one of the interior shelves. "I don't know...something..."

I padded over. "An old memory?"

"Maybe."

The blankets and sheets from inside the cabinet were stacked on the floor, along with several pieces of women's clothing. I lifted a top from the pile. The charcoal-gray material was silky between my fingers. A dainty ruffle adorned the collar. There were also a pair of jeans and a few fitted T-shirts in the pile. I hadn't thought to look in here when I'd claimed this room as my own, figuring if there was anything worthwhile, the boys would have found it. But they hadn't mentioned women's clothing. Not that any of this stuff would fit, anyway. It would be way too small.

"Whose are these?"

Sam glanced over his shoulder. "I don't know."

"Isn't it kind of weird? I mean..." I tried to think of all the reasons there might be trendy women's clothing in Sam's closet. The style didn't fit who I thought my mother would be, so I didn't even consider that possibility. These were for a younger girl. A girl my age.

I set the top down, my chest tight with something akin to jealousy, even though I had no idea who to direct it toward.

Sam ducked inside the cabinet and tugged on something in the back. A false panel popped out. He stood there, the wood panel clutched in his hands, both of us staring at it. He propped it against the wall and dug deeper.

He pulled out a fireproof box, the same kind as the one he'd dug out of the cemetery, and headed for the stairs.

Cas met us on the landing. "What's going on?"

"Sam found something," I said.

Nick was already off the couch when I hit the main floor. He followed me into the kitchen, making the hair at the nape of my neck stand on end. By the time Sam popped open the latch on the box, we had all gathered around the table.

"What is it?" Cas shifted his weight from foot to foot. "Come on! The suspense is killing me!"

Sam turned the box so we could see. Inside lay a collection of things, but the first item I noticed was the stack of money. Twenties and fifties, bunched in five-hundred-dollar bands. At least six thousand dollars' worth.

"Holy shit," Cas said with a low whistle. "We can buy food. And underwear."

Sam dug through the box. Passports. Driver's licenses. All of them belonged to Sam, but they were from different states, under different names. At the very bottom of the box was an envelope. Sam pushed open the flap and pulled out a note, along with a picture.

The note was a series of letters, none of which formed coherent words. Sam set it aside and took the old picture in his hands. The ink had faded over time. I leaned in closer.

There were two people in the photo, standing in front of a grove of birch trees. The girl was around my age, her hair the color of chestnuts. It hung off her shoulders in thick waves. She clung to the boy next to her, her eyes trained on him and only him.

The boy in the picture was Sam.

"Whoa, Sammy," Cas said, "awesome hairdo." Cas passed the picture to Trev. We had moved to the living room, the only source of light the amber glow of the fire. Sam had his back to us as he stared out the front window.

I curled into the crook of the couch, trying to forget about the girl in the picture and finding myself unable to think about anything else. Whoever she was, she'd spent time with Sam, in this cabin. Those clothes upstairs were probably hers. What else had she left behind? Did Sam have flashbacks about her?

Envy took root in my chest and I couldn't let it go. She knew Sam. The *real* Sam.

Even in profile, I could tell the girl was pretty. Freckles peppered her cheeks. Next to Sam, she looked like a slender ballerina, like he could scoop her up in his arms without any effort.

And Sam had been smiling in the picture. Sam hardly ever smiled.

"So what's it all mean?" Trev asked.

Sam held up the note, scrutinizing it. "I think this is a cipher. It'll take me some time to decode it. As for the picture...I don't know."

Nick gave the photo only a passing glance before Trev handed it back to me. I examined it again. The girl wore slim-cut jeans and tall brown leather boots. A purple sweater slimmed her even more. Sam was in jeans and a gray button-down shirt, the flannel kind that workingmen wear. The "hairdo" wasn't so much a do as it was a mess of dark spikes.

An old tractor sat in the left corner of the photo, and farther back, a couple of black-and-white cows grazed in a field. Sam looked exactly the same as he did now, except for a few superficial physical characteristics, like the hair and the clean-shaven face. He hadn't aged much since the picture was taken, which meant he must have entered the program not long after.

There was something else that struck me as familiar, but I couldn't place it. If I didn't know Sam's birch-tree tattoo so well, I'd say that it was echoed in the photo, but the placement of the trees on his back didn't match the placement of the trees in the picture.

"Mark this down as another clue to the ever growing mystery," Nick muttered as he tossed a log onto the fire.

"I think we're getting closer," Trev said.

I thought so, too. But what if at the end of this hunt, we found the girl? Would Sam remember her once he came face-to-face with her? If he'd been in love, would he fall *back* in love?

I waved the picture in the air. "Do you remember this girl at all?"

Sam turned away from the window. "No."

The worry dissipated. Maybe the picture was simply a memento. Maybe they weren't even together when Sam entered the Branch.

Maybe.

Or maybe she was out there somewhere, looking for him.

17

I THOUGHT IT WOULD BE NEARLY IMPOS-
sible to unwind enough to lie down again, but I managed to sleep for
a few more hours. When I got up, I slipped into the bathroom before
heading downstairs. I sorely needed a shower, something other than
the sponge baths I'd been taking. Maybe now that we had money, we
could buy gas for the generator. I could even cook a real meal.

One of the boys had set a candle on the vanity and I lit the wick,
the flame pulsating. I checked my reflection in the dust-covered mirror and cringed. The skin beneath my hazel eyes was the color of wet
charcoal, and what few freckles I had looked like muddy splotches on
the bridge of my nose. In just a few days my complexion had gone
from okay to crummy. I hadn't brought any of my skin products, and
I was already suffering because of it.

I had searched the bathroom when we'd first arrived, but I looked again, thinking maybe I'd missed something. Plus, I was desperate now. In the first drawer, I found an old toothbrush. I wasn't *that* desperate. In the second drawer, I grabbed the hairbrush and a stack of hair ties. I'd already used a few, but now...now I knew why they were here.

Rifling through the stack, I found a tie on the bottom with a long hair wrapped around it, like it'd been knotted when the owner undid her ponytail.

More evidence that a girl had lived here. I threw the tie in the trash can and grabbed a new one.

I fixed my hair as best I could, trying not to think about *her* as I used the mystery hairbrush. Downstairs, I found Sam and Cas in the kitchen, sharing a box of Cheerios.

The boys stopped chewing and looked at me.

"What?" I said.

Cas snickered. "Nothing. You just...look like hell."

Embarrassment spread through me.

"We'll go shopping today," Sam said, handing Cas the box of cereal. "We'll get some gas for the generator, and clothes that fit better. I want to buy a few cell phones, too."

"Awesome." Cas lifted the cereal box and poured more Cheerios directly into his mouth. He spoke as he chewed. "I could use a new pair of shoes. Nikes. The neon ones. I saw them on TV all the time, and I want them."

"Well, they won't make you run faster or look cooler, if that's what you're hoping for," I said, trying to regain some of my dignity, even if I was playing dirty.

"Oooh." Cas wrinkled his face in mock anguish. "So harsh."

I took a handful of cereal from the box as Sam breezed past me. I watched him leave.

"Trev?" he called. "Gather the guns in a bag. We're leaving soon."

"Why are we bagging the guns?" Nick said from the living room.

"In case we can't return." Sam rounded back into the kitchen and grabbed his coat from the hook. "We should take everything we need with us to be safe, and I don't want all of us running around carrying."

Ten minutes later we were on the road, my mother's journal tucked next to my seat. We drove for about an hour, until we reached a bigger city. Sam parked in front of a chain restaurant known for its buffet. Of course, the buffet was Cas's idea, but secretly I couldn't wait. It'd been forever since I'd had a real meal, and deciding on only one thing seemed impossible.

Inside, I could smell all sorts of fresh-cooked foods. Pizza. Fried chicken. Chocolate cake. I didn't know where to start.

None of us said a single word for the first ten minutes of the meal. We'd been subsisting on old food that came out of packages, and it was nice to finally have something hearty.

When the boys went up for a second helping, I dodged the lunch buffet and headed for the dessert section, my eyes filling with the sight of so many chocolaty things. I grabbed a lava brownie and headed back to our booth.

Sam had forgone the second plate. Instead of eating, he was holding the scrap of paper he'd found in the fireproof box, scrutinizing it.

When he saw me he stood up, allowing me to slide in ahead of him. "Did you decipher the message yet?" I asked.

He shoved his empty plate aside when the waitress came to clear the table. She was a tiny thing, with cinnamon-red hair tamed into a sleek ponytail. She eyed Sam with a look that was both apprising and hungry. I inched closer to him, pretending to look over the note, my brownie all but forgotten.

Sam told the waitress thank you as she flitted away. I didn't move, even though I should have, even though we were closer than was strictly necessary.

When his knee bumped mine, a shiver of delight started in my spine and raced clear up to my skull. He smelled like woodsmoke and Ivory soap. I was close, but I wanted to be closer. I wanted to press the line of my body against his.

"Mashed potatoes!" Cas shouted as he slid into the booth. "Pot roast. Butter rolls. Heaven."

I scooted back over, catching a knowing look from Trev as he took his spot next to Cas.

"Any idea what the message says yet?" Trev asked, cutting his chicken into neat, bite-size pieces.

Sam downed the rest of his ice water. "I think it's a Caesar cipher."

"What's that?" I asked.

"It's a way of coding messages," Trev said. "Julius Caesar used it when he needed to communicate with his generals. To break it, you shift the letters of the alphabet over three spaces, so *A* becomes *D*, *B* becomes *E*, and so on."

"Does that work on this message?"

Sam shook his head.

Cas, having already polished off half his meal, looked up for the briefest of moments. "Sammy wouldn't use the obvious way to decode it."

"We'll figure it out," Trev added.

Nick finally rejoined us, carrying a plate full of veggies. "Why do we even have to figure it out? I'm fine with staying at the cabin." Sam shot Nick a look, and Nick visibly stiffened. "What?" Nick said, leaning closer. "Digging this shit up is only going to make it worse. You know that, right?"

Sam didn't say anything.

"Do you think this has anything to do with the letter scars?" I asked, trying to defuse the situation.

"Already tried it," Sam said, when he and Nick stopped glaring at each other.

When we left the restaurant, we crossed the parking lot to the massive Cook Towne Mall. Our first stop was at R & J Cellular, where Sam bought two prepaid cell phones. Trev took one phone,

Sam the other. We split up. Cas and Trev headed for a sporting-goods shop, while Nick disappeared into the bookstore café, muttering something about needing caffeine more than a pair of jeans.

Sam and I went to one of the trendier clothing stores, tucked between the bookstore and an upscale candle shop.

"What am I getting, exactly?" I asked.

For the first time since we'd left the lab, Sam looked extremely uncomfortable. His hands hung in loose fists at his sides, like he wasn't sure what to do with himself. His eyes darted around, marking the exits, though I wondered whether he meant to escape potential threats or a jeans fitting.

"You can get whatever you want," he said, then disappeared behind a rack of T-shirts.

I went to the jeans section and dug through the sizes until I found a fit I liked. I passed a wall of fall skirts and sweater dresses, coming up alongside a display of fleece scarves. A vibrant purple scarf caught my attention and I paused, thinking of the photo of my mother. In it she wore a scarf much like this one. Except hers wasn't fleece, or at least I didn't think it was. Hers was made of a shiny material that hung in billowy folds around her neck.

Homesickness overcame me, swallowing me whole. I fingered the material of the scarf, wondering about all the things that made up my old life, and how much of that life was true. My mother. My father. My house. The lab.

If I found my mother at the end of this journey, what then? I was afraid of what the reunion might uncover. I was afraid of what I'd feel when I realized my father had truly lied to me.

I picked up a few long-sleeved shirts, and on impulse grabbed the scarf, too. On my way to the fitting room, I ran into Sam. He had taken off his jacket and shrugged into a new coat. Made of a thick black canvas, with a zipper at the front and a row of buttons to double it up, it looked more like him than anything I'd seen him wear so far. The gray pants and white T-shirt he'd worn in the lab had never done him justice.

"Are you getting that?" I asked.

He straightened the collar. "I don't know. I have a coat, but this seems more practical. It's thick, but lightweight. Easy to run in."

"And it looks good."

His gaze darted up to meet mine. A question hung there between us. *What are you doing, Anna?* I was treading dangerously close to a line I knew I shouldn't cross. A line Sam had built up with bricks and cement. And KEEP OUT signs.

Retreat! the voice in my head shouted. *And quickly.*

I hoisted up my load of clothing. "I'm trying this stuff on," I said and hurried toward the fitting room.

Inside, I hung the items on the wall hooks and admonished my reflection in the full-length mirror. My cheeks were pink from left-over embarrassment. *No more thinly veiled flirting*, I told myself. *No more ogling Sam. No more.*

I stepped out of my jeans and slipped into a new pair. The flare-cut dragged on the floor, so I tried the boot cut next. They fit perfectly. I ran through Sam's listed requirements. Light. Sturdy. Easy to run in, should I need to run.

I stared at myself, wondering who that girl was, the one buying jeans according to the way she could move in them. My life had changed so drastically in a few short days.

I left the jeans on, hoping the salesgirl would accept only the tag at the register. As I pulled off my shirt, I heard the fitting room attendant greeting a customer: "Hi. How many . . . Hey, you can't—"

"Take this," I heard Sam say. "If a man comes through asking about a boy and a girl, we were never here."

"Dude, I don't know . . ." the attendant said.

"Anna?" Sam called. "Open the door."

"What?" I was shirtless, standing there in jeans and a pale green bra.

"Now, Anna!"

I let him in. He shut the door and pushed me to the far corner of the stall. He pressed a finger to my lips and breathed. "Shhhhh."

I managed a nod as his eyes flicked down, seeing my bra and nothing else. Frenzied butterflies took flight in my stomach. I could hear my heartbeat in my head and wondered if Sam could hear it, too, if he could sense what I felt. His eyes moved again to my mouth. With his finger gone, there was nothing between us. I licked my lips. My breath fluttered helplessly behind my teeth.

"Can I help you with something?" The attendant's voice carried through the fitting room.

A deep voice answered, one I didn't recognize. "I'm looking for a young man and woman. They look like this."

Sam leaned into me, bringing with him the scent of new canvas. His breath touched the curve of my neck, pouring a chill down my spine.

"You know," the attendant said, "I think I saw them...."

"Where?" the man asked.

"Um..." The attendant shuffled his feet. "They were just here about fifteen minutes ago."

"If you see them again," the man said, "call this number."

"Yeah. Sure."

The agent's shoes squeaked over the polished floor as he left. Sam retreated, and an aching cold filled the space he left behind. I grabbed a shirt and slid into it, wanting to escape before the agent returned.

"Hey," the attendant said through the door, "he's gone."

Shoulders rigid, Sam avoided looking at me as he asked, "The clothes work okay?"

In the mirror, I saw the color in my cheeks grow darker. If Sam didn't know what I felt for him before, he surely knew now. I was stupid to allow him to get to me. Stupid for wishing it had gone farther than it had. "What? Yeah. Fine."

"Then we need to leave."

Hands shaking, I tugged on my shoes as Sam opened the door. The attendant waited on the other side, eyes wide, sweat beading on his forehead. "Dude, that was heavy. I don't know if I can take this." He held out a few twenty-dollar bills.

"Keep it. And we're taking these jeans and a T-shirt and a coat. I think this should cover it." He handed over a short stack of bills.

"No, this is too much. . . ."

"Keep whatever's left."

Sam poked his head around the fitting room exit, scanning the store. He grabbed my hand, threading his fingers through mine. "Don't run unless you see one of them, but walk fast. Head straight for the store's entrance. We're going right when we hit the mall concourse."

"Okay," I said as he tugged me from our hiding spot.

My mouth went dry as soon as we reached the main part of the mall. Everyone looked like a Branch man. Every cell phone looked like the butt of a gun. I blinked back the blurriness edging my vision.

Sam called Trev on the cell. "Meet us back in the food court. They're here." He hung up and slid the phone into his jacket pocket.

We were quickly swept up in the movement of the crowd. The closer we came to the food court, the more I hoped we'd lost the agents. If there were only one or two men, it'd be nearly impossible for them to spot us.

But when we rounded into the children's play area, I froze at the sight of a familiar face, at the pressed navy blue suit and no-nonsense expression.

"Sam." I tugged him back.

The man looked up and locked eyes with me.

Riley had found us.

18

"STOP THEM!" RILEY YELLED.

The command had the opposite effect. The crowd parted. People pressed themselves against storefronts, windows, and walls, as if we were infectious. Shouts and gasps sounded around us. A second agent raced in our direction, his gun out.

Sam cut left. Gawkers gathered in the mall median, capturing video of our escape with their cell phones. A gate slammed shut over a candle shop. The median thinned out.

We barreled into a clothing store. I clipped the edge of a display, knocking it over. Tank tops spilled everywhere. I lost my momentum. The agent, a man I didn't know, pointed the gun at me. Teeth gritted, lips pursed, he slid his trigger finger into place.

Sam's hand clamped down on my wrist and wrenched me back.

We ran. Left. Right. Winding through displays, around people, gasping, shrieking.

My knees were numb; I felt like I was running on leftover adrenaline and nothing else.

Sam steered us into a back room, slammed his way through an emergency exit. An alarm cut a shrill note above us. Daylight momentarily blinded me. We emerged into an alleyway surrounded by Dumpsters and broken merchandise.

We'd just started for the parking lot when a gun clicked and Riley cut us off.

"You've caused a lot of trouble," he said, panting, as his partner smashed through the exit.

I knew Sam had a gun hidden beneath his new coat, but he hadn't reached for it yet, and I wondered if he relished the idea of taking Riley out with his bare hands.

"Arms behind your back," Riley ordered, pointing the gun at me, "or I'll shoot her."

Sam urged me behind him. "You'll have to go through me first."

I gulped down fresh air, trying to cool the burning in my lungs, ease the tightening of my insides.

"Fine," Riley said as he turned the gun on Sam. Sam launched himself in Riley's direction and kicked out a foot, forcing Riley's knee to bend in an unnatural way. Something cracked. Riley cried out as Sam wrapped one hand around Riley's gun, the other around his wrist.

The second agent started for me.

I scanned the alley for a weapon. A few cardboard boxes were broken down and stacked behind one store. Plastic crates towered near a Dumpster. Broken garden urns lay on their sides behind the home-goods store. That was as close to a weapon as I could get.

I ran, picked up too much speed, and skidded across the rocky concrete when I tried to stop. I went down on one leg, sliding over the ground, gravel biting through the material of my jeans. I reached for the urns, scooping up a chunk of broken plaster.

The man grabbed me by the ankle, yanked me around. Riley growled somewhere behind us. I rocked back on my free hand and kicked up with my other leg, catching the man in the kidney. He doubled over. I leapt to my feet and swung down with the chunk of urn, connecting with the back of his head. The flesh split open, and blood gurgled up like springwater as he crumpled to the ground.

Sam clipped Riley with an uppercut. Riley flew backward, slamming into the Dumpster. Sam was immediately on him again. He grabbed a chunk of hair with his left hand and clocked Riley with his right.

Riley went limp. Sam aimed the gun at him.

"No! Don't. Please."

Sam looked over a shoulder. "Anna," he said, making my name sound like an exasperated sigh.

"Please."

"Why?"

"I don't know." I knew Riley personally, and even though he was ready to take *my* life, I wasn't sure if *I* was ready to cross that line. "Please," I said again, "don't."

Sam let the gun drop. "Check him." He nodded at the man behind me. "ID. Keys. Weapons."

I checked the man's pockets, watching the rise and fall of his chest. I found a wallet, a set of zip ties, and keys. I handed the items to Sam. He'd taken Riley's belongings, too, and tossed everything into one of the nearby Dumpsters.

We ran around front and Sam slowed while he called the others. "You guys all right? We had to backtrack." He paused. "Meet me at the car."

To me he said, "You okay? Can you keep moving?"

I nodded, even though running was the last thing I wanted to do. I was not as resolute as Sam. I couldn't fight people, people I knew, people I thought I trusted, and keep going. I couldn't bury everything and pretend that any of this was okay. Riley had pointed a gun at me. Would Connor have done the same thing? And Dad? What would he have done if he were here?

"I'm good," I said. Because it was Sam. I wanted to prove that I could stand next to him when things got bad.

As we crossed in front of the bookstore, a gray car squealed into the parking lot. Rubber burned against the pavement as the car turned in our direction.

"Is that—"

"Go." Sam pushed me toward the Jeep.

The gray sedan cut left, racing across the parking lot, parallel to us. The other boys burst from the sporting-goods store on my right. We converged, Cas ahead of me, Trev next to me, Sam and Nick in the back. I tried to count my breaths, to control the tightness in my lungs.

The sedan whipped down the parking lot aisle as we darted across it. Our vehicle sat three rows away. We weren't going to make it.

Brakes screeched behind us. I looked back but Nick urged me on. Footsteps pounded after us. Cas reached the Jeep first. Sam tossed him the keys and Cas snatched them from the air before sliding in behind the wheel. Trev ripped up on the back door handle. Nick rushed to the passenger side.

"Get the girl first!" someone shouted.

My throat constricted. The footsteps closed in as Sam rounded to the other side of the Jeep. I clambered inside. Trev fumbled in behind me. A hand snaked in at the last second and I screeched as one of the agents tangled his fingers in my hair, yanking me back. Sam wrapped an arm around my waist.

"Go! Go!" Nick yelled.

Cas jammed the vehicle into drive.

My head felt like it was on fire, the hair ripping from my scalp.

Trev hoisted the gun bag from the floorboard and swung it at the agent. The bag hit him and he lost both his grip and his footing. He stumbled backward. Cas punched the gas and the vehicle shot forward. Trev slammed the door shut.

"You idiot!" Nick screamed. "You lost the guns!"

"They had Anna!" Trev fired back. "It was the only thing I had close by."

I blocked out the argument as Sam pulled me toward him, tucking me in close to his side. The fear crowded out the pain in my leg and in my head.

Five minutes ago, he'd asked me if I was okay. Five minutes ago, the real answer had been no. But we'd narrowly missed capture, and in this new life, that seemed as much like success as anything.

Was I okay? I was as okay as I was going to be, and here, so close to him, feeling the rise of his chest, I felt safe. I was devastatingly thankful and relieved that I was here, with him, and not left behind in the parking lot with Connor's men. They were not the good guys like I thought, like Dad had taught me. Connor, Riley, the Branch. How could I have been so stupid to trust in them?

"Thank you," I said to Sam and Trev, the words coming out muffled.

"We wouldn't have left without you," Sam said.

And I believed him.

19

IN THE HOUR IT TOOK US TO REACH

the cabin, Sam never moved. I pushed closer, finding a comfortable niche in the crook of his arm. His right hand was splayed over his leg, and I traced the curve of his long fingers with my eyes, the sharp edges of his knuckles, wondering what it would feel like to take his hand in mine. I wanted him to anchor me to the real world. I felt disconnected from everything.

The words *Is this happening?* kept spiraling through my head.

I had been so sure of my life and Sam's role in it back at the lab. Maybe I'd spent every single day pining for him, wanting his attention and his affection, but I knew that glass wall would never move.

Now here I was, pressed against him again, and I was having a hard time separating how I felt about the Sam of my past and the Sam here in the present. They were the same person, obviously, but liking the Sam of my past was safe. Liking the Sam of now wasn't.

He could escape from a locked room with only straws and tape. He'd killed people right in front of me. How could I have feelings for someone like that? And what did it say about me if I did?

Cas pulled into the driveway and stopped. Sam opened his door and slipped out. Immediately I missed him. Nick followed quickly behind.

"What are they doing?" I asked.

Cas drummed his fingers against the steering wheel. "Checking the house."

Right. I hadn't thought about that. If Riley had found us in that shopping mall, how long would it be till he found the cabin?

I watched Sam disappear into the woods to the right of the driveway. One minute he was there, slinking through the trees, and the next minute he was gone. It felt like I held my breath the entire time. When Trev's cell chirped from his pocket a few minutes later, I jerked in surprise.

"Everything clear?" Trev asked. "All right." He ended the call, then slid the phone back into his pocket. "We're good."

I exhaled in relief.

Thanks to Nick, a fire was already crackling when we walked into the house. I folded myself into one of the easy chairs, tucking my legs beneath me. The heat felt good, but it made my torn-up leg burn more. It wasn't too bad, as far as scrapes went, but it was still annoying. Plus, my brand-new jeans were already ruined.

"Let's talk about the guns," Nick said once we were grouped in the living room.

The room went icily still. I had the overwhelming urge to back into a corner, far from the others. It was partially because of me that the guns had been lost.

Sam leaned a shoulder against the wall near the windows, his eyes downcast. "We can't go without guns. I know you were protecting Anna," he said to Trev, "but it's left us vulnerable."

Trev scratched at the back of his head. "I'm sorry. It was the first and only thing I saw that I could use."

Nick rose to his full six feet plus. "How about unzipping the god-damn bag and, I don't know, using one of the guns!"

"Hey, come on." Cas stepped into the middle of the argument, arms outstretched, as if he meant to hold Nick back, despite their four-inch height difference. "We can get more guns. Right, Sammy?"

Everyone turned to Sam and his shoulders sank an inch. "Yes, but it's not in the budget, and going around asking about guns is only going to draw more attention."

"We have a budget?" I asked. The boys ignored me.

Cas gestured toward Sam with a quick lift of his chin. "How many bullets we got?"

Sam was the only one with a gun now. He retrieved it from beneath his new coat and removed the magazine. "A full ten."

"Not going to get us very far," Nick said. A few rogue curls stuck out from behind his ears. It wasn't fair that he could look so good after going so long without a shower. He had that perfect kind of wavy, bordering-on-curly hair that looked presentable even when unwashed. Silently I wondered if he was dying without his organic shampoo. I hoped so.

Trev scrubbed his face with his hands. "I'm sorry I tossed the guns, but guns are a liability, anyway. We can get by without them."

"Don't be a fucking idiot." Nick propped himself up with a hand on the fireplace mantel. "We can't go without weapons. Ever."

"So what now?" Cas said.

Sam pushed away from the wall. "Now we go find some guns."

We stuck to back roads on the way to the seedier part of Whittier, in case Riley or Connor was around. Staying so close to the town where they had found us was dangerous. It was only a matter of time before we'd have to leave, and I dreaded the idea. I liked Sam's cabin.

Sam parked in front of an empty flower shop and got out, everyone but me following. They grouped at the front of the vehicle, their voices hushed and urgent. A few minutes later they broke apart, and Sam came to the passenger-side door. I opened it.

"So, where are we going?"

"*We* are not going anywhere. You are staying with Cas."

Cas cocked his head to the side and gave me an innocent look. "You were voted in as my babysitter. Sorry."

I snorted, knowing it was really the other way around. Better him than Nick, though.

After the others left, following the draw of loud rock music to the bar it blared from, Cas turned to me. "You got me for sixty long minutes. What do you say we get to know each other better?"

I screwed up my mouth. "Very funny."

"I kid, I kid." He laughed, the sound reminding me of so many moments shared in our basement, of Cas goading me from the other side of his glass wall. He was a pain in the butt, but he was also extremely easygoing.

"Actually, I'm starving."

He dug in his coat pocket. "I have…seven dollars. Want to see if we can find something close by?"

"Please."

"You got it, babe."

We set out on foot and found a gas station a few blocks away. Inside, the hum of the fluorescent lights felt oddly comforting, like I'd stepped out of one world and into another I knew well. We each grabbed a cola, but we decided to share an egg-salad sandwich.

Two blocks away, we found a little marina that butted up against a large lake that faded into the darkness. Since it was mid-October, most of the boat slips were empty, but tiny green lights still glowed on the end of each dock.

"Food always makes me feel better," I said, eating a chunk of egg off the tip of my finger. "Thanks, Cas."

"No problem. I know how the Big Dog gets. No time to savor the good things in life. Don't worry—I got your back."

I smiled. "What was Sam like in the lab? *Really* like?"

Cas popped the last of his sandwich into his mouth and leapt from the bench. "Sammy is hard to explain." He sauntered over to a maple tree that stood between a pair of benches. He started climbing as he went on. "Let me put it this way: Sammy has the intensity of a Rottweiler and the stubbornness of a mule." He grunted as he hoisted himself up into the heart of the tree. "Expects everyone to do exactly what he wants, when he wants. Except..." He trailed off, his silence piquing my interest more than his words had.

I went to the base of the tree. "Except what?"

"Well..." Cas propped himself in a fork in the branches and looked down. "Are you pumping me for gossip? Because that's what it feels like."

I warmed. "What? No!"

"Come on, Anna, you're in love with him, aren't you?"

I could barely make out his facial features in the darkness, but I didn't have to in order to hear the sly smirk in his voice.

If Cas knew about my feelings for Sam, did Sam know? Of course he did. I wasn't exactly secretive about the whole thing. But hearing it out loud changed everything. I suddenly felt nauseous.

I put my face in my hands. "Oh my God."

The tree branches rustled. Cas dropped to the ground next to me and patted my head. "It's all right. Go ahead and admit you're in love with me, too. Let's get everything off our chests while we're at it."

I swatted at him but he dodged away. "You're not making me feel better."

"Who said I was trying to make you feel better? Fact: Sam's got swagger. Fact: I'm straight. Fact: Even though I'm straight, I sorta love the dude. So I can't say I blame you."

A sliver of a smile touched the corners of my mouth. "All right. Maybe I feel a *little* better."

He hooked an arm around my neck and messed up my hair. "You're so cute when you're upset." He let me go after I shrieked.

"God. You're so annoying!" I said between bursts of laughter.

"But charming." He fell into step with me. "Let it be known that if you're ever in need of a good make-out session, I happen to be available Tuesday nights."

"Only Tuesdays?"

"Maybe Thursdays, too."

"Yeah, all right," I said with a fair amount of sarcasm. "I'll let you know."

"Come on." He ushered me in the direction of the vehicle. "We should probably get back."

We crossed the street. "One more thing?" I asked.

"Yes?"

My insides knotted just thinking about asking Cas what I wanted to ask him, but I couldn't help it. He knew Sam better than Nick and Trev. They were closer. So if anyone knew the answer to my question, Cas would.

"Does Sam...ah...does he—" The words didn't want to come out.

"Does he like you?" Cas filled in.

I cringed, completely mortified. "Um...yes?"

In the glow of a streetlight, Cas's expression blanked, and he cocked his head to the side. "Do you really want to know the answer to that? At a time like this?"

Did I? When we reached the end of this, whatever it was, I couldn't stay with Sam. He'd move on to his new life, wherever that might be, and I'd return to mine. I couldn't have him in the way I wanted. And that killed me.

"In the immortal words of the Magic 8 Ball," Cas continued, the wind flattening his blond hair to his forehead, "'Ask again later.'"

But I wouldn't. I couldn't. If Sam had no feelings for me, I didn't want to know.

20

"I GOT A NAME," NICK SAID WHEN WE met up. "And an address."

"Where?" In the darkness, Sam looked impatient, as if being in one spot for too long had already gotten to him.

Nick sunk his hands into the pockets of his new black fleece, which he'd either bought or stolen at the mall. It wasn't what I would have pictured him in, but then again, I didn't think he cared what he wore as long as it functioned properly. He had specific tastes when it came to specific things, but clothing apparently wasn't one of them.

"Ten miles east of town on a dirt road: 2757 Ax Lane," Nick said.

Cas snorted. "Well, that's pleasant."

Sam shifted, the glow from the street lamp highlighting the planes of his face. "What's the contact's name?"

"Tommy. That's all I got. No last name."

"Tommy sounds like the name of an illegal arms dealer to me," Trev said.

"Sure does." Cas nodded.

My teeth chattered as we slid back into the Jeep. I held my hands in front of the vent after Sam started the engine, wishing I had grabbed a pair of gloves at the mall. I would have loved to have the scarf, too. It might have been in my possession for all of ten minutes, but in that amount of time I'd come to think of it as an extension of my mother. Like owning that scarf would somehow bring me closer to her.

But maybe I wouldn't even need it. Maybe the miles were bringing me closer to her.

I grabbed her journal and flipped to the very back, to her recipe for garlic mashed potatoes. In red pen, she'd drawn a heart at the top of the page and scribbled a message below. *Arthur's favorite*, it read. I couldn't help but analyze everything now, looking for hidden meanings.

What I really wanted to find was an answer. Why she left. If she thought about me.

If she is even alive, I reminded myself.

With Nick navigating, Sam drove. The vehicle jolted as we exited the highway and turned onto Ax Lane, the pavement giving way to dirt. A truck passed us on the opposite side, shooting gravel into the driver's door.

"Damn rednecks," Nick grunted in the back.

"Keep that kind of thing to yourself when we get there, all right?" Sam said and Nick went quiet.

Number 2757 was a mobile home, the white sheeting on the outside sliding off in places like loose window shutters. Several cars and trucks filled the front yard. Farther back, taking up most of the lot, was a garage twice the size of the trailer. Smoke curled from a stack jutting out through the roof.

Sam parked alongside a black truck.

"We all going in?" Trev asked, eyeing me. I appreciated his concern, but I was not staying in the vehicle. Not in the middle of nowhere.

"Since we have no idea what we're dealing with," Sam answered, "it's probably best if we stick together."

The trailer in front was dark, but music pumped from the garage, so we went straight there. Sam knocked on the metal access door. I counted the seconds it took for someone to answer, hoping that the classic rock blasting inside had drowned out the sound of the knock. I started to fidget.

Sam was reaching to knock again when the door opened. A man in his late forties peered out at us, scraggly gray hair hanging in a ponytail over one shoulder. His bloodshot eyes lingered far too long on me. I should have felt uncomfortable under his stare. Old Me would have. New Me just felt angry. I straightened my shoulders and held my chin high.

Look confident. That's what my instructor used to say. *Predators prey on the weak.*

"Yeah?" the guy spit out. "What can I do for ya?"

"Are you Tommy?" Sam asked.

The man's brows knitted together in suspicion. "Maybe. Why?"

"We need guns."

He snickered. "Kid, I ain't got no guns. Now run home to Mommy." The man, obviously Tommy, started to shut the door, but Sam blocked it with his foot.

I braced myself for a fight.

"What the hell do you—"

"See that Jeep out there?" Sam said.

Tommy craned his neck. "Yeah, what about it?"

"It's stolen." Sam pulled the cell phone from the inner pocket of his jacket. "Not only do I think you're an illegal arms dealer, I think you're also a drug dealer. Is that weed I smell?" Sam gave the air a sniff. "What else will the police find if I call to report a sighting of that stolen vehicle?"

Tommy jabbed his finger in Sam's direction. "Now listen here, you little punk—"

"We just want a few guns."

By the look of his trailer, Tommy needed money, and he certainly didn't want the police prowling around this place. He readjusted his hold on the door. "Well, you got any cash?"

Sam pulled a clip of money from his pocket and held it up.

Tommy snorted. "Fine. This better not bite me in the ass."

Permitted entrance, we filed in. I counted a total of ten people inside, including Tommy. A few guys stood around a computer watching Internet videos. Another group played poker at a foldout table. Two of them were women, somewhere in their thirties. The one on the left hunched forward, allowing her cleavage to spill out of her low-cut shirt. The other woman flung a hank of kinky brown hair off her shoulder, catching a few wisps of it in the big hoop earrings dangling from her ears.

They studied the boys—*my boys*—then settled their attention on me.

"Tommy!" one of the guys at the computer said. "Hurry up. You got to watch this."

"Later," Tommy said.

The guy turned around. "Oh," he said when he saw us. "Didn't know we had company. You need me?"

"Yeah, get your pansy ass over here."

Tommy's friend joined us as we approached a closed door in the back. His eyes landed on me. "So, what's your name?"

"Anna."

"Name's Pitch. And it's a fine pleasure to meet you."

Pitch was younger than Tommy by about ten years. He shared Tommy's long, thin nose and pronounced chin, but his hair was some shade between brown and red, cropped in a short shag around his face.

In another life, Pitch might have been cute, but in this garage, he gave off a sordid vibe that made my insides scuttle. With Sam's earlier suggestion running through my head, I stayed close to him and pretended to be flattered by Pitch's attention, wanting no hard feelings or trouble.

Tommy unlocked the closed door with a ring of keys attached to his belt loop and pushed through, flicking on an overhead light. The room looked like a library, which seemed so out of place here that it was obvious it was a cover. Three bookcases lined the walls. Car manuals took up most of the shelf space.

Tommy shoved aside a manual on Ford Mustangs and revealed a silver lock embedded in the back of the bookcase. He pulled out the same ring of keys, undid the lock, and swung the bookcase out.

Behind it was an entire rack of weapons. Handguns, shotguns, knives, brass knuckles.

"So what can I do you boys for?" Tommy said, revealing the weapons like a street dealer holding out his suit coat, showing off a load of watches pinned to the inside.

"Browning Hi Power?" Sam said.

Tommy pulled a sleek black pistol from two pegs on the pegboard and handed it to Sam. "How's that?"

Sam nodded at a little folding table open against the far wall. "May I?"

Tommy shrugged. "Be my guest."

Sam removed the clip and set it on the table. Next he pulled back and locked the slide, checked for bullets. He wiggled something and a piece popped out.

Even though he'd told me he remembered using guns, it still amazed me to watch him dismantle this one like it was something he could do in his sleep.

He pulled out a spring, then the barrel, and inspected the pieces with the keen eye of someone who knew exactly what to look for.

"Hasn't been cleaned in a while," he concluded.

Tommy snorted again. "This isn't fuckin' Martha Stewart."

"Any gun owner would know that cleaning a gun ensures its accuracy and gives it longevity."

Pitch stepped up. "Do you want it or not, Cupcake?"

The boys and I shifted closer to Sam. "How much?"

"Nine hundred."

Sam reassembled the gun and fired a dry shot, making sure to point it at the ground. "I can buy a brand-new one for a thousand."

"Then go buy a brand-new one." Tommy hitched up his pants. "Something tells me you need that gun tonight, or you know you'll fail the background check. Whichever it is, it means you ain't getting a brand-new one, now are ya?"

"Four hundred," Sam said, ignoring the goading, even though Tommy was right.

"Seven," Tommy countered.

"Five apiece. I'll take four."

"I ain't got four the same, but I can give you something close to it for twenty-two. That a deal?"

Twenty-two hundred dollars for guns?

"Ammunition included?" Sam asked.

Tommy shrugged. "Sure."

"Deal." Sam handed over the money.

Pitch selected three other guns and a few boxes of ammunition. He passed one of each to Trev, Cas, and Nick.

"Pleasure doing business with you, boys," Tommy said.

I let out a breath once the bookcases were locked behind us, the guns put away. I wanted out of there. The whole place felt off, and a discomforting sensation crept along my skin like spider legs.

We passed Tommy, Cas leading the way. I stayed in the back, close to Sam, but we had to go single file through the door and Pitch came up behind me, slinging an arm around my shoulders.

"So…Anna…you staying close by here? Can I get your number?"

I tensed beneath his touch, assaulted with the smell of cheap cologne and stale cigarette smoke. Pitch's flannel shirt rasped against the back of my neck and I moved to shove him off.

"Pitch!" one of the girls called. "Keep your goddamn hands to yourself, and try to remember who you're engaged to."

The bottle-blond woman stood next to the card table, cigarette smoke curling around her face, her mouth tense with fury. My hands started to sweat.

"Shut up, Debbie!" Pitch yelled.

Sam hung back. "Anna."

Pitch cocked his chin. "Is she your girlfriend or something? I don't see your name on her."

"Pitch," Tommy said, the warning ringing out loud and clear.

"Pitch, goddamn it!" Debbie said again.

"You broke up with me last night," Pitch shouted. "Far as I'm concerned, I'm a free man."

Debbie gave her metal folding chair a shove. She dropped her cigarette, ground it out with the toe of her boot, and stormed in our direction.

"You little piece of shit," she said, slamming Pitch in the chest. Pitch stumbled back. She turned to me.

"Get your people in line," Sam said to Tommy.

"Don't tell me what to do, kid." Tommy flicked his ponytail off his shoulder. "Maybe if your girlfriend wasn't a whore—"

In one quick move, Sam slammed the bigger man to the floor, getting in a punch before one of Tommy's friends jumped between them.

I backpedaled and held my hands up. "I'm not going to steal your boyfriend!"

"You're damn right you're not!" Debbie slapped me across the face. The shock hit before the heat did, and I went motionless.

Nick reached for me, but a burly blond guy grabbed him by the forearm and swung him around. Pitch sidestepped us and dove for Sam. Tommy's other men swooped in. They cornered Cas near the poker table and slammed Trev up against a freestanding toolbox.

Debbie hooked a leg around mine and pushed, slamming me to the floor. The air rushed from my lungs and I gasped to get it back.

"Anna!" Sam yelled.

Debbie climbed on top of me, pinning me. Her eyes were bloodshot, like she was drunk or high or both. Air trickled into my lungs. I gritted my teeth. I was not going to be bested by a sleazy hick.

I bucked, dislodging her, and got to my feet. She wrapped her arms around my legs and my knees hit the concrete. I threw back an elbow, cracking her in the sternum. I found my footing again, twisted, grabbed a hunk of frizzled blond hair and rammed her face into my knee. Something snapped. Debbie screeched as blood poured from her nose.

"I don't want your stupid boyfriend!" I yelled.

"Anna?"

I whirled around.

Tommy and Pitch and all the others lay scattered, unconscious. The boys were bloodied and bruised, but looked all right.

"That was effing hot," Cas said. "Didn't know you had it in you, Anna."

I looked at Debbie, who was curled in the fetal position, her friend cooing at her side.

I didn't know I had it in me, either. I knew the moves, I knew how to defend myself, but I never thought it'd feel so . . . satisfying.

Sam was staring at me when I turned back to him. There was a slant to his green eyes, a question on his face. Like he was finding it difficult to read me. Little Anna, so predictable. Until now.

"It might be best if we're gone when they wake," Trev said.

I wiped the blood from my face with the sleeve of my coat and led the way out the door.

WITH EVERYTHING THAT'D HAPPENED,

Sam decided it'd be best if we ditched the Jeep and stole something new. Cas was the one who was good with hot-wiring, or whatever it was he had to do to start a vehicle without keys. He, Trev, and Nick dropped Sam and me at the cabin first.

When I protested that I was fine, that the boys didn't have to make a special trip home for me, Sam silenced me with a look that said otherwise. And then Cas added, "I'm not going home for you, Banana. I want to start up the generator now that we have gas. Get that water heater going."

Once we were inside, Sam lit a small candle and left it on the kitchen counter. The room filled with pulsating light.

Sam tore off his coat with a wince, and nodded at the table. "Sit."

I pulled out one of the chairs and fell into it. I was too exhausted to even think about arguing anymore. Apparently fighting made for hard work. Sam sat next to me, turning his chair so that we faced each other. He reached over, grabbed the bottom of my seat, and dragged me closer. So close that I was practically wedged between his legs.

A shiver threatened to rock my shoulders, but I tamped it down. I didn't want to show Sam what his close proximity did to me. Though I suppose he probably already knew. And maybe on a sub-conscious level, I *wanted* him to know.

He ran quick, gentle fingers over my jaw, then my forehead. I hadn't had a chance to examine the damage Debbie had doled out, but my face hurt all over. I must have looked like a mess.

"Your eye hurt much?" he asked.

"The left one? Yeah. It's throbbing."

"Close it."

I closed both eyes and breathed in deeply when his fingers inched up the side of my face, tilting my head at different angles, examining me in a way no one ever had.

"Stay right here," he ordered.

He crossed into the kitchen. I noted the way he favored his left leg, the stiffness in his back.

He returned a minute later with a dampened washcloth.

180

I winced when he pressed it to my face. Not only did it hurt, but the cloth was freezing cold from the water. Without Nick to tend the fire, the cabin had gotten considerably chillier in the hours we'd been gone. And Sam didn't like to use power unless he needed it, despite the far-off chugging of the generator.

"You're just bruised, and a little cut."

"So I'll survive?"

"Of course." He pulled the rag away. "I'm sorry that you had to go through that. It's my fault. I should have left you in the car with one of the others."

I tsked. "No, it was Debbie's fault, and Pitch's. Don't blame yourself. Really. I mean, look at you. You're in worse shape than I am. Your eye is bruised, and your lip is split, and you keep hunching over funny, like your ribs hurt. How are *you*?"

He stood up, the wet rag still in his hands. "It doesn't matter. What does matter was your reaction in there. What were you thinking?"

"What do you mean? Why did I fight back?" He didn't respond, but I didn't need him to. The look he'd given me as Debbie lay in a ball at my feet came back to me. Like I'd changed into something else right in front of him.

I rose, hands on my hips. "Is it so far-fetched to believe that when I needed to act, I acted? I'm not going to let you admonish me for it. I liked it. I felt strong. You're not going to take that away from me. I finally put all those combat lessons to good use."

"That was more than basic fighting, Anna." He leveled his shoulders, pointed at his chest. "You could feel it here, couldn't you? Something more than instinct."

I hadn't taken the time to label exactly where the feeling had come from, but he'd described it perfectly.

"That worries me," he said, knowing my answer before I spoke it. "Because that's how I feel it."

"What?" I tried to make sense of what he was implying. "Do the others..."

He nodded.

"But..."

He threw the rag in a bin near the door and started to pace. "Did you ever meet with Riley or Connor outside the lab?"

I frowned. "What kind of question is that? No. Never."

He sighed, another crack in his hardened exterior, a tiny and barely perceptible tell on his emotions. "Did they ever approach you about anything outside the lab?"

"No."

"Think, Anna."

I thought back to all the times Riley and Connor had come to the farmhouse. We saw Riley maybe ten times a year, and Connor even less than that. They usually sidestepped me, rushing down to the basement to check in on the boys—or, as they called them, the "units."

The only time I'd been alone with one of them was...

"Wait," I said.

Sam stopped.

"The first time I found you guys, Connor showed up unannounced, three days later, while Dad was at the store. He sat me down at the kitchen table and told me I couldn't be allowed in the lab until you guys were ready." Bits and pieces came back to me. "A few years later, he came out for a regular check, and I remember hearing him and Dad whispering outside in the driveway. They were arguing. I heard Connor say my name."

"What else?"

"I don't know for sure. I was too far away to hear the whole conversation. That was the same night Dad asked for my help in the lab."

Sam thought for a second. "Or Connor ordered your father to allow you in."

"Why?"

"I don't know."

A vehicle pulled up the driveway, and Sam moved to the windows. "It's Cas," he said, relieved.

When Cas walked in a few minutes later, I was shocked to see how terrible he looked. In the hour since we'd left him, a bruise had darkened around his left eye, another on his right cheekbone.

Nick and Trev had fared better, but then Cas was the kind of person who leapt into things without fully thinking them through. I wasn't surprised he'd taken a few more hits than the others.

"I hope that water heater is full," he said. "I want a shower. I'm so effing sore."

"Let Anna," Sam said.

Trev's gaze immediately went to me. "You all right?"

I nodded, but I was not all right. Sam was calculating something, trying to put the pieces together into a working theory. That's why he'd questioned me about Connor and Riley.

I just didn't know what that theory was.

"Fine," Cas groused. "I guess I'll stuff my face instead."

Every inch of my body hurt, and I wanted to scrub the feeling of Pitch and Debbie and that whole place off my skin. But one look at Sam, the way he dodged my gaze, told me the real reason behind his insistence that I go first. He wanted to talk about me.

The water was plenty hot, but instead of climbing into the shower, I stood at the bathroom door, one ear pressed to the wood. I could barely make out the boys' voices. Biting my lip, I twisted the doorknob one millimeter at a time until the door eased open. I waited, listening. The boys kept talking, so I opened the door wide enough to slip through and tiptoed across the upstairs landing.

I strained to catch something.

"Barter with Connor for her," Nick said. "She's more trouble than she's worth. None of us would have been in that fight tonight if it weren't for her."

I went down a few steps, getting as close to the kitchen as I dared.

"Dude," Cas cut in, "you can't blame Anna for what happened with that d-bag."

"Forget about the kid that started the fight," Nick said. "Why did *we* fight? It's like I *needed* to protect her, even though I can't stand to look at her. She reminds me of everything I hated about that lab, all those goddamn years locked in that little glass bubble while she got to go in and out whenever she wanted. Think about it. Why the hell do we want to protect her so damn badly?"

"She's like family," Trev said earnestly.

"It's not that and you know it," Nick snapped back. "That agent at the mall said to get Anna first. Why would he say that?"

I'd forgotten all about what the agent had said in the chaos that followed our escape. I'd thought it weird at the time, but now it seemed damning.

Silence settled in downstairs.

"Stop looking at her like a defenseless little girl," Nick went on, "and start looking at her like a liability."

I stomped down the remaining stairs, my temper flaring. I rounded into the kitchen, fingers curled into fists at my sides. Sam's gaze met mine. I could sense the shift in the room. Would they turn on me? Would Sam?

I had never been more aware of my vulnerability than I was at that moment. I was in the middle of Michigan, with no directional bearing, at the whim of these four boys who could kill me with a toothpick if they wanted to.

And they were looking at me like they didn't know me.

"I am not a liability," I said. "I am your friend."

The corners of Sam's mouth tightened.

Nick ignored me. "We could ditch her at the next town over."

He could be persuasive when he wanted to be, and the thought of being left alone in some town I didn't know made my stomach knot. I lunged at him, fear and anger and a million other things propelling me forward. I caught him off guard and he rocked back a step before finding his balance. He grabbed me tight at the arms as he swung around, slamming me into the wall.

The others leapt to their feet in one rush.

"Nicholas!" Sam growled.

Nick and I met eyes, the animosity between us almost visible, like a heat wave.

"Jesus Christ," Trev said.

"You attack me and still I can't hurt you." Nick's voice was punchy with accusation. "Logically, I should be protecting myself; instead I'm protecting *you*. Tell me that's not a liability, Anna. Tell me that makes perfect fucking sense."

"Back off her, Nick," Sam said.

For once, Nick ignored Sam's command. I wrapped my hands around his forearms, bracing myself in case I needed to fight. "Let. Me. Go." I put as much vehemence in my voice as I could muster.

Flexing his jaw, Nick let up, and I slid down the wall a few inches. "I'm not whatever you think I am." I looked from him to the others, hovering just inches away. They all had the same uncertain expression on their faces.

"Do you all feel that way? Like you inexplicably need to protect me?" No one said anything. "Are you kidding me? And you didn't tell me?"

"We weren't sure," Sam said.

"Oh my God." I exhaled as the fight rushed out of me.

"Hey." Trev came to my side and took my hand as I fumbled to the chair. "It doesn't necessarily mean anything, and no one is leaving you behind."

I desperately wanted Sam and Cas to agree. But they didn't. They didn't say anything.

Did Sam think I was some Branch tool? *Was* I a Branch tool? But how? Why? It didn't make sense. None of this made sense.

Sam's attention came to rest on my hand, intertwined with Trev's. He blinked. "Why don't you go take that shower?"

I choked back a sob. He didn't trust me.

Trev had to lead me toward the stairs. "Come on. I'll go with you."

Inside the bathroom, the hot water still ran, filling the tiny space with steam.

"Don't let the others get to you. Everyone is on edge."

I bowed my head. I couldn't *not* let them get to me. There was more going on here than any of us understood. In the lab back home,

I used to feel like I was part of something good. Like I was helping change the world. But now I felt ashamed and guilty. The boys had every right to doubt me. Nothing was as it seemed. Maybe every shred of my life in that lab had been a lie. Maybe everything I knew about the program was, too.

"Anna?" Trev ran his fingers down the side of my face and nudged my chin up with his thumb. "They're just grasping at straws."

I practically threw myself at him, wrapping my arms around his neck. There was no hesitation as he hugged me back. What would I do without Trev? He was my best friend. Loyal. Trustworthy. He kept me sane and grounded. That was what I needed right now, more than anything.

"Do you have an inspiring quote for me?" I asked when I pulled away. "They always help."

He laughed and ran a finger over his lips as he thought. The lightbulb expression winked on. "'Faith in oneself is the best and safest course.' Michelangelo." He looked down at me, his amber eyes heavy with exhaustion but still present, still seeing me.

"Thank you," I said.

"Don't mention it. Take as long as you want. Or at least until the hot water runs out. I'll be out there when you're done."

He left me alone. On my way back to the shower, I caught my reflection in the foggy mirror. A bruise bloomed beneath my right eye. A scrape ran across my collarbone. My lip was split in two places, and a scratch sliced my temple at the right side, blood matting my blond hair.

I was a mess. And I just wanted to forget about everything. I climbed under the showerhead, letting the drum of the water drown out my thoughts.

22

LATER THAT NIGHT, I LAY IN BED OVER-
analyzing the slant of moonlight on the trees outside, hoping the act
of mentally sketching would overpower everything else crowding my
head. It didn't.

Now I knew why Sam had asked about meeting with Connor
outside the lab: He was questioning why that agent in the mall parking lot had ordered the other men to grab me first. Nick wasn't the
only one who was suspicious, and I didn't know how to convince the
boys that I wasn't the bad guy. That I cared for them like they were
family.

The wind shifted the trees, wiping away my mental sketch-
in-progress.

A floorboard creaked and I lurched upright. Sam stood in the doorway to my room, half hidden in shadow. He wore jeans, a T-shirt, boots. He'd been hanging around the house fully clothed since we'd returned, just in case we needed to leave at a moment's notice. I had on an oversized T-shirt I'd nabbed from Trev. It was the only thing I wore other than my bra and underwear. What if Connor ambushed the house right this second?

I tugged the blanket closer as Sam crossed the threshold.

"I didn't mean to startle you."

"You didn't," I lied. The truth was, I was on edge. I knew what he was capable of, and I wasn't sure if I was considered an enemy at this point.

He dropped into the window seat, rested his elbows on his knees. "How are you?"

"I'm okay."

"Sore?"

"A little."

"Do you need anything?"

I swallowed. "Why are you here, Sam?"

He ran a thumb over the knuckles on his opposite hand. Moonlight pooled on his back. "Remember when you got your first black eye, in your class?"

My combat class. I remembered—it was something I would never forget. While I'd hated that my opponent had bested me, that fight had made me feel strong. Like a warrior. I wore the bruise like a badge and barreled downstairs as soon as Dad fell asleep so I could show it off.

But Sam's reaction had not been the reaction I'd hoped for. I'd wanted him to be impressed. I'd wanted him to look at me with reverence.

Instead, he had questioned me excessively over how it happened, who did it, whether my opponent was bigger, stronger, faster. Boy or girl. Arrogant or nice. That was the first time I saw a glimmer of his protective side, and I thought, well, I'd take that, too.

When I left the lab that night, I felt like I'd gained some ground with Sam, earned something from him, just not in the way I'd expected.

"I remember," I said now.

He folded his hands together. "That was the first time I realized there was more to our relationship than I'd thought." He sat back, and I lost sight of his face in the shadows. "It frustrated me in a way nothing else had since I'd woken in that lab. Because I couldn't protect you the way I needed to."

Needed. Like it was something he couldn't control. I dared not move. I couldn't stand it if he stopped talking now.

"I knew it was odd to feel that way for someone who was on the other side of the wall, but I never questioned your involvement in the program. You made our lives bearable in that lab. I won't forget that. No matter what."

My throat thickened. My eyes burned.

"So whatever's going on, I will do what I can to keep you safe. I won't leave you. I won't barter with Connor for you. I don't care what Nick says."

I clamped my mouth shut against the stinging in my sinuses. I would not cry. Not now.

"I wanted you to know that," he said. Even though I couldn't see his eyes, I felt the weight of his gaze.

"Thank you." My voice came out in a quiet hush.

He rose to leave. Inside I was screaming: *Stay. Stay. Stay.* I didn't care if we talked or not. His presence was enough.

At the door, he paused.

"What color would you use?"

I frowned. "What?"

"When I came in, you were staring out the window."

Drawing, was what he didn't say. *You had that look on your face like you were drawing.*

That familiar burn came back and my vision blurred. It seemed like forever ago that we'd last discussed the weather, the outside world, and how I would draw it. I missed it. I missed it so much. "Lavender gray."

He nodded and turned away. "Good night, Anna."

"G'night." I let out a breath of relief as his footsteps thudded down the stairs. I hadn't realized until that very second how badly I wanted him to trust me. No matter what we'd gone through, I was on his side. Always. Even if it killed me.

The house was eerily quiet when I woke late the next morning. I put a hand up to hood my eyes from the daylight that blasted through my window. My head pounded on all sides. The trek down the stairs seemed to take forever; every step was agonizing. Every joint in my body creaked in misery. I felt like I'd taken a week's worth of combat courses.

In the kitchen, I barely registered Trev at the table as I shuffled past him. I pulled the bottle of ibuprofen out of a drawer and downed two pills with a gulp of water.

When I turned around, Trev was barely a foot away. "You okay?"

"No. I feel like hell."

"You look like hell."

I managed to part my lids a fraction, only enough to glower. "Geez. Thanks." I started to move around him, but he stopped me with a tug on my wrist.

"Hey. Come here." He wrapped me in a hug, and I melted instantly. He smelled like tea and pinesap, probably from gathering wood. I stalled there for a second, loving how comfortable and familiar he felt.

"Where is everyone?" I asked, my voice muffled against his sweatshirt.

"Sam went for a run. Cas and Nick are in the garage messing around with the generator. Something shorted out last night."

I pulled away. "And you? What are you doing?"

A lock of black hair fell across his forehead. "Me? I am tending to you."

I sighed. "No need for that." I peeked over his shoulder and saw the table covered in loose sheets of paper. "What's all that?"

"That is what Sam spent most of the night doing."

I dropped into a chair and picked a page from the pile. Sam's handwriting, a barely legible scrawl, filled the paper. None of the notes made sense to me.

Trev rooted around in the kitchen and came back a minute later with a steaming mug of liquid. "Drink this."

"Thanks." I sipped gingerly, expecting coffee but tasting freshly brewed green tea. I didn't drink tea a lot, except for when I was sick. Dad would brew up a cup using loose tea leaves and a little metal basket with a chain on the end.

"Your mother liked doing it the old-fashioned way," he'd say.

Trev slid into the chair next to mine. "I just pulled the kettle out of the fireplace. It's not quite the same as putting it on the stove—it tastes like burning wood, if you ask me—but it's something."

"It's perfect. Thank you." I held up Sam's notes. "Did he crack the cipher?"

"Ah." Trev plucked a page from the stack. "This is what he has so far."

There was a series of letters running along the top of the paper. A lot of *X*s and *I*s, and a few other letters. Then, at the bottom, *Retrieve evidence from Port Cadia. Use scars and tattoo to find your location.*

Once you find it, the tattoo marks the spot. When you find the spot, it'll be the third tree, sixty north.

The back door burst open and Sam sauntered in, his dark hair glistening with sweat. He wiped his forehead with the back of his sleeve and disappeared into the pantry, returning a second later with a fresh bottle of water.

I gave the paper a shake. "You broke the cipher. So now what?"

Before answering, he examined my face with a quick sweep of his eyes. I hadn't bothered to check my reflection in the mirror before coming downstairs, and now I wondered if I really did look like hell.

My face felt puffy in spots. I was sure I sported new bruises that'd formed while I slept.

"How are you feeling?" he asked.

"Fine." I shook the page harder.

Trev rose to his feet. "Now that you're back, I think I'll go out for a run."

"You got a cell?" Sam asked, and Trev patted his pocket. "Stay alert."

With a nod, Trev left through the front door. Sam sat at the head of the table, the water bottle crinkling in his grasp. "The first portion doesn't make any sense. So I don't know if it's deciphered."

"How do you think you have to use the scars? Or the tattoo? Maybe the UV light—"

He shook his head. "Cas checked me again this morning."

I slumped. "Oh." Not only was I disappointed that that wasn't the answer, I was disappointed that he hadn't asked *me* to check him. Though I suppose at that stage, he wanted to be as thorough as possible, which probably meant...

I blushed thinking about what "thorough" meant.

"But you know where you're supposed to go," I said, flattening the page in front of me. "*Port* was mentioned in your file. Whoever wrote those notes, they must have been talking about Port Cadia, right?"

He shoved the mess of discarded paper aside and set his elbows on the table. "Maybe. But I can't go there without knowing where to look." He scrubbed at his face with his hands. "The first part of the note could be a warning for all I know. I need to have a clear plan before making a move."

I looked at the mixed-up letters at the top of the paper. The *X*s and *I*s seemed vaguely familiar, but I couldn't place them. And the longer it took us to decipher the rest of the message, the closer Connor and Riley would be to finding us.

23

I LOOKED AT THE CLOCK HANGING ABOVE

the fireplace. It'd been six hours since my last dose of painkillers. I'd spent most of the day in one of the easy chairs in the living room with my mother's journal. I alternated between sketching a new picture of Trev, analyzing my notes about the boys, and rereading my mother's passages.

One of the very first recipes she had added to the book was one she titled "Dinner for Two on a Rainy Night." It was a tuna casserole that seemed all right, but at the bottom she'd written,

DISASTER. Arthur hated it

Dad. It seemed like I hadn't talked to him in weeks. I didn't even know if he'd had his wound tended to, if he was out of the hospital. And still I wondered about the house: Who would take care of it now that I was gone? The leaves needed to be raked and dumped in the woods. The winter rug had to be dug out of the garage and unfurled in the mudroom. The windows in the living room needed to be weatherproofed. Would Dad remember to do those things on his own?

I wished I could call him, hear his voice, know that he was okay.

I set the journal aside and pushed myself out of the chair. My body grumbled and my head swam. The headache had returned in full force. I was not built for real combat, apparently.

I shuffled across the living room and froze midway to the door.

The clock.

I looked at it again. It was an older model, with Roman numerals for the hours. *X*s and *I*s and *V*s. The first half of Sam's coded message was in *X*s and *I*s.

"Sam!" I called and instantly regretted it as the vibration of my voice intensified the pounding in my head.

He came tromping down the stairs, eyes heavy with sleep. I hadn't realized he'd been napping and felt a pang of guilt for waking him.

"What is it?" He held his gun loosely at his side. The others crowded in the doorway between the living room and kitchen.

"I think I know how to decode the rest of the message."

I saw the message in a whole new way once I knew what to look for. Sam hovered over my shoulder. Cas had been excited about my revelation for all of five seconds, until his dinner was ready. Now he sat across from me, stuffing his face. Trev was next to me, and Nick had pulled himself up onto the counter at my back.

"I think these are Roman numerals," I said, pointing at the beginning of the message. "So if we translate them into actual numbers, maybe it'll give us an address or coordinates or a phone number."

Sam put his hands on the back of my chair and leaned forward, sending a wave of nervous flutters down my back. I held tighter to the pen. "There were breaks in the code," he said. "I thought it meant a space between words, but it might be a break between numbers."

I read the first set: XXIII. "Twenty-three."

Then XV. "Fifteen."

We went down the row until we had 23 15 55 85 82.

"Ten numbers," I said.

"I don't think those are coordinates."

"I think the obvious answer is that it's a phone number," Cas said around a mouthful of rice.

I broke the numbers into a phone number: 231-555-8582.

"Should we try it?" Trev said.

Nick slid off the counter and landed with barely a sound. He was wearing another of the found button-down shirts with a pair of jeans. "We should pack everything before we do. Be ready to run."

It took us all of ten minutes to gather everything that was important enough to take. We regrouped at the table. Everyone tensed with trepidation as Sam punched in the numbers.

The kitchen sink dripped in the open drain. *Plink. Plink.* The generator chugged in the garage. Sam paced. He made it from one end of the room to the other, then froze.

I could faintly hear a voice pick up on the other end. Sam looked right at me, his eyes wide and incredulous. "Yes," he said. He rubbed his face with his free hand and then rattled off the address of the cabin.

"How long?" he said. Then: "All right." He hung up.

I pounced. "What did they say?"

"She knew who I was."

She? Please don't let it be the girl from the photo.

"Do you know who it was?" I asked.

He picked up his gun from the counter, pulled out the clip, checked the bullets. He'd done that once already, before making the call.

"Sam?"

"I think it's best if we wait till she gets here, in case...."

I rose steadily, rocking my shoulders back with resolve. "Who was it, Sam?"

He blinked slowly, like he meant to close his eyes and sigh but thought better of it. "Sura. She said her name was Sura."

My vision dimmed. The air in my chest retreated to a place where I couldn't seem to find it.

My mother was not dead. And she was on her way here.

24

MY HEAD POUNDED EVEN HARDER.
Sura—*my mother*—told Sam she was four hours away. Four hours. In four hours I would see my mother. The butterflies in my stomach wouldn't quit. Did she know I was with Sam? What did she know about me at all?

I couldn't understand why she'd left. I couldn't understand why my dad had lied to me almost my entire life. I couldn't understand why my mother knew Sam, why she'd left him that first clue in her Pennsylvania house.

That clue should have been mine. If she wanted to lead anyone to her, it should have been me. Only an hour into the wait, the questions fueled the hurt, calcifying it into a lump in my throat. Mothers were not supposed to abandon their daughters. I'd needed her. And I'd mourned her. And she'd been only hours away, living a secret life as Mrs. Tucker.

The excited butterflies burned and fizzled.

Nick opened the gun bag, the zipper making a sharp-edged sound, followed closely by the *snick*-rack of a gun being loaded. What if this was an elaborate setup? What if Connor had gotten to my mother? There were a million *what if*s, and one wrong decision would cost us so much.

But it was my mother. *My mother.*

The boys rotated through a watch of the front and back windows. They each had a gun nearby, if not in their hands.

Four and a half hours into the wait, Cas shifted at the front window and snapped his fingers. It was somewhere close to eleven PM, and we'd been sitting in the dark for a while.

Headlights flooded through the canvas curtains, and Sam leapt off the couch. I ran to the window in the dining room, despite Sam's earlier instructions to stay put. I had to see. I had to know if it was her.

An old, dented pickup truck parked next to the latest SUV Cas had stolen. The engine cut out, the lights shut off, and the driver's-side door opened. I could just make out her silhouette and the shape of a thick braid hanging over her shoulder. A dog barreled out of the truck behind her and dashed for the cabin.

The woman came up the steps, still shrouded in darkness; I

couldn't make out her facial features. A knock sounded on the cabin's door. I started for the living room, but Sam held me at bay with a wave of his hand. He raised his gun, motioned to Nick. Trev. Cas. They formed a loose circle around the door, guns up.

My knees went cold, numb. Sam twisted the knob. My heart felt like it might leap from my chest.

The door opened.

She stepped in.

"Hands up," Sam said. Even tone. Cool as ever.

She did as he asked, but the dog—a chocolate lab, from what I could tell—trotted in, uninhibited.

"Are you armed?" Sam asked.

With a nod of her head, she pulled a gun from a shoulder holster tucked beneath her fleece jacket. Then she pulled a knife from her boot. She placed both weapons on the floor, and Nick swept in, kicking them out of range.

"I am a friend, Sam," she said.

While she didn't sound old or haggard, I could tell she wasn't younger than thirty. Her voice had a depth to it, an authoritative edge, like she'd seen a lot and wouldn't take crap from anyone.

Sam motioned to Cas and Trev. They squeezed past us and left through the back door. Checking the perimeter, as planned.

Turn on the lights, I thought. *I want to know if it's really her, see her with my eyes.* But we stayed in the dark as Sam gestured her forward.

"Sit," he said. She sat. I peeked around the doorway from the kitchen. When she saw me, I swear something flashed in her eyes, but whatever it was, it was gone before I could name it.

The dog came to her side and lay on the floor, tail swishing.

No one said a word.

When the boys returned with the news that the perimeter was clear, Sam finally flicked on the lights. It took me a second to adjust, and I blinked the light burn from my eyes. When my vision cleared, a woman came into view. Black hair. Willowy. Eyes the color of summer grass. Wrinkles at the corners of her mouth like wind cutting through sand.

I sucked in a breath and the air crystallized in my lungs.

"Oh my God," I breathed.

It was her. My mother. Alive.

The words didn't seem to want to come together in my head. She'd never been more to me than pages and words in a journal. A woman in a picture. But she was flesh and blood. Real. *Alive.*

This woman might have been older than the woman in my photograph. Her hair might have grayed around the temples. Her cheeks might have looked thinner than those of the twentysomething woman at that lake's edge. But it didn't matter. I knew it was her.

"Sura?" Sam said. The name sounded foreign spoken aloud there in the cabin's modest living room.

She nodded. The dog sat up.

A million questions washed through my head and I couldn't grab on to one of them long enough to ask. Why hadn't she ever gotten in touch with me? Did she recognize me?

Sam sat on the couch and dragged me down next to him. He threaded his fingers with mine. His hand was cool and dry and sturdy. Mine trembled, slick with sweat.

"I've been waiting for you boys to contact me for days," she said. "I caught word through the line that you'd escaped. I was going to wait for you in Pennsylvania, but I got spooked and took off." She shook her head. Her braid shifted. Why wasn't she looking at me?

"So, tell me, what is going on? I had no idea...." She trailed off, wringing her hands in her lap. "I'm sorry, Samuel. I really am. I tried looking for you for a few years after you disappeared, but I couldn't find you."

I fidgeted, and Sam's hold on me tightened. *Not yet*, was the message, loud and clear.

"One of the clues led to your phone number," Sam said.

She nodded. "That was the plan, in case they cleaned you out. You gave me a phone and asked me to keep it on, always. I didn't know about this place." She gave the room a cursory glance. "But then, you never were forthcoming with details."

"How do you know me?" Sam asked.

"You and Dani came to me a little over five years ago and asked for my help. I knew Dani through her uncle." Her eyes lost focus for a second, but she quickly shook it off. "Anyway, you stole something from the Branch that you were going to use to buy your freedom. But then Dani disappeared. You planted the clues as a backup plan before going after her." The dog whined. "You never came back."

"Hold on a minute." Cas held up his hand. "I'm having trouble keeping up. Who is Dani?"

Sam dug the picture of himself from the back pocket of his pants. It'd been folded in half, and the edges were worn to the white paper beneath the ink.

An odd, nameless emotion stirred in me. What did it mean that he kept the picture folded in his back pocket, like a memento?

He showed Sura the picture. "Is that Dani?"

Sura didn't need more than a second to decide. "Sure is."

"I don't remember her." Sam took it back, hid it away. "Why was I going after her?"

"Well...you loved her. It's as simple as that. And Connor took her from you."

The nameless emotion intensified, brittle and tangy on the tip of my tongue. And suddenly I knew what it was: heartache. If she was the whole reason Sam had planted clues, the whole reason he'd eventually been caught, that meant that if not for her, Sam would never have been locked in the lab. I never would have met him. I both loved and hated this girl.

"I don't know what happened to her," Sam said. "But sometimes I have flashes of a girl."

I looked over at him. He'd never told me that.

"I don't see a face," he went on, "but maybe it's her?"

208

If he'd done everything in his power to find this girl five years ago—tattooed himself, scarred himself, gone up against the Branch—what would he do now?

He'd made me a promise that he would always have my back, but when it came down to choosing between Dani and me, who would he choose? If it meant sacrificing one of us to protect the group, I wasn't sure which side he'd pick.

Sura clasped her hands together. "They really cleaned you out, didn't they? Tell me what you do remember."

Nick grunted. "Try fucking none of it."

Her gaze swept to Nick. "Well, Nicholas, I can see not much has changed with you. All brass and balls."

Cas choked on a laugh, and Nick gave him a hostile look.

"We woke up in a lab five years ago," Sam explained. "We have only vague memory flashes of our lives before that."

Sura nodded, like that made sense now that she knew the facts. "All right. So let's start over. Tell me about your escape. I'm vaguely familiar with him"—she pointed at Trev, then turned her attention on me—"but I don't know this young lady."

Sam tensed. I tensed. Everyone tensed. "You don't recognize her?"

Sura deepened the V of her brow. "Should I?"

Trev fidgeted in the doorway. Nick cracked a knuckle. I wasn't sure what they'd expected, but sixteen years had passed since my mother last saw me. I'd changed a lot in that time. Couldn't they give her a second before they jumped to conclusions?

Sura examined me. Dad had told me I had her eyes, but now I wasn't so sure. Hers were dark green, and mine were hazel. She'd been too far away in the picture I had of her for me to see before that the comparison wasn't right.

"This is Anna," Sam said.

"Anna," she repeated, like she was trying out my name, like it felt familiar, but she wasn't sure why. "Well, Anna, it's nice to meet you."

I stared at her, the greeting saying all there was to say. And the longer I stared at her, the blurrier she became, as my vision clouded with tears.

"Sura, Anna is your daughter," Sam said. But even he didn't sound convinced.

A ringing noise filled my head as she looked at me, *really* looked at me, the fine lines around her eyes deepening. "What exactly did they tell you?"

"You don't recognize her?"

She sighed when she turned back to me. "Honey, I've never been pregnant."

The weight of so many days of fear and uncertainty abruptly overcame me. The ringing grew louder, and a choked sob escaped me. I leapt from the couch. The dog lifted his head, jangling the tags on his collar. I hurried through the kitchen. The dog barked behind me. I burst outside, the wind too cold now as tears streamed down my face.

"Anna!" Sam's footfalls pounded the ground behind me as I ran, unsure of where I was going—anywhere was fine, as long as it was far from here. All those years I'd wished I'd known my mother, and now here she was, and I wasn't her daughter?

"Anna, stop!"

Brittle ferns whipped against my knees. A branch snagged my hair. I lost my momentum and Sam caught up, spinning me around.

"She doesn't know me!" I screamed, pushing him away, because I didn't want him to see me fall apart, and because I couldn't stand still for one second longer.

"We have to find out why," he said. "Stop!"

I buried my face in the crook of his neck. He smelled like Ivory soap and clean, crisp air. He smelled like home.

I just wanted to go back, even if none of it was real. I missed the predictability of everything. At home I knew what to expect, and Sam would always be there and I would always be Anna with a mother who was dead and a dad who spent every waking minute working.

That was my life. It might not have been much, or even true, but it was mine.

We stood there in the middle of the woods as Sam let me cry. He held me tightly, like he was afraid that, given the opportunity, I'd run again. And maybe I would have. Maybe I would have run as far as my legs would have taken me.

"She's not my mother," I said finally, wiping the tears from my cheeks. Speaking the words aloud made them seem truer. Maybe deep down I'd known this was a possibility—ever since I'd found that sticky note, her handwriting there in the present, matching the handwriting in the journal from the past. Maybe I'd known since then.

My dad might have lied about a lot of things, but lying to me about whether Sura was my mother seemed too devious even for him. So why did he do it? What purpose would it serve?

"If she isn't my mother, then who is?"

A gust of wind shook the trees. "I don't know," Sam said. "But I promise you, we'll find out."

25

GROWING UP, I'D DESPERATELY WANTED
to know my mother. It was probably why I drew her so often, as if my
pencil would somehow fill in the blanks. And now here she was in
front of me, and she wasn't even mine to know. That hurt worse than
anything. I thought I'd been given a second chance, only to have it
snatched away.

Trev handed me a mug of instant coffee. Sura got one to match.
Sam sat next to me, so close we touched. He'd already made it clear
he wasn't going anywhere.

"We'll be out in the garage," Trev said, "tending to the generator."

I caught Sam's half nod out of the corner of my eye. He'd dismissed Cas and Nick earlier with some discreet gesture I missed. To
give me as much privacy as possible.

When I came back inside, I'd wanted to retreat to my bedroom and curl into a ball and mentally dissect everything I thought I knew about myself. Memories of my father, the things he'd said about my mother. I wanted to flip through her journal, looking for clues that I might have missed before. It was Sam who insisted I sit down with Sura.

Flames crackled in the fireplace and the chill in my hands dissipated.

"Why don't you tell me about Arthur?" Sura said. "About you."

"Um..." I licked my lips, brought the coffee mug down to chest height. "I don't even know where to start."

"Maybe I should start with me?" she offered. "About me and Arthur?"

"He told me you died when I was one, but obviously that isn't true."

She shook her head and tucked her feet up into the chair. "We divorced thirteen years ago."

I frowned. "But that would have made me four at the time. Did he...um...you know..."

"Have an affair?" she filled in. "Not that I'm aware of, but I guess it's possible. We were two different people by the time we divorced. Arthur had always been more focused on his career than anything else."

So who *was* my mother? Where the hell did I come from? More questions. Fewer answers. I needed to talk to my dad.

"Did you ever work for the Branch?" Sam asked.

"Yes. By accident. I found myself fresh out of college with a journalism degree and no available job openings. Arthur got me into the Branch."

I thought of her journal and said, "Oh, I have something of yours." I picked the book up off the table beside the couch and handed it to her.

She raised her brows. "Is this the one with all the cookie recipes in back?"

"Yeah. I've tried them all."

She flipped through the pages. "Wow. I wondered where this thing had gone. A lot of angst and soul-searching in here, but the recipes are good. Most of them I got from my mother. She knew cuisine like no one else."

Hearing her talk about her own mother filled me with despair. "You can have it," I said, gesturing to the book.

"Oh, no." She gave it back. "It's yours now. I see you added to it. Besides, I've since started a new one."

Secretly, I was relieved. Maybe the journal no longer had the same meaning it once did, but it still reminded me of home, and I didn't want to part with it.

"So, tell me about Arthur. How is he?"

Sam and I exchanged a glance. Bringing up the fact that he'd shot Dad didn't seem like a great way to start the conversation. "He's good. Like you said, he works a lot." I picked at the corner of the journal. "What did you do in the Branch?"

"I worked in the med department. Before I left, they were experimenting with mind manipulation. They'd already perfected the memory wipes, clearly."

"Is the Branch a wing of the government?" Sam asked. He looked calm, his hands casually clasped in the space between his knees, but his body was tense. And when he readjusted, I noticed that his shirt was tucked in in the back, giving him quick, easy access to the gun there.

Sura set her mug on the table. "No, but they're largely funded by it, and there's a mutual agreement between them. They let the Branch do whatever they want, and whatever they develop, the government gets first dibs."

"Like the boys?" The thought made me ill.

"Yes." Sura looked right at Sam. "You boys were designed to be soldiers of the highest caliber. But when you start making men stronger and smarter than men should be, it's hard to control them. I'm assuming that's why they locked you up. That, and the fact that you stole something from them that pissed Connor off."

Sam edged forward. "But what?"

She shrugged. "I was out of the Branch by then. I don't know the particulars. And you were never the sharing type."

That was true even now.

"Did I give you any other information?" Sam asked. "A code word? A clue about my tattoo?"

She shook her head. "I was only supposed to stand by as a safe contact, to fill in some of the blanks if they wiped your memory."

A pause, then Sam said, "Were they working on something new when I stole whatever it was I stole? Further alterations? A different drug?"

"I really don't know, but"—she untucked her legs—"I did hear they were moving a lot of money around. I had contacts—still do—within the Branch."

"People you trust?" Sam asked.

"Oh, yes."

The dog rolled over onto his side and let out a snuffle. The fire crackled in the hearth. Sura twisted toward me, her thick braid swinging off her shoulder. "I'm sorry you had to find out this way. I know it must be hard to trust anyone right now, but if there's anything I can do, let me know."

I offered a smile. "Thanks."

"It's getting late." Sam stood. "You can stay here, if you want. There's a bedroom upstairs you can have."

"Thank you." She snapped her fingers and the dog climbed to his feet. "Which room?"

Sam started to answer, but I beat him to it. "I'll show you," I said. He gave me a guarded look. In response, I nodded, as if to say *I'll be fine*.

Upstairs, I led Sura and her dog to the first room on the left, one of three bedrooms on that level. The second one was all mine. The third, the boys shared. They never slept at the same time, anyway, so sleeping arrangements weren't a problem.

"What's your dog's name?" I asked as I pulled an extra pillow out of the closet.

"Coby." Sura went to the windows and gazed out. "The boys treating you okay?"

I paused halfway between the closet and the bed. "Yeah. I mean, Nick and I don't get along all the time, but that's pretty typical."

Sura took the pillow I offered her and fluffed it. "Give him time. Maybe he'll come around."

"I doubt it."

"Well, he's had a hard life, that boy. Been broken as long as I've known him. So don't take it personally."

I went back in the closet and rummaged around inside, pulling out two blankets. "What do you mean?"

Despite the fact that Nick and I didn't get along, I was intensely curious about him; I wanted to understand him, to figure him out.

"The whole reason Nick got involved with the Branch," Sura explained, "was because he left home at the age of sixteen and had nothing to lose. His mother left him with his father when he was two. His father was an alcoholic. He beat Nick every chance he got."

The blankets suddenly felt too heavy in my arms. Was that what he'd had flashes about? His abusive father? I sat on the edge of the bed as the horror of Nick's history settled in. I'd had no idea.

"Nick is the way he is because he grew up that way," Sura added, "and no amount of memory wiping could change that."

The things he'd said to me in the cemetery made more sense

now: *I might not remember who I was before all this, but I can bet it wasn't all sunshine and fucking roses.* Maybe a part of him had always known that keeping the memories buried was better than digging them up.

"What about Sam?"

Sura came around and took one of the blankets off my hands. "How did he enter? His mother gave him up. The Branch took him in."

"They're allowed to do that?"

"They get away with a lot worse."

I moved so she could make the bed. "If you know about the boys' lives before the memory wipes, why aren't you telling them now?"

The corners of her mouth curved into a wry smile. "I just got here an hour ago. This is Sam we're talking about. He's wary of everything. Sam only trusts himself, and anything I said would have to be taken with a grain of salt."

I nodded. She was right, of course.

I helped spread the second blanket over the top of the thinner cotton one. They both smelled like a musty closet, but she'd need them in the early-morning cold.

"Well, I guess I'll let you get some rest."

She inclined her head as I started for the door. "Anna?"

"Hmm?"

"You seem like a strong-minded young woman. You're very beautiful, too. I would have been proud to call you my daughter."

That's all it took. My vision went hazy, and I had to clamp my jaw to stop my lips from trembling. Even though I knew it wasn't true, I still wanted to hold on to the belief that she *was* my mother. I didn't want to let her go.

"Thank you," I said and closed the door behind me.

26

LATER, IN MY ROOM, I KICKED OFF
my shoes and lay back on the bed. After the radiating heat of the fire
in the living room, the cold air of the bedroom raised gooseflesh on
my arms. I tugged the blanket over my shoulders and took a second
to listen to the natural sounds of the house—the creak of floorboards
downstairs, the scuffling of dry leaves outside.

In one day I'd learned so much. My mother was not my mother.
Sam had been in love. And I now saw Nick in a whole new light. I
was having a hard time finding a place for the new information in my
already jumbled head.

I closed my eyes, thinking I'd spend a minute warming up,
but before I knew it I was out. I woke in the middle of the night, the
blanket askew, my feet exposed to the cold air. The first thought

to come to me was that I needed to sneak down to the lab to see Sam. It took me a moment to get my bearings, to remember that I wasn't at home and that I didn't have to go down to the basement to see him.

I planted my feet on the floor, the old habit ingrained in my body, every nerve, bone, and cell telling me to go. As I descended the stairs, the amber glow of the fire flickered through the banister, casting spindly shadows on the wall. Outside, tree branches scraped and tangled with one another, while the house itself had settled into that eerie nighttime silence when everything stood still.

I found Sam lying on the couch on his stomach, eyes closed, hands buried beneath a pillow. I realized with a hazy sort of wonder that I'd never seen him asleep before, except when it was induced by gas. If I had, I would have been mesmerized by how ordinary and peaceful he looked. When he was awake, he was anything *but* ordinary.

I got within a few feet of the couch and stopped, training my eyes on the rise and fall of his shoulders, assuring myself that he was still breathing. Assuring myself that nothing had changed in the hours since I last saw him.

I'd just started for the chair, thinking I'd warm myself by the fire for a few minutes, when Sam leapt from the couch, pushed me into the wall, and thrust a gun in my face.

I gasped and said, "Sam. It's me."

"Anna." He relaxed his hold.

"I'm sorry," I managed to say.

He shook his head. "No, I shouldn't have—"

"I snuck up on you. I know better."

He set the gun on the table to my right. "I didn't hurt you, did I?" He took my face in his hands, and my skin tingled.

"No. I'm fine."

In the muted light, his muddy green eyes seemed bewildered, lost. *Like he'd seen a ghost.* He took a step back.

"What is it?" I asked.

A sigh forced its way past his lips. "The longer I'm outside the lab, the worse I feel."

"Is it the memory flashes?" He didn't answer, which clearly meant yes. I hated myself for asking what I was about to ask, but I couldn't stop the question from sprinting past my lips: "Are they about Dani?"

He looked away. "I failed her."

An overwhelming sense of possession washed over me until I felt like I'd been crushed. I wanted him to be mine, not someone else's. What did this girl have that I didn't? Could she reach across the years and steal Sam back?

And had he ever been mine to begin with? I hadn't thought Sam capable of love, at least not in the unreserved way every girl wants, but maybe the old Sam had been. Maybe the old Sam bought roses and wrote sappy poetry and held hands with the girl he loved. He'd only learned about Dani a few hours ago, and already he remembered pieces of her. If he was on his way to reclaiming who he was, it was only a matter of time before I lost him for good.

I pulled away. He stopped me with a hand on my wrist. "Wait," he said. "I know what you're thinking."

"What?"

His lips looked redder, wetter. My pulse thumped against my ribs.

"It's written all over your face." He pushed a lock of hair out of my eyes. "I'm not going anywhere."

"I never said you were." But my voice came out an uncertain whisper.

His hand went to my waist as his eyes met mine. His fingers found bare flesh beneath the hem of my T-shirt. Every nerve ending in my body thrummed in response.

"Sam," I said, though I couldn't pull together the rest of what I wanted to say, all the things I should have said.

He leaned in and brushed his lips against mine, feather-light at first, then more eager. My heart thundered as he exhaled, like he'd been holding the air in his lungs for far too long.

My hands walked up his biceps as his fingers threaded through my hair, sending ribbons of heat down to my skull. He pressed into me as if he couldn't get close enough, and I pressed back. Because I *wasn't* close enough. Because I'd spent the last several years of my life wishing I could be closer.

As his hands slid up, mine slid down, exploring the swell of muscle in his sides. I slipped my hands beneath his shirt and a voice in my head said, *No, slow down, what are you doing?* And every part of me ignored it.

His body felt fevered beneath my touch, and when his mouth found mine again, I leaned back into the wall, unsure of my ability to stay upright.

If he wanted to, I was ready to do anything. *Anything.* And as my mind opened to the possibilities, he pulled back.

"Anna," he said. His voice was hoarse but firm.

The way he looked down at me, his fingers still pressed against my cheeks, I knew what he was thinking without him saying it.

We shouldn't.

And maybe he was right. But I still wanted so much more of him.

I slid away, tugging down the hem of my shirt and smoothing it with a shaky sweep of my hand. I tried not to look at the sliver of hard stomach still exposed under his hitched-up shirt, but failed. If I couldn't touch him with my hands, I wanted to touch him with my eyes and never let go.

"Anna," he said again, but nothing else came out and I thought maybe, for once, he was the one at a loss for words.

"I'll see you in the morning," I said, my tone sharper than I meant it to be.

I didn't wait for a reply. I hurried from the living room, from the fire, from Sam. The cold snuck back in, crawling up my arms.

What was I thinking?

I wasn't. I wasn't thinking, and that was the problem. If I'd learned anything about Sam in the years I'd known him, it was that he calculated everything he said and did.

And that kiss... that wasn't in the plan.

I just wanted to retreat to my room, lock myself inside till dawn. But when I was halfway up the stairs, Sura came barreling down, eyes wide, hair wild and unbraided.

"Grab your stuff," she said. "Connor found you."

27

SAM HOISTED HIMSELF UP AND OVER the banister, landing on the stair above me. He drove Sura into the wall and pressed the barrel of his gun under her chin, forcing her head back.

"Did you bring him?" he asked.

Sura tried to shake her head, but Sam held her firmly in place. "No. I swear it. I am on your side, Sam."

"Then how do you know Connor is coming?"

She swallowed. "I just got word from one of my contacts. I called to ask for help."

"Who is this contact?"

"No one you know."

A bead of sweat rolled down Sam's temple. "How long do we have?"

"Ten minutes."

"Shit." He put the gun away and took the stairs two at a time, hurrying to rouse the others. One of them was probably outside somewhere, on watch, but I didn't know which one.

Sura and I locked eyes. "I didn't set you up," she said. "I would never."

"I want to believe you...."

She came down a step. "It doesn't matter. Listen. There's something else my contact told me. Something about you."

I backed into the banister. "Me?"

Her hair hung in thick waves over her shoulders. "What's your earliest memory?"

Nick darted across the landing on the second floor. Somewhere upstairs a door banged open.

"Anna! Think."

I refocused. "What does this have to do with anything?"

"Where did you live before the lab? Before you knew the boys?"

Cas sailed past us on the stairs. That meant Trev was the one outside.

"In town. In an apartment." I started up the stairs. "I have stuff to grab. I should—"

Her hand circled my forearm. "Was it an upstairs or downstairs apartment?"

"Upstairs."

"What color was your room?"

"I have to go!" I shook out of her grasp.

"They're false, Anna!"

I froze.

"Your memories. If you sit and think about them, you'll realize you don't actually know what color your room was. Or where you ate breakfast."

Uncertainty cemented me in place. "I know the color of my old room."

"Then what was it?"

A dog barked outside. Sura's dog?

"It was..." I tried to picture the room in the apartment. Where the bed was. The closet. What color were the walls? Purple. Weren't they?

The dog yelped. I heard a bag *thunk* against the landing above me.

"Anna," Sam called. "Move it!"

"When I left the Branch," Sura said in a rush, "they were testing a new way of wiping memories and planting false ones. I think that's what they—"

A window shattered in the living room and blood sprayed across the front of me. Sura pitched forward, taking me down with her. I hit the hard edge of the stairs and felt the unnatural crunch of muscle against bone.

"Sura?" I gave her a shake, but she didn't respond.

When I pushed her away, her wide-open eyes stared back at me, unblinking. Unseeing. There was a gaping bullet hole in her forehead, and I doubled over, retching.

Someone grabbed me beneath the arms. Dragged. Lifted. Hauled me to my feet. The blood had soaked into my shirt. Blood and other things. Meaty things. I screeched and swiped at the mess, trying to erase it. *Get it off.*

Cas swung into the stairwell as the front door exploded in a burst of splinters. Another gun went off and Cas dropped to his knees.

Sam pulled me back as I shouted down the stairwell, "Get up! Cas! Get up!"

Another bullet hit him in the shoulder, and he toppled back down the few stairs he'd made it up. Men barged into the cabin, gas masks concealing their faces. Another window shattered and a black cylinder *whump*ed to the floor, hissing as it let out a cloud of gas. Behind me, Nick shouted.

"Cas!" My voice was lost in the sound of pounding footsteps. I fought against Sam's arms, wrapped around my waist. Cas lay on the floor, blood leaking from his wounds, eating away at the white of his shirt. His eyes closed.

Sam carried me into my bedroom. Nick was already there, a bag slung over his shoulder. He opened the window. The wind caught the curtains and they ghosted out. Sam pushed the dresser in front of the door, while someone banged on it from the other side. What if it was Cas? And where was Trev?

Nick jerked me toward the window. "Out," he said, and I scrambled onto the roof. The gritty shingles dug into my hands and the wind bit at my exposed arms.

"We can't leave Cas," I protested.

Nick climbed out behind me. Sam came next. Staying low, they steered me forward, to the edge of the roof. We peeked over. An agent stood between the cabin and the garage. Sam pointed to him and Nick nodded. *What does that mean?* I wanted to ask.

Sam rose to a crouching position and jumped off the roof. I gasped. Nick clamped his hand over my mouth, catching the sound before it fully escaped. He pressed his lips against my ear. "If you don't keep your goddamn mouth shut, we're all dead."

I forced a nod and he let me go. We both looked down to where the agent lay sprawled in the dirt. Sam motioned us down.

He wanted me to jump? No. No. I couldn't jump. It was two stories. I backed away.

"He'll catch you," Nick whispered.

"I can't."

His flame-blue eyes narrowed. "Fine. Don't scream." He placed his hand on my back and gave me a shove. I staggered over the edge, arms pinwheeling, hair whipping in my face. The sky blurred around me, and then I was in Sam's arms and he was swinging me to my feet.

Nick came down with a graceful, almost silent *thud* as a second agent rounded the corner of the house. Nick attacked with a knee to the gut and an elbow to the back of the head. The man collapsed. Another agent appeared. Nick distracted him as Sam moved in from the other side and snapped the man's neck with a quick twist of his hands.

My stomach churned.

Go, Nick mouthed.

"Outside! Outside!" someone yelled.

We ran through the woods, disappearing in the dark and the twist of trees. It didn't take long for my lungs to burn, for my legs to cramp. Sam wasn't even breathing heavily.

I tripped on uneven ground and staggered forward.

Nick caught me. Sam looked over his shoulder and asked, "Can you keep going?"

I sucked in a breath, trying to catch up. No, I couldn't. I couldn't even breathe. "Yeah...I'm...okay."

The land descended the farther we went. I could just make out the line of the road, the barren stretch of dirt cutting through the woods. Sweat gathered at the small of my back. I wasn't sure how long I could keep up this pace. Probably not long enough.

Headlights swung out of the driveway and Sam stopped running. Nick pulled me down to a crouch. Whoever was behind the wheel punched the gas and the back end fishtailed.

"Sam!" someone shouted.

"That's Trev," I said.

We cut across the woods to the road as Trev stomped on the brakes, the SUV swinging sideways. "Get in!"

A shot rang out. The bullet hit the back door a foot away from my hand, the metal folding in like a sinkhole. I stared at it, at the closeness of it.

"Anna!" Sam said.

The sound of his voice broke my trance and I ripped the door open, scurrying inside as Trev shifted into drive.

"Shut off the headlights," Sam ordered. Trev did as asked and the lights cut out, the night swallowing us.

I stuck my head between my knees, sucking in air, and along with it the stale smell of an old fast-food bag that lay crumpled on the floorboard.

Cas had been shot. *Shot*. Was he dead? Sura was. She was *truly* dead this time. My shirt still felt hot with her blood. The material stuck to my chest.

Had she betrayed us? Her last warning rang through my head. My memories. My memories weren't real. Had Sam overheard our conversation? Nick? No; if he had, he'd have already turned against me. He couldn't find out.

"How did you escape?" Sam asked Trev.

Nick slid closer to me, putting himself in the middle of the bench seat so he could better see Trev and Sam in the front.

Trev messed with the radio. "I was taking Sura's dog for a walk when I *literally* ran into an agent. We fought"—he pointed at his eye, the lid swollen and bruising—"but clearly I won. So I went to the truck and tore out of there. I saw you guys running from the house, but I lost you when you hit the woods."

I sat up, watching Sam over the rise of Nick's broad shoulder. Sam clenched his fist, then relaxed it, then clenched it again, the tendons dancing in the half light of the dashboard. "How many were there?"

"Fifteen, give or take."

"Did you see Riley or Connor?"

"Riley's there. I didn't see Connor."

Sam propped an elbow on the center compartment, running a hand over his chin, the stubble rasping.

"What are you thinking?" Nick said.

Sam closed his eyes, the dark fan of his lashes resting against his cheeks. He looked so worn out. "Maybe they held back to flush us out." He opened his eyes. "That way, Riley can follow us to Port Cadia and retrieve whatever it is I left behind. Maybe that was the plan all along."

"You mean"—I twisted in my seat—"they deliberately allowed you to escape the lab? Is that what you're getting at?"

He sighed. "I don't know. Maybe."

"No way. Think about it. If that was the plan, Connor and Riley wouldn't have been there to begin with. They wouldn't have risked themselves."

"Anna's right," Nick said, surprising me. He gave me a look. "Well, it makes sense. We were never supposed to escape, and now that we have, they know the information Sam stole is at risk of being found. This is them scrambling to prevent more damage."

Trev set the radio on a classic-rock station. If Cas were there, he would have demanded a pop-hits channel. I felt the loss of him suddenly and acutely. He'd been so close to escaping. Maybe if I had helped him...

I put my face in my hands and tried to force the image of Cas lying on the floor, blood pouring from his wounds, out of my head.

Please don't be dead, I thought. *Please*.

"Are we headed to Port Cadia then?" Trev asked.

"Yes," Sam said, "as fast as we can. Before they catch up with us."

28

"GET UP." I OPENED MY EYES. SAM leaned in through the door of the SUV. His hand lay gently on my shoulder. Exhaustion still held me in its grip, and I had a hard time keeping my eyes open as I righted myself on the bench seat, arching my back to stretch my sore muscles. I'd never before used my body in such a brutally real way, and it was starting to catch up to me. I felt like a pretzel, knots included.

I had no idea what time it was, but it was still dark, so I couldn't have been out for too long. "Where are we?"

"Port Cadia. I got us a room."

Behind us, an orange motel sign buzzed, but the street was dead and quiet. It was such an anticlimactic arrival. We'd been pushing to reach this place for what felt like forever, and now we were here, and there wasn't anything to see. And Cas was gone. I closed my eyes again, thinking that if I hoped hard enough, maybe it wouldn't be true.

"We'll get him back." Sam tried to sound positive, but his voice echoed my distress.

"They shot him."

"Cas is strong." He held the SUV door for me as I slipped out, shivering in the cold. He forced me to look at him with a nudge of his thumb. "We'll get him back," he said again. "I promise."

All I could do was nod.

Trev, still in the driver's seat, cleared his throat. "We'll be back in a few minutes." To me he said, "We're going to the gas station to fill up. You need anything?"

"No, thanks."

The boys pulled away and I followed Sam down the motel's open breezeway, passing brown metal doors with the room numbers tacked above the peepholes. Sam stopped at room 214 and wiggled the key into the lock. The door opened with a pop. He flicked on the light and I squinted, still too tired to see clearly.

I dropped into the chair at the table, slouching, arms crossed over my chest. I missed my jacket. I missed Cas. I missed Dad and the farmhouse. I missed being normal.

Sam sat across from me and dug a few sheets of loose paper from his pocket—the clues he'd left himself. We still didn't know the answers to those mysteries. We had no idea where we were going or what we were looking for.

I lay my head on the backs of my hands on the table, too exhausted to even think about it anymore.

"What did Sura say to you? On the stairs?"

I jolted upright and met Sam's eyes. He regarded me with open sympathy. I swallowed. "Did you hear any of it?"

"Enough to be interested."

So I told him everything. I wanted to get it out before Nick came back and formed his own opinion. I still didn't know how I felt about it.

I vividly remembered a sketch I'd done not too long ago, of a girl in a snow-covered forest, pieces of her separating and dissipating. Was it my subconscious, trying to tell me something?

"What if I *am* a Branch tool?" I said once I'd finished. "What if you can't trust me? What if..." There were too many *what ifs* to list them all.

I bowed my head. My hair swung forward in a curtain. "This doesn't even feel real anymore."

Sam ducked his head to better see my face. "I trust you. You got it?"

"Okay." The pressure in my chest lessened. "Thank you. Really."

"We need to figure out what I stole from the Branch. Maybe some of your answers will be in there." He disappeared into the bathroom and came out a minute later, shirtless. My eyes went to the *R* scar on his chest, then down to the hard planes of his stomach.

"Can you look over the tattoo again?" he asked. I had to drag my eyes up to meet his. "If you see anything unusual, tell me."

"Sure." I climbed on the bed from the opposite side as he sat on the edge, waiting. I scooted up behind him. I started at the trees' leaves, checking the veins, counting the clusters, looking for any sort of symbolism.

Finding nothing, I moved to the bark, examining the fine lines. On the third tree to the right, a line in the bark caught my eye. I stifled a yawn. I was exhausted and not seeing clearly, so whatever it was wasn't immediately evident.

I got in closer. Something definitely seemed out of place. I ran a finger over Sam's skin. He felt warm to the touch, warmer than he should have been in the cold room without a shirt.

"Did you find something?" he asked.

"Maybe."

He got up from the bed and dug around inside the drawer of the bedside table. He found a pad of paper with the motel logo on it and a pencil and handed them to me. "Can you redraw it?"

I nodded and he settled back on the bed. My knees were sore from my sitting on them for so long, so I unfolded myself, keeping one leg up and putting the other alongside Sam's. Being so close to him sent my heart skittering, and I wondered if he felt it, too.

My lips tingled as I remembered the feel of his mouth on mine. I worried my lower lip with my teeth, trying to squash all the emotions running through my head.

I re-created the peels and texture in the tree bark with my pencil, enlarging it so it was easier to see. As I worked, a pattern started to emerge. When it was finished, several striations in the bark came together to form what looked like numbers. Since the work had been done in a light gray color, from afar it looked like nothing more than expert shading.

Sam twisted around. "Let me see."

I handed him the pad of paper.

"Numbers." He squinted, took my abandoned pencil, and started to sketch lines around the bark. "Two-six-four-four."

I nodded. That's what I'd read, too.

He studied the drawing with a furrowed brow. "There wasn't anything else?"

"No. I mean, I can look again, if you want."

"Yes. Please."

We resumed our positions, even though I knew I'd find nothing. And as I thought that, I couldn't help wondering if he just wanted me near, if searching the tattoo was an excuse. Of course, that was a stupid idea. Sam wasn't the type to waste time with excuses.

I eyed the tattoo again, running my finger down the bark, over the trees and the grass, as if using a part of myself to memorize the lines would somehow reveal a new clue I hadn't seen before.

Sam shuddered beneath my touch. I was no longer looking for clues so much as I was pushing for a reaction. He hung his head for one quick second before twisting around to meet me face-to-face. We were inches apart. I slid closer.

"Anna," he said.

The door burst open and I leapt away. Trev and Nick stared at us. Blood rushed to my cheeks. I had never wanted to disappear more than I did at that moment.

Nick tsked and shook his head as he came in. He set a paper bag on the table and unpacked what they'd bought.

"We got sandwiches and chips," Trev said. "Two turkey, two roast beef. Iced tea for Anna. Sam, I got you a water."

Sam ignored him, keeping his back to the rest of the room, his shoulders taut.

"Roast beef is mine," Nick said. He turned on the TV and flipped through the channels with the remote. "You lost your shirt, Sam?"

"Anna was looking over the tattoo."

"Yeah." Nick grunted. "It looked like it."

Sam took one quick step and snatched the remote out of Nick's hands. He tossed it toward the bathroom, where it smashed against the wall, shattering into a dozen pieces.

Nick spread out his arms. "What the hell?"

"I don't answer to you."

Nick rose to his feet. "I never said you did, but in case you forgot, we're in the middle of a clusterfuck, and we lost Cas. And instead of, *I don't know*, focusing on figuring this shit out, you're practically sticking your tongue down Anna's throat—"

Sam's fist cracked against Nick's jaw. Nick flew back into the bedside table, causing it to judder against the wall. Sam was instantly on him, taking a fistful of Nick's shirt and hauling him up.

"You think I don't know what's at stake?" Sam barked.

I glanced at Trev, hoping he'd step in, but he looked as shocked as I was.

Nick wiped the blood from his face and wrestled himself free. "You're supposed to be the goddamn leader, so fucking lead!"

Sam let out a guttural growl as he swung again. Nick ducked at the last minute, and when he came back up, he landed a punch to Sam's gut. Sam doubled over. Nick seized the opening, swinging his foot, almost catching Sam in the face before Sam crossed his arms in a shield.

Nick stepped back, picked up the glass bottle of iced tea, and started after Sam.

"Nick! Stop!" My voice bounced off the walls, cutting through the fight, and Nick went rigidly still. "Put the bottle down."

Sam struggled to his feet, spat blood on the floor.

Eyes molten with annoyance, Nick set the tea down and started for the door. "I think I need some air."

"No." Sam eased into his T-shirt, then threw on his coat. "I'll leave. I *need* to leave."

Without saying another word, he walked out.

29

I SHOULD HAVE STAYED IN THE MOTEL
room, should have quieted the rumbling in my stomach because I
was starving. But I didn't. I chased after Sam, dodging potholes in
the parking lot. I met up with him as he crossed the street.

"What was that all about?" He didn't answer me. I hurried ahead
and cut him off. "Talk to me."

He met my gaze with a disquieting look. A broken blood vessel had
turned the white of his left eye dark red. "I didn't mean to fight him."

I paled. They'd fought because of me, and I hated it. Or at least
the fight had *started* because of me. "I know. He probably knows
that, too."

"Nick and I have never seen eye to eye, and—" He disconnected
again and focused on his hand, rubbing at the knuckles.

"And what?"

A clench of his jaw. A shake of his head. "Nothing." He started forward.

"Sam. Don't shut me out."

He paused. His head sank back, and with a sigh, he said, "I can't seem to concentrate anymore. I feel like shit all day long. I can't tell what's real, or what's a flashback, or if it was something I heard on TV, read in a book, saw in a dream."

"And it's putting you on edge," I concluded. He didn't deny it. "Any more flashbacks about Dani?"

His guarded looked told me what they were about even as he said, "They aren't specific."

I couldn't help wondering how far back the flashes went and how long he'd kept them from me to spare me the heartache. In the pantry, our first day at the cabin, he'd mentioned a memory brought on by that dent in the kitchen wall. When I'd questioned him, he'd dodged me, like he was doing now.

I couldn't help imagining the story behind the damage. Because he was angry. And scared. And heartbroken. Because he'd lost someone he loved so much, he didn't know what else to do but start throwing things.

I wrapped my arms tight around myself, hoping to ward off the chill night air. "You shouldn't be alone right now."

"I'm fine. Go back to the room, where you'll be safe. And get something to eat, too. You'll need your—"

"Energy. I know. Except I'm not going back. So I guess you're stuck with me."

Sighing, he slipped out of his coat and handed it to me. "At least put that on, then."

"I'm okay."

He considered me warily. "Just put it on."

I took it. The arms were too long, the shoulders too baggy, but it smelled like him, like crisp autumn air. We walked for a good fifteen minutes before coming across a twenty-four-hour waffle house. Interior lights shone through the windows and spilled across the sidewalk.

Sam must have read the hunger on my face, because he went straight for the entrance and held the door, motioning me inside. The place was heavy with the scent of freshly brewed coffee and waffle batter. My stomach immediately growled.

The tables were pretty full despite the hour and we ended up choosing a booth in the back corner. When the waitress arrived, Sam ordered eggs with orange juice, and I got the full waffle treatment and a cappuccino. It was almost like we were normal people, ordering normal food, late on a . . . God, I didn't even know what day it was.

I fidgeted with the saltshaker, picking the dried salt off the metal top as Sam scrutinized the people and our surroundings.

"Do you think Sura set us up?" I asked.

Sam swung his attention back to me. "Why?"

I shrugged. "Seems awfully convenient that the Branch showed up at the cabin the same night she did."

"They found us at the mall."

"Yeah, it's just..." I trailed off, trying to make sense of the theories I had going. Something didn't feel right about how we had been ambushed, but I didn't know what it was, or how to relate it to Sam. "Never mind."

Our food showed up a few minutes later. Despite the fact that we were in a cheap twenty-four-hour diner, my waffles were the best I'd ever had. I was suddenly thankful for the late-night walk. *I'd take this over a gas-station turkey sandwich any day*, I thought.

I sopped up the last of the syrup on my plate with a chunk of waffle. "So, that clue you left at the cabin—it said to use the tattoo with the scars, right?"

Sam pushed his plate away. "Yes. I thought it might be a more complicated cipher—"

"Or maybe it's something as simple as an address. The numbers are the house numbers, and the scars spell out a road."

He started to protest, but then thought better of it. "Maybe, but I've spent years working on those letters, trying to get them to spell something useful. It's not there."

I drained the rest of my cappuccino, the heat of the liquid warming my throat. I felt better than I had in a long time, and while it might have been due to the caffeine, I tried telling myself it was because we were *this close* to solving Sam's clues. We just needed to analyze the scars a little more.

"Excuse me?" I called out to the waitress. "Do you have a pen I can borrow?"

The older woman offered me a capless BIC with teeth marks in the barrel before scurrying off. Using the underside of my paper place mat, I wrote out the letters of the scars again, organizing them by boy.

Sam—R O D R

Cas—L V

Nick—I E

Trev—R R E E

"There are twelve scars," I said, tapping the end of the pen against the table as I thought. "If you'd divided them evenly, each boy would have three scars. Instead, you and Trev have four, and Nick and Cas have two. Why?"

Sam frowned. "If you're asking me what my reasoning would have been, I'd say I would have taken more to spare the others some pain."

"But Trev has four, too," I reminded him.

What other reason would there be for Trev to have as many scars as Sam?

Sura had said she was only vaguely familiar with Trev, which would have meant he wasn't around when she interacted with Sam five years earlier, when he planted the clues. Which meant, possibly, that he hadn't been around when Sam, Nick, and Cas devised the plan, cutting the scars into their skin.

I relayed my thoughts to Sam. He folded his hands on the table. "If Trev's scars were added later—" he said.

"Then maybe they don't even fit the clue."

"A decoy." A flash of excitement warmed his eyes. "Give me the paper."

He started writing and rewriting the remaining letters in different sequences.

R O D R L V I E

LOR DIVER

LORD RIVE

RIVER DOL

"Old River," I whispered.

"So 2644 Old River," he said. "If it's an address."

I looked around the diner. A few twentysomething girls sat kitty-corner from us, discussing their boss. An older couple sat at another table, reading separate newspapers. In the opposite corner, a boy clicked away on a laptop, a pile of textbooks open beside him.

I swept out of the booth, and Sam followed. The guy looked at us over the top of his thick, black-framed glasses when we approached. Acne covered his chin. Overgrown dark hair hid what looked like overgrown eyebrows.

He frowned. "Can I help you?"

"Do you have Internet access on that?" Sam said.

"Um, yeah."

"Would it be possible for us to borrow it for a few minutes? I'll pay you." Sam put a twenty-dollar bill on the table, and the guy's eyes widened.

"Seriously?"

Sam nodded. "Seriously."

The guy scooted over, letting Sam slide into the booth in front of the computer. I sat on the other side. Sam tapped a few keys, navigating the Internet effortlessly despite the fact that he'd been in a cell for five years with no Internet access at all. The boys didn't even have computers.

"So, what are you looking for?" the guy asked. "Anything I can help with?"

Sam hit enter. "I'm looking for an address. I'm not sure about the street name. Old something? River, maybe?" Sam read the computer's display. "Nothing came up in the search." He tapped in a few more things, clicked the mouse.

"Old River?" The guy rubbed the back of his index finger across his mouth. "Hmm. Do you know if it's in town? Farther out?"

"No."

I straightened. "What about the address 2644?"

The guy repeated the numbers. "I know of a 2644 Old Brook Road. Could that be it?"

Sam and I locked eyes across the table. "You know the place?" he said.

"Do I?" the guy echoed, like that was the stupidest question he'd ever heard. "Everyone knows that place. It's only the site of the town's biggest unsolved murders. There was even a crime documentary filmed there a few years back. Where have you guys been?"

Sam wheeled to face him. "Tell me about it."

The guy shrugged. "Well, the O'Brien family lived out there for a long time. They had two daughters. Then the O'Briens fell on some hard times. The oldest daughter went off to school on scholarship. She was the family's star. Was supposed to become a doctor or something. At least that's what Mrs. O'Brien told everyone.

"Anyway, it turned out the daughter ran off somewhere and never came back. About a year later, Mr. and Mrs. O'Brien were found dead in their home, and the youngest daughter disappeared. Never did turn up."

The empty file in the third drawer in my father's filing cabinet had had the name O'Brien written across the top.

A rushing noise filled my ears. Sam said, "What were the daughters' names?"

The guy shook the hair out of his eyes as he looked over at Sam, having no idea his answer would change my entire life. "The girls were Dani and Anna. Dani and Anna O'Brien."

30

I FELT NUMB ALL OVER AS I TRUDGED down the sidewalk. Sam kept his distance behind me. I hadn't said a word since we'd left the waffle house, because I couldn't. The boys had been right. My entire life was a lie. The Branch had planted me. How or why, I didn't know, but they had. They'd wiped my memories and filled the void with made-up truths. And I'd believed every one of them.

According to that boy in the diner, my parents were dead. Dani was my sister, and no one had seen her in years. And if that was true, then Sam and I must have known each other before all of this, long before the memory wipes and the farmhouse. There'd always been something about Sam, some unseen thread that connected me to him. This explained a lot. If it was true. If I chose to believe it.

The boy in the diner had given us directions to Old Brook Road, and we headed that way on foot, despite the fact that it was a good five miles south of town. Raindrops wet my face. In the far distance, lightning lit the sky.

"Anna?" Sam caught up, his arms tight against him to hold in the body heat because he'd given me his coat. I could make out the butt of his gun bulging beneath his shirt at the small of his back. "We need to talk about this."

"What are we supposed to talk about? That my dad lied to me? That my real parents are dead? That I apparently had a sister who you were in love with?"

"You can't go running to that address if you're not thinking straight."

He was right, of course, and that only annoyed me more. "I'm thinking just fine, thank you."

Suddenly he was in front of me. "We need to talk about you and me. About this entire thing. About the answers you might find at that place, and whether or not you're even ready for them."

"What is that supposed to mean?" I stepped around him. "This is my life. I'd like to know a thing or two about how I got here and why I'm *here* to begin with." There had to be a reasonable explanation for all this, right?

But even as the thought crossed my mind, the rational side of me argued that we were far past reasonable.

A small truck chugged past and I shoved my hands into the pockets of my jeans, turning my face away in case the person behind the wheel had any connection to the Branch. Paranoia had taken hold of me and wouldn't let go. Every corner of my life had been altered by the Branch.

Nothing seemed real anymore.

The truck kept going and my shoulders sank with relief.

When all of this had started, I thought I was a bystander, swept up in the boys' problems, and that I only had to survive. But if what that guy at the diner said was true, I'd always been a part of it.

How did I fit into it now? What purpose did I serve? Somehow, all of this—the stolen evidence, the house at 2644, me, Sam, the others—was connected. And nothing would be solved until we knew what Sam had buried five years ago, at the house that used to be mine.

———

My feet ached. My legs felt like rubber. The rain had let up, but thunder still rumbled in the distance. I shivered inside Sam's coat. He hadn't complained yet, but his lips were blue and he looked paler than he should.

Two hours after leaving the diner, we turned right onto Old Brook Road. Gnarled branches of mammoth oak trees laced together overhead. I could smell the earthy scent of farmland—overturned dirt, hay, manure. It should have been revolting, but it stirred something deep in my memory.

The first mailbox we passed had the number 2232 nailed to its wooden post. A broken-down truck sat in the driveway, its back fender rusted out.

Rain started falling again, fat drops making a pattering sound on my already soaked jacket. Sam ran a hand over his head, flinging water from his hair. My shoes squeaked and gushed with each step I took.

We passed a working farm with a rambling Victorian out front and a cluster of barns out back. Cows mooed in the field. A dog barked at us from the front porch.

We passed another house. And another.

And then we were there: 2644 Old Brook Road.

The abandoned house was a squat one-story place. Once white, the siding was now a dusty gray. A few of the front windows were broken out, shards of glass still clinging to the frames. An old remnant of the driveway remained, partially hidden by the overgrown lawn. Cedar trees hugged the property on the left, blocking out the view of the neighbor down the road. Woods took up the other side of the lot, the ground coated in dead pine needles.

The rain fell harder now, plastering my hair to my face. Water dripped from Sam's nose.

"Are you sure about this?" he asked.

I took in the sight of the house. "We don't have much of a choice, do we?" I cut through the grass and darted up the steps to the front porch. The neglected wood creaked beneath me. Under cover of the roof, I took a second to wipe the rain from my face as Sam pushed through the warped front door. He let me take the lead.

We entered into a foyer, its hardwood floors pitted and dusty. Cobwebs hung from the ceiling corners. A torn couch sat in the family room, to the right. I crossed to the back of the house, to the kitchen, where the cupboard doors hung from the cabinet frames like broken wings. An old-fashioned stove butted up against a window that looked out on the cedars. I tried to picture the family that had inhabited this space. Dad at the table, reading a newspaper. Mom at the stove. Two daughters chasing each other through the house.

It was almost as if the memories hung there among the cobwebs, waiting for someone to pick them free. And if I could, could I make them mine again?

We backtracked and followed the hallway to the very end, to a bedroom. A four-poster bed sat in the middle of the room without its mattress. Cobwebs made their own canopy on the frame. I looked in the closet, finding the hanging bar empty, a pile of forgotten things in the back corner. I crouched, dug through the belongings.

A hairbrush. A shoestring. A torn newspaper. A tiny decorative box.

I pulled the box out, flipped the saffron lid open. Inside lay an origami paper crane, a knotted beaded necklace, and a picture, the edges crisp and torn, the photo itself folded into a crescent.

In my hands it felt brittle with age, and when I straightened it out, a corner fell away, fluttering to the floor. I sat back on my butt, in line with the light coming through the window, so I could better see the image.

A breath danced in the hollow of my throat. The girl in the picture was me.

A ten-year-old version of me. My hair was tied back in a high ponytail, but a few loose strands hung in front, hiding my hazel eyes. Dani stood behind me. She must have been fifteen or sixteen, and where my hair was fair, hers hovered between dark brown and auburn. We didn't look alike, not in the way you would expect sisters to. But we shared the same smattering of freckles, the same narrow nose.

I held the picture tightly in my hands, feeling something stir. A memory, a wish, an emotion, I couldn't tell. But what I did know was that it was a connection. "She was really beautiful."

Sam dripped rain on the floor and said nothing. He leaned against the wall between the door and the closet, his shoulder the only thing holding him up. His eyes were closed tightly, as if the very sight of Dani had brought on a new wave of memories and the emotion attached to them. His mouth twitched and the fine lines at the corners of his eyes deepened.

I wrapped my arms around his neck.

"Do you remember her yet?" I said, my voice muffled against his chest.

"I can remember the way she made me feel."

"Tell me."

He shook his head, as if the new emotions were alien to him, and he wasn't sure how to put the feeling into words. "Happy. Safe."

I wanted to ask, *How do I make you feel?* But it was selfishness and jealousy that fueled the question, and no amount of bravery would pry the words from my mouth. I was too afraid to find out the truth—that I couldn't make him feel the things Dani had made him feel. And what did it matter now, anyway? Dani was my *sister*. Sam had *loved my sister*.

A flash of lightning filled the dark corners of the room, and a crack of thunder followed.

"We should keep looking," Sam said, his voice leaden in the quiet between thunderclaps.

I looked once more at the picture still clutched in my hand. I could sense the ghosts of the house around me, welcoming me home.

Sam started for the door. I folded the picture and put it in my jeans pocket, hoping the rain wouldn't ruin the only image I had of a life I couldn't remember.

31

SAM AND I SPLIT UP TO CHECK THE
rest of the house. I looked in the kitchen cabinets and the pantry. It
was hard to guess where we might find a clue, and I wasn't about to over-
look something, no matter how inconspicuous it might have seemed.

Back in the foyer, I checked a coat closet and found it empty. I
was making my way through the living room when I heard a crash
from the bathroom.

"Sam?" I hurried down the hall and found him lying on the floor
on his back. "What happened?"

He blinked several times, like he couldn't see straight, and then
rolled over and rose to his knees. "Shit," he muttered as he got to his
feet. A bolt of lightning illuminated his face for a split second. He
looked ashen and wary.

"Was it a flashback?"

He rubbed at his eyes with his thumb and index finger. "I'm fine." He ushered me back into the hall.

"You're sure?"

He finally looked at me. "Yes. I'm just tired."

We had been up all night, and though I'd slept in the car on the way to Port Cadia, he probably hadn't.

We made our way back to the foyer. "So now what?" I said. "There's nothing here I would consider suspicious. We're missing something."

"The clue said that once I found the location, the tattoo would mark the spot. I thought it was the address, but maybe it means the tattoo is a depiction of the spot."

"The birch trees seem to be a running theme."

We headed outside. The rain had stopped since we'd been in the house, but the dark clouds hadn't cleared up. The boards of the back porch creaked worse than the ones in the front, so I took as few steps as I could.

When I reached solid ground, I looked up and gaped.

Birch trees. Everywhere. At least a hundred of them.

"How are we going to find anything that matches your tattoo in this?" I said.

Sam stepped up beside me. "There has to be something else."

I went over everything in my head. The scars. The note Sam left himself. The clues I'd found in the tattoo. When I came up with nothing, I went further back. The UV light. The cipher. The picture...

"Do you still have the picture of you and Dani?"

Without questioning my line of thought, Sam dug the picture out of his pocket and handed it to me. In it, Sam and Dani stood in front of four birch trees. Sam's tattoo was of four birch trees. That seemed like more than a coincidence. I held the picture up to the woods in front of us. The trees here were too thick, and while I tried to account for years of growth, nothing seemed to match. I examined every other tiny detail and felt a pang of excitement when I noticed the cows in the background.

"Here, look. We passed a farm on the way here. The woods in this picture—maybe they're back that way." I gestured to the left. "It would make sense that you wouldn't hide whatever you stole in the one place the Branch would look. It'd be close, but not that close."

"It's worth a shot," he said, and we started through the woods.

I didn't know how long or how far we walked, but it seemed like forever, like we were walking in circles. Finally, the trees thinned out and the farm we'd passed earlier came into view. Cows grazed in the field. The old tractor in the picture was gone, but the landscape itself looked similar.

We walked parallel to the farm fence until we reached the farthest corner. From there, we headed north, trying to match our surroundings to the picture of Sam and Dani.

A few birch trees dotted the landscape, but none in a group of four like in the picture or the tattoo. We walked until we almost couldn't see the farm anymore before we found something that might match. We moved around the cluster of trees so that we could see them from the same angle as in the picture. Over the years, they'd gotten bigger, widening at the trunks. The branches were bare now, the bark peeling in lengthy ribbons.

Sam and I stood shoulder to shoulder, staring at the scene in front of us. He held up the picture and, sure enough, it was a match.

"They don't match the tattoo, though," he said.

"But it still feels familiar, doesn't it? There's something..."

The dozens and dozens of drawings I'd done of my mother at the lake came to mind. I'd spent a crazy amount of time analyzing every detail in her photo to get the sketches right—the shadows, the highlights, the angle of the trees. I knew what to look for, how to see a pattern that I could copy onto paper. And something about Sam's photo and the tattoo seemed off.

Think, Anna.

There was nothing wrong with the photo. It hadn't been altered, as far as I could tell. All the angles were right, the proportions, the shadows—

"The shadows!"

Sam frowned. "What about them?"

The pattern started to form in my head. The trees in front of us went large tree first, slightly in front of a skinnier tree, then a space of three feet, then a crooked tree. One more foot, and then another skinny tree.

I knew that pattern.

"Turn around," I said. "Let me see the tattoo."

Sam grasped the sides of his shirt and lifted it up to his shoulders. I looked to the shadows the trees cast. They were wrong. I'd thought they were an error on the artist's part, but maybe not.

I put the photo against Sam's back, checking the shadows from left to right.

Large tree in front of a skinnier tree. Space. Crooked tree. Space. Skinny tree.

"The shadows in the tattoo match the trees here," I said in a rush. "The tattoo itself is reversed."

Sam hesitated for a sliver of a second before going to the third tree and from there counting out the steps to meet sixty paces. That's what the clue said, the one he'd found at the cabin: sixty paces north from the third tree.

The path led us away from the cluster of trees and farther into the woods. Soaked ferns left trails of fresh rain at our calves. Sam reached sixty steps quickly, and we stared down at the dirt. This was the spot where all the answers lay buried.

"We need a shovel," I said.

"Stay here. Don't move." He ran off toward the farm. I lost sight of him when he disappeared over a hill.

In the quiet, every thump sounded like a footstep, like boots crushing twigs. I made a complete circle, checking for signs of trouble. Thankfully, I found none, and when Sam reappeared, I exhaled with relief.

"Where did you get that?" I asked, nodding at the shovel in his hands.

"Does it matter?"

"No, I guess not." I stepped aside as he plunged the tip of the shovel into the dirt.

The earth came up easily and he snagged only a few roots, the shovel snapping through with a *crack*. It took him at least a half hour to dig a hole deep enough to stand in. I stood at the top and fidgeted, shifting my weight from one foot to the other, every tiny little noise putting me on alert.

What would we do if Riley or Connor found us now?

Sam grunted, heaving another shovelful of dirt onto the pile.

"Are you sure you counted right? We could try another hole. I'll dig for a while."

Sam looked up at me, dirt and rain covering his forehead. "I counted right. I just don't know how far down to go. Or whether it's even still here."

The sky brightened to a grayish shade of yellow as the sun rose. We were running out of time. Trev and Nick were probably worried by now; we'd been gone for hours. And Cas? *I hope he's all right.*

Sam swung down with the shovel and the sharp *clang* of metal hitting metal answered back, just like in the graveyard. An unwieldy sense of déjà vu rose in me. Sam scraped away the earth with his fingers, revealing a thick metal safe stuck in the ground, its door facing up. He tried lifting it, but he had trouble getting it to budge. He must have had help lowering it down there five years ago.

"Can you open it?" I asked. There was a simple combination lock on the door above a levered handle.

He grabbed the shovel and swung it down again. Sparks exploded from the safe as the shovel made contact. He swung again and the lock crunched in on itself. Another swing popped the lock out entirely.

He tossed the shovel aside and wrenched the door open. Loose dirt avalanched through the open door and Sam swiped it away, revealing a package. It was wrapped in tattered cloth, tied tight with twine. He handed it to me before hoisting himself up onto level ground.

After wiping his hands on his pants, he tore off the twine and unwrapped the cloth, revealing a plastic zipper bag stuffed with papers and a curled notebook. He pulled the contents out and started flipping through them.

"Does it mean anything to you?"

He scrutinized the loose papers. "They're logs and graphs, similar to what you and Arthur used in the lab. Blood results and logs of mental tests, but the names... Look."

I read over his shoulder.

Matt. Lars. Trev.

"Trev was part of a different group?"

I held the files as he inspected the notebook. It was a simple spiral-bound book with a black cover, no writing on the front. He opened it, revealing lined paper on the inside, the pages yellowed.

The first page read:

> ### February 14
>
> Results going well. New group showing promise, abilities are similar to Sam's. Control still an issue. Cohesion only stable throughout the unit. They will not listen to commander or me.
>
> Thoughts: If we can alter units to work as one, can we alter them to take orders from a "programmed" commander? Must explore.

Sam and I looked at each other.

"Keep going," I said.

He turned another page.

> ### March 22
>
> After interested parties grew impatient, released three of the units. Sam grew agitated when he realized they were missing. Will monitor situation closely.
>
> **Operation ALPHA under way**

Sam flipped through a few more pages, to May 2.

Outsourced units not performing well.
Memory flashes render them useless. Must
look into more permanent memory wipes.

Will send one of the others for cleanup.
Sam is out of the question. Aggression
has gotten worse. Will listen to no one
except Dani. Are these attributes
we can relate to ALPHA?

**Arthur has agreed to undertake
Operation ALPHA**

"I don't know whose handwriting that is," I said.

"It's not Connor's." Sam shifted his weight so that he could prop the notebook open on his lap. He flipped through several more pages, but the rest were blank.

I searched through the logs, looking for Trev's files. In the middle of the stack, I stalled. "Look at this."

Sam's name was written across the top, and next to it, SUCCESSFUL MISSIONS.

There were names listed below that, with titles and statuses. A scientist in Texas—Eliminated. A U.S. senator—Eliminated. A CEO based in New York—Eliminated.

I stifled a horrified shudder. "You had *a résumé.*"

Sam snatched the pages away and scanned the info. "There are kill sheets for all of us. Nick. Cas. Trev. There are several other names here, too." He flipped to another sheet. "Bank account numbers. Wire transfers from foreign countries." Anger notched the space between his brows. "They were taking deposits on us."

"Sura said the Branch has immunity from the U.S. government, provided they're given first pick on whatever they develop. This"—I nodded at the evidence—"promising the 'units' to other countries, taking money from them, would probably strip them of that immunity."

"Worse than that," Sam said. "They'd be shut down. I must have stolen this, with Dani's help. And when they found out, they took her."

"With the intent to use her to get to you," I added. "So you came here five years ago to retrieve the evidence, but they must have apprehended you before you could make it back to this spot."

"And then they cleaned out my memories." He snapped his head up, like he'd heard something.

I jolted. "What is it?"

He tucked the evidence beneath his arm. "Run."

We were up on our feet and running in a heartbeat. We headed north, away from the farm, away from my old house. I trailed behind Sam by two or three feet, but came to a jarring stop when Trev stepped out from behind a tree.

Sam hunched over. "Damn it, Trev. I thought you were one of Connor's men. I almost shot you."

Trev slid a gun out from beneath his shirt and pointed it at Sam. "I'm sorry," he said, so quietly I wasn't sure I'd heard him.

I took a step back, but Sam held his ground. "What the hell are you doing?"

I cast a glance over my shoulder and gasped. "Sam."

Riley was behind us, along with two of his men. Nick was there, too, arms pinned behind his back.

"Trev?" Sam said.

Riley spoke first. "Number one rule of an operation, Samuel: Have a man undercover."

As I looked at Trev and he looked at me, several things clicked into place. Trev was the one who'd lost the guns. He was the only one who escaped the cabin unscathed, having been conveniently outside with the dog. And he was the one who had the other cell phone, who could call whoever, whenever he wanted, to alert them to our location.

"No." The word came out strangled.

I'd trusted Trev the most out of all the boys. He was my best friend.

I stumbled back. My eyes blurred. "Trev?"

"Quit stalling," Riley barked.

Trev made a grab for me. Sam moved, too, but not fast enough. And I wasn't ready to fight. I didn't want to believe it.

Trev swung an arm around my neck, positioning the gun at my head.

I felt like I was breaking in two. He'd deceived me. And he'd done a good job of it, too. I'd never, ever questioned his loyalty.

"Toss your guns," Riley said. "And the documentation."

Don't, Sam, I thought. *Run. If anyone can escape, it's you.*

But he didn't. He didn't even hesitate. He dropped the evidence at his feet, then pulled the gun out from beneath his shirt and tossed it to the soggy ground.

Riley nodded at one of his men. The taller, balding agent retrieved Sam's gun and the evidence we'd dug up before resuming his position at Riley's side.

I shifted, looking for a weakness in Trev's hold, but he only drew me closer.

As Riley barked out more orders, Trev whispered in my ear: "It's the alterations. Sam and the others are powerless when it comes to you. Don't you see, Anna? You're the whole reason we're here."

I tried to digest what he was saying. Was he trying to feed me more lies? My mind raced through all the things Sam and I had read in the files we unearthed.

The Branch had always had an issue with controlling Sam. So they started Operation ALPHA, hoping to implement a "programmed" commander. They wanted to program him into cooperating.

As Riley tapped in a few numbers on his cell phone and one of the men came around to handcuff Sam, Sam's words came back to me: *If you're trying to make the ultimate weapon, you don't lock it in a basement for five years. You put it on the field and test and alter it until it's perfect.*

Realization washed over me. The lab had been the field. And every interaction between the boys and me had been a test. We'd been living and testing and altering the program right there in the farmhouse.

I was the "commander," and the boys were programmed to listen to and protect me.

"I'm the key to Operation ALPHA," I said.

Riley went silent. He slid his phone into his pocket.

"When I ask the boys to stop, they stop," I said. "They listen to me without fail." I thought back to everything that had happened in the last few days. At the house in Pennsylvania, I'd asked Nick not to hurt that cop with the wastebasket, and he hadn't. I'd asked Sam not to kill Riley behind the mall, and he hadn't, even though in Sam's position it made total sense to do it. And last night, Sam and Nick stopped fighting when I told them to.

Of course they had an overwhelming urge to protect me. Even if they found out I had the ability to control them, they wouldn't turn on me. Because somehow the Branch had programmed them not to.

The Branch, Connor, Riley—they'd covered all their bases.

"But why me?"

Riley tilted his head to the side, analyzing me, picking me apart with his eyes.

"Because the only person Sam listened to was your older sister. And then she died."

I sucked in a breath. Dani was dead? Pain crept into Sam's eyes.

Riley didn't pause to let the news sink in. "We'd already dumped too much money into Sam to let him go. So, Plan B. Dani wasn't the only O'Brien sister, was she?"

The notes said that Operation ALPHA was supposed to explore the possibility of replicating the control attributes between Dani and Sam. And they'd done it. They'd produced an artificial link between the boys and me. They'd taken something that was human—love, respect, trust—and made it into something scientific, valuable.

Biological control.

It was no wonder they'd gone to such lengths to lock Sam away and clear out his memories, to keep the evidence he'd stolen hidden. The alterations—strength, intelligence, a slower rate of aging, obedience—would be worth millions.

A dog barked in the distance. Sam's nostrils flared and his shoulders tensed. He looked ready to leap at Riley, and that wouldn't be good for anyone.

I twisted, trying to face Trev. "Your name was in the file," I said. "Five years ago. You were altered, and they tried to sell you like a weapon."

"She's lying." Riley swept forward and whacked me across the face. Pink and yellow dots filled my vision.

Trev's hold loosened. Sam made a low sound that rumbled in his chest as he tried to rip himself away from the man holding him.

"I'm telling the truth," I sputtered.

"Stop," Trev said to me. "Please."

"But—"

"Don't try to redeem me, Anna."

I would not go down like this, held in place by the one person I'd thought always had my back. Not with the evidence so close at hand, the documentation we'd fought for days to locate.

This was not my end.

If I was as much a part of this program as the boys were, I wasn't some weak girl caught in the middle of a top secret program. Like Trev said, I was the whole reason we were here. And if I was the key, then I had the power to send the plan off course.

Sam and I exchanged a glance.

On three, I mouthed, and he gave a barely discernible nod.

One.

Two.

Adrenaline raced through my veins. I felt stronger than ever.

Three.

I grabbed Trev by the wrist and shoved his arm up, forcing the gun away from my head. Caught off guard, he didn't fight, giving me just enough time to whirl around, set my hands on his shoulders, and drive a knee up between his legs. He collapsed to the ground.

Nick jumped, swinging his tied hands beneath his feet. He lunged for one of the men at Riley's side and they went down, tussling.

Riley reached for me but I dodged him, plucking the shovel off the ground and brandishing it like a club. Riley and I danced back and forth and I swung. He ducked.

A gun went off. The other agent stumbled backward, clutching at his side. Sam barely stopped to see if his shot had hit the mark before he aimed for Riley. He pulled the trigger, but the gun didn't fire; either it was jammed or the magazine was empty. He tossed it aside.

I tightened my grip on the shovel as Trev stood up. It was me and Sam against Trev and Riley, and I wasn't sure if I could best Trev. My only hope was the shovel. I stayed light on my feet, my anger at Trev's deception all the fuel I needed. I would slam that shovel in his effing face and have no qualms about it.

"I'm sorry," he said.

Out of the corner of my eye I saw Riley pull something from the interior pocket of his suit jacket. I realized too late that it was a gun. He pointed it at Sam and shot.

"No!"

The gun made a light *thwoop-thwoop* sound, and two darts hit Sam in the chest. He looked down at them, then back up at me.

I dropped the shovel—*I had to get to him*—as he collapsed to his knees, his eyes glassy and unfocused. Nick cut me off and shoved me in the opposite direction. Trev stole a gun from one of the downed men.

"Sam!" I screeched. Riley shot again, and a dart hit the tree next to me.

Nick took hold of the collar of my jacket and dragged me toward the woods. "We don't have time!"

I staggered back, saw Sam struggling to send me one last message, his finger pointing at something off to my left.

The notebook and logs—they'd been abandoned by Riley's man.

I tore away from Nick.

"What the hell are you doing?" he shouted.

"We can't leave it." I scooped up the evidence as another dart whizzed past. Riley yelled. A gunshot rang out. Nick tugged me in front of him and away from the bullet. He staggered forward, and blood began to soak through his shirtsleeve at an alarming pace.

"Oh my God," I said.

"Go."

We crashed through the woods. The sky opened up with a downpour. I slipped in the mud, regained my balance, and kept on even though I had no idea where I was going, even though I didn't *want* to go.

We'd left Sam behind. He couldn't even fight back. They could do whatever they wanted with him. They could wipe his memories again, and he'd have no idea who I was or who he was or what had happened between us.

Branches pulled at my hair. Ferns whipped my legs. Nick ran next to me, but he was slowing down. "Are you okay?" I asked.

"Yes." But he didn't sound good.

We passed a hunting shack, and then an abandoned farm wagon, its big wheels rusted out. We crossed a creek, stomping through the water. Finally, the trees ahead thinned, and we saw a dirt road. An abandoned barn sat in a field across the road, the structure leaning dangerously to the left.

Nick pushed me toward it. "What about you?" I asked.

"I'll leave a false trail."

He ran the other way, purposefully dripping blood on the surrounding brush.

Checking to make sure the road was clear, I hurried to the other side, keeping the evidence we'd dug up tight against my chest. Despite the rain, the brown field grass crackled beneath me. When I reached the barn, I poked my head in through an empty window. The interior was dark and smelled of wet earth and rotting wood. I danced on my feet, unsure of what to do with myself, worried about Nick.

He reappeared a minute later, a branch from a pine tree in his hand. He darted across the road, sweeping the branch as he went to clear our footprints. I forced my way through the door and Nick came in behind me.

"Now what?"

He looked around. The barn's loft had collapsed, and the old wood hung from the rafters, cascading down to the first floor. A few stalls sat empty in the back corner. There was a tack room directly across from us, but the fallen loft blocked the entrance.

"Over here," Nick said, taking careful steps across the floor to the very middle of the barn. He dropped down on one knee and ripped up the floorboards, revealing the barn's framework and the earth below it. The boards came away easily, the nails rusted and useless.

"Get in."

"Are you kidding me? What if the barn collapses and we're trapped?"

"And what if Riley finds us?"

Voices shouted from the road outside. Someone yelled, "Check the barn!"

Nick lowered his voice. "Get in the goddamn hole."

I climbed in and he squeezed in next to me, stuffing the pine branch around us. He pulled the floorboards back into place until they settled.

My heart raced. I couldn't catch my breath. It was dark and dank in our hiding place, and I felt like I'd been buried alive.

I twisted onto my side to make room for Nick, because he was injured and we were practically on top of each other. The voices outside closed in on us. I laid my head in the dirt, trying to stop my body from shaking.

The floor creaked overhead.

"Check over there," Riley said.

A second set of footsteps thudded across the barn. There was a rustling of debris, the snapping of wood. "Nothing here," the other man said. Not Trev. Riley had backup already?

A cell phone chirped. Riley answered it, paused, and then said, "We're on our way back." To his partner he said, "Trev found a blood trail in the woods."

Dirt rained down through the cracks above us as they retreated. Next to me, Nick sighed heavily. Something scuttled several feet behind us. I cringed, biting back a scream. *It's just a mouse*, I told myself. *Nothing to be afraid of.*

Ten minutes must have passed before I could breathe evenly again. I waited at least ten more before nudging Nick.

"I think they're gone," I said. When he didn't respond, I rose up onto one elbow. "Nick?" His eyes were closed, and he seemed colder than was normal. "Nick. Wake up." Frustrated tears bit at my eyes. "Nick!"

I was alone in the middle of nowhere and buried beneath a barn. Nick was unconscious. The Branch had Sam and Cas. Trev had turned on us. Riley was somewhere out there, still searching. I didn't know where to go. I didn't know what to do. I couldn't very well carry Nick out of there.

Let them find us, I thought. *I give up. I can't do this anymore.*

Sam was the one who kept us together, who barked out the orders we followed, because he knew what he was doing and when to do it. Now I was supposed to be the commander? I didn't deserve the role.

I put my ear to Nick's chest, praying for the sound of his beating heart. I heard it, faintly, and it was pumping slower than it should be. What was I supposed to do in a situation like this? Was I supposed to keep him warm?

His hands were still tied together, so I started there, working against the zip ties, but with little success. I gave up and wrapped an arm around his torso, dragging him closer to me to lend him my body heat. As I did, my hand rapped against something hard in his pocket.

I dug inside and pulled out the prepaid cell phone. I sighed in relief. I'd thought Trev had the cell. Or maybe Nick had stolen it when Trev wasn't looking, when he realized Trev was on the Branch's side.

I flipped the phone open and found enough bars to get out a call. Except I didn't have anyone *to* call.

I didn't have any friends, and even if I had, I was several states away from home. And my dad...

Dad.

I wasn't his daughter and he had no ties to me, but he'd promised me when I left that he'd find me, and I wanted to believe in him. I wanted him to be the man I'd known all those years.

I didn't have anything left to lose.

I punched in his cell number and hit send.

32

DAD ANSWERED HIS CELL PHONE ON
the third ring.

"Dad?" I said.

He exhaled in a rush. "Stay at this number. I'll call you right
back."

The line went dead. I stared at the phone, thinking he was going
to turn me in, that he hung up so he could call Connor and tell him
he'd found me—

The phone beeped. The number registered on the screen as
THORTON GAS & GO.

"Hello?" I said.

"My line isn't secure," Dad explained. "Don't ever assume it's safe
to call it."

I clutched the phone harder.

"Are you using a listed number?" he asked. "Cell phone? Is Sam with you?"

"They have Sam. And Cas. And Nick's been shot and he's . . . I don't know. He's not responding to me."

I rested my head on Nick's chest, one ear listening to Dad, the other listening to the beating of Nick's heart.

"And . . . did you find Sura?"

I caught the faint glimmer of hope in Dad's voice. My shirt was still stained with Sura's blood. A flash of her dead eyes came back to me and I didn't have the heart or the energy to tell Dad what had happened.

Maybe he understood what my hesitation meant anyway, because he surged on before I could fake an answer. "I never wanted you to find out like this."

"Dad," I started, then cut myself off. He wasn't Dad anymore.

"I didn't mean to hurt you."

But you did, I wanted to say. *You and Trev both.*

I summoned a thread of dignity and hardened my voice. "We can talk about that later. Right now, Nick needs your help."

"Are you in Michigan?"

"Yeah," I said after a pause. If he turned me in, he turned me in. It was a gamble I was willing to take. "We found the house. *My* house. We're in the woods behind it, at the next road over. In a barn."

"It'll take me a while to get there. As soon as I was discharged, I went straight to the Pennsylvania address and found the house swarming with police officers."

I groaned. "Oh, yeah. Sam sorta knocked out an officer by accident."

Dad sighed. "That sounds like Sam."

"How long before you make it here?"

"A few hours. Six, maybe."

Six hours? Nick might not have much time. And I couldn't stand to sit in that hole any longer. Claustrophobia had set in the moment I'd climbed down there, and the longer I sat, the worse it was going to get.

"Hurry, please."

"I will. I promise. Don't move."

I looked down at Nick. "Don't worry. I'm not going anywhere."

————

I watched the clock on the cell phone and waited forty-five minutes after hanging up with Dad. I figured if I wasn't safe now, I wouldn't ever be, so I might as well risk it. Plus, I had to go to the bathroom.

It took me a few tries to pry the floorboards up, but once I did, I burst from the hole like I'd been drowning, sucking in fresh air as if my lungs had been starving for it. I checked on Nick once more before climbing out. He hadn't woken, but he was still breathing all right.

I went to the bathroom behind the barn, then hurried back inside. I sat on the floor near the hole and gave Nick a nudge. He muttered something before going quiet again. I stood watch over him for a while. When the cell phone said it was close to four PM, I went to the broken windows at the front of the barn. The storm had finally passed, leaving the earth soggy. Mentally, I drew my surroundings, like it was important to name all the colors so I could share it with Sam later. But what if I couldn't? What if I never saw him again?

The thought left me nauseous.

When I heard the slow crawl of tires over gravel, I slunk away from the window and peeked through a gap in the siding. I thought to call Dad's cell, then remembered his warning and pocketed the phone. Instead I watched. He parked on the shoulder of the road and shut the engine off. I was relieved to see that he was alone, though I still half expected Riley to jump out from behind a tree.

Dad made his way across the field sporting a limp. Inwardly, I winced, remembering that day in the lab, the horror of watching Sam shoot him.

"Anna?" Dad called.

I poked my head out the door. "In here."

When he squeezed inside, an uncomfortable staleness surrounded us. If ever there was a time for hugs shared between family, this was it. But Dad wasn't my dad, and we'd never been big on hugs to begin with.

I gestured at his leg. "How is it?"

"It wasn't as bad as it looked. Are you okay?"

I lifted a shoulder in a half shrug, wanting to say all the things crammed in my head. I was sore and broken and sad and scared. But I wanted Dad to know without me telling him. I wanted him to read me, like dads are supposed to do. To dispel all the stories I'd heard so far, to make things right again.

But he didn't.

"Where's Nick?" he asked.

I deflated. "Over there."

Nick had moved since I'd last checked on him. That seemed like a positive sign.

Dad set to work, because that was what he was good at—working, fixing things. He climbed in the hole and pressed his fingers to Nick's neck. "Pulse is still good, but it's slow. Can you climb down here, too? Get his legs so we can lift him out? I don't know how much weight I'll be able to carry."

I did as Dad asked, wiggling into the hole near Nick's legs. I grabbed him beneath the knees, Dad counted to three, and we lifted. Dad gritted his teeth in pain. We swung Nick to the side, laying him on the floor so we could climb out of the hole.

It took us a good ten minutes to navigate outside and through the field to the car, carrying Nick between us. I tried to bear as much of the weight as I could so Dad wouldn't have to, but I was only half Nick's size.

"I can manage him if you'll open the door," Dad said when we reached the car.

I lifted up on the handle, but my fingers slipped, tearing a nail in half. I cursed and tried it again, my hands all but useless. Finally we managed to get Nick onto the backseat.

"The files," I said as Dad eased in behind the wheel. "I forgot to grab them. There's information in there about the program, about the Branch. It's the only leverage we have."

"Hurry," he said and started up the car.

I raced back to the barn, ducked into the hole, and came up with the evidence. Dad didn't waste a second when I returned. He slammed the car into drive before I had the door closed.

The rain had gathered in puddles, hiding potholes. We hit one and Nick groaned in the back. I clambered over the seat as we hit another, and I almost fell on top of him.

Maybe Nick and I had never gotten along, but I owed him. He'd put himself in front of a bullet for me.

"Nick? Can you hear me?" His fingers tightened around mine and I let out a breath of hope.

We drove for a while before Dad stopped at a drugstore to grab the supplies he'd need to treat Nick. About thirty minutes later, we found an out-of-the-way motel and Dad rented a room, using cash so the Branch couldn't pick up on the transaction.

By the time we got Nick inside, his eyes were fluttering. We laid him on the bed, and Dad carefully peeled away his bloody clothes.

He worked with the quick precision of a professional, as if he'd done this before. And maybe he had.

Using the rubbing alcohol and travel sewing kit he had bought, Dad managed to patch up the bullet wound, which turned out to be only a deep graze.

I sat in the chair, wringing my hands in my lap as I waited for something, some update, wondering where Sam was and whether he was all right. I was getting restless. We were wasting time. At any moment, Riley and Connor could wipe Sam's memories, and nothing we'd accomplished would matter.

When Dad finished, he washed his hands, took a swig of the bottled water he'd bought along with the medical supplies, and scooped up a straw. "He'll be all right, I think. I didn't find any major damage. He just lost a lot of blood, and he's exhausted on top of that. Dehydrated, too, I think."

"Why are you doing this?" I'd been bouncing the question around inside my head for the last hour, wondering if calling him had been a mistake. I was still waiting for Riley to come crashing through the door.

Dad brought the straw up and jammed it into his mouth. "I'm doing what I should have done a long time ago." He went to the window, pushed aside the thick orange curtain, and checked the parking lot. "I agreed to take on the boys' project because I was in a bad place at the time. Your mother and I—" He cut himself off. "I mean, Sura and I...we'd been divorced for a while, but she was still a large part of my life, and we were fighting again. . . . Anyway, I wanted to get as far away from everything as I could. I heard about the project at the farmhouse and agreed to take it on before I knew what it entailed."

He ran his hand over his graying hair, smoothing it down. "And then when you came along . . ." He shook his head, the hair falling out of place again. "Well, I was stuck at that point. I didn't think you'd ever find out. At least not the way you did."

"Riley said I was altered, too. Is that true?" Dad looked at me grimly, confirming it with a nod. "When did I have treatments?"

"You had treatments twice a month, in your food." He eyed me, waiting for the information to sink in.

"The lemonade." He'd given me treatments in my lemonade, the only tradition we had. Sam and the others had been going through withdrawal since they'd left the lab. I'd had headaches, too; I'd thought they were from the stress.

Dad continued. "The alterations you went through were minimal. I suspect you might be stronger than the average girl of your build. But mostly you are connected to the boys on some level even I can't understand. And they will listen to you without fail."

"What about Trev? Was he altered the same way? Do I have sway over him?"

"Why do you ask?"

I told him about Trev turning on us. The news hit him the same way it had hit me.

"Wow. I had no idea. Trev's treatments were different, yes. I thought they were testing a different drug on him, to see how he would interact with you and the others. I never would have guessed he was working for the Branch."

"It explains a lot, though. I can't ever remember him listening to me when it made more sense not to. The Branch wouldn't have wanted him to be under my control." I rubbed my eyes with the heels of my hands. "Why were they taking the boys from the lab in the first place?"

"They were going to move them to another facility and leave you at the farmhouse to test the connection across states. Connor wanted to push the program to the limit before—"

"Before selling it."

Dad sighed. "I try not to get involved in all that. I just like the science. Or, at least I did."

He pinned his straw between his index and middle fingers. "I knew what he was doing, you know."

I looked up. "What?"

"Sam. I knew that he was trying to escape. The straws. I knew." He massaged the bridge of his nose. "All those years I kept them down there, and there wasn't a single day that went by that I didn't imagine what it would be like to let them out and let you go.

"It took me a long time to even accept what I was doing. It helped that Sam and the others didn't remember a whole lot. And you helped. You kept my mind off things. I'd come upstairs and you'd be there waiting for me, and for a second I'd forget about the boys in the lab." Dad eased into the chair in the opposite corner of the room, propping his elbows on the armrests. "I owe you all. I wish there was some way I could make it up to you. I really do."

"We have to get them back," I said. "Sam and Cas."

Dad shook his head. "I don't see how we could, Anna. I'm sorry. The Branch will try to clean out their memories again, and with Sam..." He shook his head.

"What?"

"They've already pushed him to his limits. His memories have been altered more than the others. He was having memory flashbacks even in the lab. I didn't record that, though. I worried about what they'd do to him if they found out. I suspect that without the suppressant, the flashes will get worse...."

I went cold all over.

Dad must have noticed the look on my face, because he said, "They *have* gotten worse, haven't they?"

"What will happen if they try to wipe him again?"

Dad shook his head in a way that said he wasn't sure what the answer was, but it wasn't a good one. "It's best if we don't get involved. You are free. Nick's free. That's more than I could have ever hoped for."

I got to my feet. "Tell me what will happen to him, Dad. You have to tell me."

"It's only a theory," he sputtered. He brought the straw back up to his mouth, paused, then said, "It could be debilitating. It could render him useless. Uncontrollable. Volatile. I don't know. There could be any number of consequences."

I sucked in a breath, trying to stall the tears pushing against my eyelids. "I can't just leave him."

"There's nothing we can do."

I looked at the notebook and the files sitting on the table by the window. Sam had pushed me to grab them because he knew they were important. That information was the only bargaining chip I had. "Maybe there is something."

Nick woke with a groan sometime after two in the morning. I'd been watching TV and dozing for the last hour, waking myself every ten minutes or so to make sure he was still breathing.

He eased up to a sitting position, grinding his teeth against the pain. "Sam?" he muttered.

"Hey," I said, going to him. "Be careful."

He caught sight of me in the half dark and tensed. "Anna."

"Yeah. I'm here. And you've been shot. So you need to lie back down."

He grunted. "Probably isn't the first time."

"Do you want some water?"

"Tylenol."

We had that, too. I filled a plastic cup with water from the sink and shook out two pills from the new bottle. I handed them over, watching Nick in the flicker of light from the TV, checking for any signs that he was *not* okay. He seemed all right, but that didn't mean he was.

He popped the Tylenol and drained the cup of water. He looked around the room. "Where are we?"

"In a motel outside Traverse City."

"Who's that?" He nodded at the lump that was my dad in the next bed over. When I told him, he lowered his voice and snapped, "What the hell is he doing here?"

"I called him. You passed out, and I didn't know what to do. You didn't leave me with very many options."

"Is he on our side now?"

I shrugged. "Honestly, I don't really know. I think so."

"Any word on Sam?"

I thought about telling Nick what my dad had said, about the memory flashes, the consequences of another memory wipe, but it'd only fuel Nick's anger. "No word yet. My dad seems to think he's gone for good."

Nick bowed his head. The TV switched to a commercial. "We can't leave him there."

"I know."

"He's always had my back."

More so than your own family, I thought. Sam had taken care of all of us.

And I knew what he'd say about us coming to save him: *Don't.*

Get as far away from the Branch and Connor as possible. Use the evidence against them if they ever come after you.

But I couldn't just forget about him. I couldn't let Connor ruin Sam with another memory wipe so they could use him to their advantage. There was an undeniable wrenching in my chest, like being away from Sam, even for a few hours, tore me apart. I wanted to go, go, go, right now. I didn't want to sit in the motel room for another second.

As if he sensed my train of thought, Nick met my stare. The glow of the TV only amplified the brilliant blue of his eyes. "Sam would say it's a stupid idea. Rescuing him."

"But what other option do we have? My dad..." Dad shifted beneath his blanket, stirring at the sound of his name. I whispered, "I think I have a plan. I don't know if it'll work, but at least it's something."

Nick stood. He made his way to the bathroom, his progress slow and stilted. "Whatever the plan is," he said, "count me in."

33

THE CLOSEST BRANCH OFFICE WAS IN

a shoreline town—Cam Marie, Michigan. That's where Riley had taken Sam. A chill westerly wind pushed the hair from my face as we strode down the sidewalk, the crosswalk signal beeping behind us.

Next to me, Nick had gone surly. His shoulders were tight, his hands hidden inside the pockets of his jacket. That morning, over a cup of coffee and a bagel, he'd said, "This is crazy. You know that, right?"

And I'd said, "Yes. A new brand of crazy. But what do we have to lose?"

"Well…" He'd taken a bite of his onion-and-garlic bagel. "Our heads. Our freedom. Or something more creative, like our fingers—"

"Okay. I got it."

But now we were here and I wasn't turning back. Dad was pretty sure we wouldn't be hurt. We had measures in place if anyone threatened to harm us, though none of it would matter if Connor wanted us badly enough.

The Branch building had a cover at the front. MESSHAR AND MILLER ASSOCIATES, the sign read in thick gold letters. A red-haired girl at a circular desk greeted us. Behind her, tall windows revealed an expansive view of Lake Michigan, the waves swelling to whitecaps. To her left rose a staircase, the railings glass, too, so as not to obstruct the view. An elevator bank spanned the wall to our right.

"Good morning, Arthur."

Nick pulled his hands from his pockets, flexing his fingers as if he meant to draw his weapon at the first sign of trouble.

"We're here to see Connor," Dad said.

The woman nodded and hit a button on the control panel. "You're set to go down."

"Thank you, Marshie," Dad said. He motioned us over to a door beneath the staircase.

Nick leaned in. "'You're set to go down'?" he echoed. "That's comforting."

The door opened on a stairwell that wound belowground. I tightened my grip on the legal-sized folder in my hand, the one that held all the information Sam had stolen five years earlier. A nervous chill ran up my spine. I didn't feel great about this, and Nick's comment only made it worse.

Waltzing in and handing over a bunch of papers in exchange for our freedom seemed too easy, but I didn't know what other choice we had. I had to get Sam and Cas out. Sam especially, before they broke him.

Our footsteps echoed down the stairwell as the soles of our shoes hit the metal treads on the stairs. We twisted around and around, passing four floors before Dad stopped at the door labeled B5.

Hand on the doorknob, he turned to us, a span of wrinkles deepening on his forehead. "Let me do the talking. Okay?"

Nick grunted. I nodded. Dad pushed the door in. We emerged into a small receiving area, where a man sat behind a mahogany desk, a hands-free phone device latched to his ear.

"Arthur," he said, smiling. "How nice to see you."

Dad fidgeted. "Yes, you, too, Logan. Is Connor here?"

"He'll be right out."

"We can't go in?" Dad asked, and Logan shook his head.

So we waited. Nick cracked the joints in his hand one finger at a time. I had to bury the urge to pace. And just when I thought I might go stir-crazy, a door behind Logan swung open and five men entered the room.

"About time," Nick muttered, pushing off from the wall with one foot.

Dad placed a hand on Nick's chest, holding him back. "Is Connor ready to see us?" he asked the agents.

The man in the front, who had a scar that ran from his chin to his ear, smiled. "He's ready." He pulled out a gun and hit Dad with a tranquilizer dart. I barely had time to register what had happened before Nick shoved past me and started throwing punches.

The gun flew behind the desk. Scar Man went down, but there were four more men to get through. Nick started for the next agent, but a tall blond guy came from behind and punched him in the right side. Another fist slammed into Nick's face. His eyes rolled back in his head and he toppled over.

"Stop!" I screamed. "Please, we're here to see—"

Something heavy and solid whacked me in the forehead, cutting me off, and the light winked out.

———

The ache in my head reached me first, before anything else. Next came the nausea. I winced and avoided opening my eyes. I touched the spot that hurt the worst and groaned when I felt the lump on my forehead.

Everything came back in a rush, and I snapped my eyes open.

I was in a square room with no windows, one door, a bed. A glass of water stood untouched on a small bedside table. Riley sat in a chair across from me.

"You're awake," he said. "Finally."

The sound of his voice made my head vibrate, and I fought another cringe.

"Why—" I started, but Riley interrupted me.

"Did you set up a media spread of the evidence in case of an emergency?"

I put my hands over my eyes, like shutters, blocking out the glare of the fluorescent lights. I put my feet on the floor.

"Anna. I'll only say this once more. Did you set up an emergency spread?"

"Yes," I muttered.

"What are the particulars?"

"Where is he?"

"Excuse me?"

I squinted. "Where's Sam? Where are the others?"

Riley fixed his hair, taming the front. "In a cell. Where they belong."

"I won't tell you anything until you take me to them."

He crossed one leg over the opposite knee. "That's rather unfortunate, because I'm not taking you anywhere until you tell me the particulars of the media spread."

He spoke in slow, drawn-out syllables, as if he wasn't sure I understood English.

Anger boiled in my chest. "Well, that's rather unfortunate," I spit back, "because I'm not telling you anything until you take me to the boys."

He sighed. "Fine. Then I guess we'll wipe your memories and hope that Arthur spills the details." He stood.

Dad. He'd come here to help me, put himself at risk. Would they torture him for the answers? Yes, they would.

"Wait."

Channel Sam, I thought. *What would he do?*

"Yes?" The line of Riley's eyebrows arched high on his forehead as he waited.

I had to get out of there. I had to find the others. I had to find Dad. Going to Riley and Connor had been my idea, and I'd put us all at risk. I needed the quickest, safest solution. I needed a plan.

One door. No windows. Bedside table. Glass of water. One chair. One vent in the ceiling. Bed made of metal.

Were there more guards outside? Was there a camera anywhere? I darted a glance around the room. No cameras that I could see. I needed a distraction.

"I don't have all day, Ms. O'Brien."

"Is there a bathroom?" I swallowed and blinked back the pain blooming in the center of my head.

"There's one down the hall, and you can use it after—" As he spoke he twisted slightly, nodding toward the door, and I seized the opportunity.

With my left hand, I wrapped my fingers in the bed sheet. With my right hand, I scooped up the water. I tugged on the sheet until the corners popped off the mattress. I swept to my feet and tossed the sheet as Riley reached for his gun. The sheet wrapped around him. I brought the glass down on his head and it shattered into a thousand pieces. Water ran down to my elbow. Glass sliced through my fingers so that I couldn't tell if the blood soaking the sheet was Riley's or mine.

His legs got caught up in the sheet. I kicked where I thought his knee might be and felt something snap. A hollow cry escaped his lips as he toppled over. I wrapped my hands around the back of the chair, ignoring the stinging in my broken skin.

He pushed to his knees and I cocked the chair back, swinging it upward. It burst on impact, splintering into pieces. Riley went over with a final grunt.

"Sir?" someone said outside the door.

I froze. *Think.*

"Sir?"

I grabbed Riley's gun from his shoulder holster and retrieved the sheet. I hid behind the door, bracing myself against the wall. The door opened and I kicked. It whacked the guard, bounced back. I scuttled around and struck the man's chin with my open palm. He staggered and I wound the sheet around his neck, giving it a jerk. He fell onto his back. I scrambled on top of him, jamming the gun beneath his jawbone.

"Where are they keeping the boys?"

"I'm not telling you anything," he said, but his lower lip trembled.

"You think I won't shoot? You have till the count of three to test that theory. One. Two."

Would I do it? This place had stolen my life, and anyone who worked here was as guilty as Connor and Riley. I pushed my weight behind the gun. The barrel ground against bone.

"Last chance," I said. "Thre—"

"Wait!" His forehead glistened with sweat. I let up, but only a little. "Go right. Then left. Down the stairs to the next floor. Go straight. You'll see the lab on the right."

"Do you have a walkie-talkie or a phone?"

The man nodded. "On my belt."

I pushed to my feet but kept the gun in place. I tore off everything that was attached to his belt and stomped it flat, reducing the devices to nothing but piles of plastic and wires.

I backed away, but kept the gun trained on the man. "Don't move."

I maneuvered into the hallway and slammed the door shut behind me. The knob twisted as the man tried to escape, but the lock was still engaged.

I looked both ways, tucking the gun beneath my shirt. My head still hurt. The place was eerily silent. I followed the directions the agent had given me and encountered no one. I took the stairs down two at a time, feet quick and light, hand trailing the metal railing. At the next level's door, I went still, listened.

Nothing.

I edged the door open. The hall looked deserted. I hurried forward, and just when I started to think that I'd taken a wrong turn somewhere, that I'd been given false directions, I found what I was looking for.

Through a half wall of windows, I saw a lab, and inside were the boys, locked behind another glass wall like at the farmhouse. They saw me, too, and surged to the front, all three of them in a row.

Sam. My gaze went to him first, analyzing him. Was he hurt? Had they wiped his memories?

I found the lab door unlocked and pushed through it. There were counters covered in files and beakers and trays to the right. Several computer monitors lined the back wall, the screens showing they were locked.

Cas whistled. "You are a sight for sore eyes, Anna Banana."

"You shouldn't be here," Sam said.

I sighed with relief. He knew me. Which meant they hadn't wiped his memory yet.

"I'm not leaving you guys." There was a keypad on the wall next to their room. "You don't by chance know the—"

"Seven-three-nine-nine-two-four-one," Sam said.

I punched in the numbers. The keypad beeped. The wall slid out and over, and the boys filed out. Sam wrapped me in a hug, taking me by surprise.

"Are you all right?" He scrutinized my forehead and the dried blood I knew was there.

"Are *you* okay? What did they—"

"Shit," Nick said, cutting me off.

In unison, we turned toward the door, just in time to see Connor enter, a gun in his hand. He pulled the trigger without hesitating. *Thwap.* One bullet. That's all he needed.

Blood splattered across my face and Sam dropped to the floor.

34

"I AM DONE PLAYING GAMES," CONNOR
said.

I started to reach for my hidden gun, but thought better of it
when a line of agents marched in. They were fully uniformed, wearing the same armored jackets I'd seen on the men and woman who
died in the lab. Thick bulletproof vests protected their torsos.

Riley, limping and bloodied, shoved Dad in last. I sank down
next to Sam and wiped his blood from my face with my sleeve.
"Sam?" His eyes rolled around for a second before settling on me. The
bullet had hit him somewhere between his shoulder and chest; I
couldn't tell where without ripping off his shirt. There was so much
blood.

"Sam?" The terror sent a sharp burn to my eyes. "Can you hear me?" He grunted. Coughed. Didn't say anything, and that made everything worse.

Riley knotted his fingers in my hair and hauled me back. Cas lurched for him, but he was too weak to fight. Riley knew it. I knew it. Cas knew it. And the gun already pointed at my head didn't help, either.

"Now that we have everyone's attention," Connor said, coming around to face me. Usually tan year-round, he looked paler than when I'd last seen him, and I wondered how he'd fared after the confrontation with Sam in the lab. When he took a breath, it was labored—a weakness I wouldn't soon forget.

"This is a mistake," I said and received a swift tug of my hair for the effort. I surged ahead. "We have evidence that says you were taking money from foreign countries, *selling people*. You can't get away with this anymore. You already know that we have measures in place in case we don't make it out of here."

Connor slid a hand into the pocket of his tailored pants. "Oh, you do? Well, in that case, I should simply let you go? Let you saunter right out of here?" He took two quick steps, putting his face inches from mine. When he spoke, I caught the sharp smell of whiskey. "Do you have any idea how much money I've dumped into Sam? And then, to have him run away... He's a million-dollar project with legs, and I am *this close* to shooting them off."

Something else had changed in Connor since the last time I saw him. He'd shed his charm. And maybe this was the truer form of him: ruthless, power-hungry, merciless.

"So it's safe to assume that if I'm this close to terminating *him*"—he jammed a finger in my chest—"then I've already exceeded my limit of tolerance with you."

For once, I was profoundly terrified of Connor. Maybe that was why he had turned on the blindingly white smile all those years—to soothe me, tame me, make me think he was harmless. Of course I knew he helmed the program, knew he could be cold, but I'd never feared for my life around him, not even when he held a gun to my head in the lab. This was different, because now he was losing control of us.

"Let them go, Connor." Dad, unguarded, stepped up. "In exactly eight hours, all the evidence Sam stole will be released to every major media outlet. Do you know how much money that will cost you? More than Sam's worth. The government will be forced to cut off funding, and then what? I don't think it's so far-fetched to believe they'll turn their back on you entirely. Make you the scapegoat in the public's eye."

Connor's nostrils flared. A lock of his too-blond hair fell out of place. "Don't pretend for one second that you're exempt from any of this."

"I'm not. But I also don't want to be a part of the program anymore."

Dad had always seemed so small and insignificant next to

Connor and Riley, but at that moment, I could see the strength and the wisdom of a man I'd scarcely met. I liked this Dad. I admired this Dad. "Let Anna go, for starters, and we'll talk terms."

Connor, his mouth set in a grimace, flicked a finger. Riley muttered something before letting me go. I immediately went to Sam's side. He was still breathing and his eyes were still open, but his gaze was unfocused. He looked close to passing out. His skin had taken on an ashen color, making the bruises on his face stand out even more.

He needed medical attention. I shot a glance over at Cas. He stood straight as a totem pole, not one sign of his wounds visible in his demeanor. But if we had to fight, I wasn't sure he'd stand a chance.

And Nick... he might be able to power through, but he was weak, too. If it came down to it, I knew I couldn't fight all these men on my own.

Connor clasped his hands in front of him. "All right, then, let's negotiate."

"We need to talk first about the conditions," Dad said.

Connor cocked his head to the side. "Please, regale me."

"Grant them freedom."

"Freedom?" Connor paced, the expertly pressed line of his pants in sharp silhouette. "And who's to say they won't leak the information later?"

"We won't. As long as you leave us alone," I said.

"I have another idea." He spread out his hands. "I will agree to let you all go if you cooperate with a memory alteration."

A knot formed in my gut. I couldn't let them mess with Sam's memories. "No."

Connor looked over at me. "Anna." He made my name sound like a sigh. "So surly and determined. Tell you what—you agree to work for the Branch, and I'll spare your memory. The others will be wiped and let go."

That wasn't a counteroffer. That was worse. Even if Sam survived another wipe, how could I let him go? He'd disappear, because he was good at that, and I'd be stuck with Connor for the rest of my life, knowing that Sam was out there somewhere with no memory of me at all.

Besides, if the control alterations were permanent, then Connor could use me against the boys any time he wanted, whether they had their memories or not.

"I won't agree to that, either."

Connor sniffed. "Then none of you leave. How about that?"

"Eight hours and counting," Dad reminded him, not the least bit dissuaded by Connor's rising agitation. "Stalemate, Connor."

The men behind Riley fidgeted with their guns. Riley shifted his weight around, jaw clenched against the pain he must have felt in that damaged knee. Served him right.

"You can't keep us forever," I said. I rose to my feet, but stuck close to Sam. "We're human beings. We deserve free will, the right to our own lives, without some clandestine company directing our every move, stealing our memories and—"

"I'll do it."

I drew back.

"I'll stay," Sam said, straining to swallow, as if even that small act took considerable effort. "Let everyone else go."

"No." I ducked down. "No, Sam. We're all leaving here...."

"They won't allow it, and I'm in no shape to fight." He coughed again and had to roll to spit blood from his mouth.

"We have a plan, and—"

"Fuck the plan." His eyelids hung heavy. I could barely make out the iris of his left eye under the red stain of the broken blood vessels.

Tears pricked my eyes. I'd just learned the truth about everything in my life, and I didn't want to lose it. I didn't want to lose Sam. I *couldn't* lose him.

My voice came out a desperate plea, but I didn't care. "You're all I have left." The only constant, the only person from my old life, the one I couldn't remember.

He sliced me through with that unflinching look of his. "Then let me do what's right."

I closed my eyes. His fingers found mine. I buried my face in his chest, my vision hazy. "I won't remember you."

"You will," he whispered into my hair. "Someday. I'll find you."

I wrapped my arms around him, careful not to squeeze too hard. He still smelled like Ivory soap and late-autumn air. Would I forget that? Would I forget his name? The way he felt. The way he looked at me.

I didn't know what Sam and I had, if we had anything at all, but the void opening in my chest told me that it was enough, that maybe the connection between us was real, and not something scientific, and manufactured, and fake.

It was something worth fighting for.

"I'm sorry," I whispered. As I stood, he gave me a look that said, *Whatever you're about to do, don't.*

But I had to, and the reassuring pressure of Riley's stolen gun against my back told me I could. I had a chance, no matter how small it was.

I stumbled to Riley's side. *Be weak.* I held my hands out as if I meant to let him cuff me. *Be vulnerable.* He frowned but pulled a zip tie from inside his jacket. And when the thin plastic raked at the skin on the undersides of my wrists, I kicked Riley's bad knee and pulled the gun out from beneath my shirt. I shot one of Connor's nameless men and suddenly everyone was moving.

Nick head-butted one guy. Cas punched another. Someone tackled me to the ground and I kicked, flailed, pressed the barrel of the gun up and shot at close range. Blood washed over me and I pushed the man off, scrambling to my feet.

Nick took out a skinny guy. A gorilla of a man landed an upper-cut to Cas's jaw, but Cas was still standing, smashing the man's foot with the heel of his shoe.

"Stop!" Connor yelled. He held Sam at his side, a gun pressed to Sam's temple.

"Do what he says, Anna." A vein swelled in Sam's forehead. "Goddamn it. Just listen to him and you can all go."

"Put down your weapons," Connor ordered.

I did as instructed and held up my hands. "Don't hurt him."

"Anna," Sam growled.

"I'm not leaving you," I said matter-of-factly.

Connor chuckled, but it almost sounded sad and regretful. "At least I know the program worked. Look at you two—you can't stand to be apart. If we worked together, we could make the program so much better."

I let my hands fall to my sides, determination filtering to the top. "I would rather die here than work for you."

Connor pitched Sam to the floor. The gun was now trained, unwavering, on me. "And do you know what, little Anna? You've been far more trouble than you're worth. You're just a cog in the machine. You aren't irreplaceable. Eventually it'll run fine without you." He narrowed his eyes and pulled the trigger.

Time seemed to falter. I was tensed, waiting for the blow, when Dad dove in front of me. The bullet hit him, and he took me down, too. I slammed against the concrete floor, the wind knocked from my lungs as Dad's weight landed on top of me. In his hands was a gun.

"Take it," he said in barely a whisper.

A crammed, crunched sensation filled the spaces between my ribs, but I ignored it and grabbed the gun. Dad rolled away. I sighted Connor and took the shot, not a second's worth of hesitation robbing me of the one chance I had to finally be rid of him.

The bullet hit Connor in the chest.

I squeezed out another and it tore through his shoulder.

He lurched.

I shot again.

For one single second, we stared at each other. Then a trickle of blood ran down his shirt and time sped up again. I took one last shot—one more, to make sure he never came after me again.

It tore a hole through his head and his eyes went vacant as he teetered to the side.

The entire room went still. Connor toppled over.

I let out the breath I didn't realize I'd been holding. The boys stood around me in a loose half circle, Cas with a gun in his hand and a generous bruise blooming on his face, Nick with a smug smile lighting his eyes.

The other men littered the floor around us. Riley was noticeably absent.

I spotted Sam a few feet away from Connor. I dropped the gun, scrabbled to Sam's side, and gave him a shake. He tensed, groaned. "Sorry," I said. "Are you okay?"

His eyes fluttered open. "Goddamn it, Anna, you could have been killed." He coughed. "You can't be so damn reckless—"

I kissed him. When I pulled back, I said, "Shut up, all right? You need your energy."

A genuine smile played across his face and I fell for him all over again.

"I think he's delirious," Cas said.

"Don't die on me," I ordered.

"I wouldn't dream of it," he said right before he passed out.

––––––––––––

We managed to reach floor B1 by taking the stairs. Nick carried Sam slung over one shoulder. Cas held on to Dad the same way. Nick had tried to check Dad for a pulse earlier, rationalizing that leaving him would be easier for all of us, especially if he was dead. But I wouldn't let him. Because I didn't want to know if he was okay or not. Because I wasn't going to leave him there, anyway.

We'd just started for the ground floor when the door on B1 pulled open.

Cas had a gun trained on the person before whoever it was even made it over the threshold.

Trev stared back at us.

Nick deposited Sam on the floor and slammed Trev up against

the wall. "You try to stop us from walking out of here and I'll kill you."

Trev held up his hands. "I won't, but you should know that Riley is waiting in the lobby for you, and he's summoned more men. I can help you get out."

"And we should trust you?" I asked.

"You're a traitor, dude," Cas added.

Trev looked crestfallen. "I was never one of you. I was always undercover."

Cas readjusted Dad on his shoulder. "You conned us."

"I thought I was doing my job. I thought..." He blinked, regret pinching the corners of his eyes. "I hacked into the files here, and I think you were right. I started out like the rest of you, but somewhere along the line they made me think I was on their side. I thought I was working to save someone I loved. That's what they told me. Being undercover was never supposed to last this long. I was as much a prisoner in that lab as you were."

"Whose side are you on now?" I asked.

"No one's. But I can help you get out of here."

Nick released Trev and gave him a shove. "I'm not following you anywhere."

"You'll be stopped the second you enter the lobby." He took a step, then paused. "Through this door"—he motioned behind him—"is a hallway that will lead to a parking garage. There's a car there you can take."

The boys looked doubtful.

I tugged at the hem of my shirt, the urge to move overwhelming. I wanted to get out of there. I wanted to look every inch of Sam over to make sure he was all right. And the longer I stood there listening to them argue, the longer it'd take me to get to Sam.

"We don't have anything to lose at this point," I said. "And for what it's worth, I believe him."

Nick snorted, but he hefted Sam over his shoulder again. "Fine, we'll go. But if you screw us over again, I swear to God…"

Trev raised his eyebrows. "Let me guess: You'll kill me?"

"Consider that a promise," I answered and meant it. Trev shot me a look threaded with dejection, and I did the best I could to ignore it. "Show us the way."

———

The car Trev led us to was a nondescript, smoky-gray sedan with tinted windows. The keys hung in the ignition, waiting.

With Trev's help, we put Dad in the backseat and placed Sam next to him. Nick got behind the wheel and I went around to the other side, Cas on my heels.

"Wait." Trev dug in his pants pocket and pulled out a black flash drive. "I don't know if you want the information or not, but everyone's files are on that drive. From start to finish. It might shed some light on the blank spots in your memories. I figure you deserve that much."

"Thanks," I said and took the offering.

Cas slapped Trev on the back, the hard sound of the contact echoing through the parking garage. "You're still a dick."

I went to duck inside, but Trev stopped me. All my senses went on alert. It said volumes about how quickly my relationship with him had shifted. I hated it. I hated what he'd done.

"Yeah?"

A bruise colored the skin around his left eye. He looked so tired and forlorn. "All those years...I wanted you to know..."

"Come on!" Nick growled.

Trev moved in closer, his head down as if the words he was about to say were too raw and true to face. "You really were the bright spot of that lab. I wanted you to know that. Whatever I said or did, it was real, even if my identity wasn't."

"You were my best friend." I let all the tension flood out of my shoulders. "I can't ever look at you the same. Ever."

"I know."

I wrapped him in a hug, catching him off guard. He stumbled backward before leaning into me and squeezing. "Take care of yourself," I said.

"You, too. They won't stop coming after you, you know."

Now that Connor was dead, I wasn't sure who "they" were, if Trev meant Riley, or someone higher up. At the moment, I didn't really care. I tipped my head in a silent good-bye before sliding in the back beside Sam and taking his limp hand in mine.

"I'll open the exit door," Trev called, "and you'll be on your own."

"Sounds swell to me," Nick muttered, turning the engine over.

Trev punched in a code at the exit. The garage door rattled as it rose, gliding up its metal brackets. I held my breath, because while I wanted to believe in Trev, I half expected Riley to be waiting on the other side.

Daylight spilled in through the opening, gleaming off the polished hood of our borrowed sedan. Nick pulled the car up the slight concrete incline and merged into traffic.

Dad woke up with a wince ten miles later. He had one gunshot wound to the back. His skin was the color of egg whites and his eyes were ringed in black.

"Take me to a hospital," he grumbled, and we didn't argue. Nick found one in minutes.

"Do you want us to stay?" I asked as Cas went in search of a wheelchair.

Dad shook his head. "Get as far from here as you can."

"But—"

"Anna." He regarded me in a way that was more fatherly than ever before. "Go. Please."

Cas appeared with the wheelchair. With the boys' help, I got Dad out of the car and into the chair, though it took a lot of effort on everyone's part. We were all damaged in some way.

"What's the story?" Cas said. "Homeless man?"

Nick shoved up the sleeves of his shirt. "We found him that way?"

"I'll do it," I said, taking control of the chair. "You guys will be here when I get back?"

Cas grinned, showing his dimples. "We're not going anywhere."

The automatic doors opened with a *whoosh*, and it reminded me instantly of the entrance door to the lab in our old farmhouse. I wondered what would happen to it now. Where would Dad live? And what of my belongings? I couldn't think of anything I'd miss. My sketches, maybe. That was about it.

"Excuse me," I called out. "This man has been injured." I figured *injured* was better than *shot*. I didn't want them questioning me, too.

A woman behind the desk pushed a button on the elaborate call center and said, "The nurses are on their way."

I came around to the front of the chair and took Dad's hand in mine. "You'll be okay?"

He inclined his head. "I'll be fine. You go on now."

"Will I ever see you again?"

"Do you really want to? After everything I did..."

"I want to. You're all I know. You'll always be my dad."

He shook his head, avoiding looking at me, and I wondered if he felt like crying, too. "I never thought I'd hear you say that. Not after you found out the truth."

A nurse rushed up, claiming the chair. "What happened?"

"He's hurt. I...ah..."

"She found me lying in the street like this," Dad said. "If it weren't for this young lady, I might be dead."

"Let's get him to the ER." Another nurse punched the door's auto-open button. The wide door swung in, revealing the bustling ER beyond.

Dad winked as the nurses rolled him away.

Outside, I slid into the waiting car, next to Sam. His eyes were open a slit.

"You're awake. Thank God. I don't suppose I can talk you into seeing a doctor, too?"

"Cas can fix me," he croaked.

Cas snorted. "I don't know, dude. That could be dangerous. You might end up with fewer organs than when you started."

As Nick pulled away from the curb, Sam threaded his fingers with mine. I smiled a real smile that touched every corner of my soul. Because the boys were back by my side. Because we'd made it. We were free.

35

THE BRITTLE GRASS CRUNCHED BENEATH

me as I sat in front of the headstones in the middle of Port Cadia
Cemetery. Leaves had collected at the bases of the massive stones and
in the lone pot of dead flowers.

I read the names on the headstones over and over again.

CHARLES O'BRIEN

BELOVED HUSBAND AND FATHER

MELANIE O'BRIEN

BELOVED WIFE AND MOTHER

"Hi," I said to the stillness, feeling weird, but somehow closer to
them, my *real* parents. "It's Anna. It took me a long time to come
back home. But I'm here." I ran a hand down the raw edge of my

father's headstone, then patted my mother's. "I wish I could remember you."

I waited for something to come to me, for some old memory to dislodge itself from the deep hole the Branch had created. But nothing came. I didn't even know what color my mother's hair was. Or if my father had my hazel eyes.

Maybe I was expecting too much. Just seeing their final resting place was enough for now. I was here, and they were real, and that was at least a start. I had all the time in the world now to find out whom they had been, or if I had any other remaining family, maybe an aunt or uncle who could help to fill in the blanks.

Sam eased down beside me, still healing from the wounds he'd suffered two weeks earlier. His hair was longer and darker now, nearly matching the black of his thick canvas coat. It was early November and snow fell in soft flakes around us, not yet managing to stick to the ground.

"I found them," I said.

Sam waved his hand in the air, signaling to the others that the graves had been found. Cas and Nick headed for the car parked outside the wrought-iron fence, leaving us alone.

"Do you think Dani has a gravesite?" I asked.

Sam looked outward, past the cemetery. "I don't know. We can look into it."

I nodded, feeling a pang of sadness for her. From what little information we'd found on the flash drive, we knew that she'd died right before Sam was moved to the farmhouse lab. We didn't know how it happened. Another question left unanswered.

It was still odd to think of her as my sister, because I couldn't remember a single thing about her. Instead, I thought of her as a long-lost relative I never knew, but who clearly meant a lot to Sam once. She must have been great in some immeasurable way.

"Now what?" I said, picking the leaves from the flowerpot, mentally promising myself I'd come back in the spring with something new. "Where do we go from here?"

We'd been staying in a motel in the Upper Peninsula the last few weeks while Sam healed, but we'd checked out yesterday. Stopping in Port Cadia on the way south had been Sam's idea. "To give you closure," he'd said, and now that I was here, I was thankful for it, but being in this town made me uneasy.

"We'll find a place to settle for a while," Sam said. "Something more permanent so we can sort through the rest of the information on the flash drive. We need to know if there are others out there like us, and if so, what the Branch plans to do with them."

We'd started digging into the files immediately after we escaped the Branch. Already we'd gathered information on the Altered drug, as it was referred to in the files, and how it affected all of us. But there were hundreds of files. It'd take us a while to organize everything.

"And you're sure that I'm not putting you in danger?"

Sam tilted his head to the side and gave me a look that said I was being absolutely ridiculous.

"Well"—I shrugged—"I wanted to ask rather than assume. With everything we learned, Nick wasn't so far off. I *am* a liability, and maybe it'd be safer—"

"Stop." He climbed to his feet.

I said a silent good-bye to my parents as Sam offered me his hand and hoisted me up. But even when I stood firmly on the ground, he didn't let go.

"You're not a liability. I read through the treatment file a dozen times. The control elements aren't permanent."

"But we don't know how long they'll last. Don't you worry that the Branch might get to me and use me against you?"

He started walking and took me with him, our hands still entwined. "Even more reason for us to stick together. You're the only person I trust. That's not something you waste."

I smiled. "You trust me more than Cas?"

"Cas would choose a case of beer over me."

My laughter echoed through the cemetery. "That's not true!" I brushed the hair from my face. "The others have your back."

"Yet you were the one who saved my life."

A warm feeling, like sunshine on bare skin, filled me. He was right, of course. I couldn't argue that. I'd always cared for him, loved him even, but risking your life for someone changes things. It wasn't just love. It was a million other things all woven together. Emotions I couldn't even name.

When I said I would die for him, I meant it. And now I knew he'd risk his life for me, too.

A breeze kicked up, scattering leaves across our path. The snow was no longer soft but steely as it hit our faces. I moved closer to Sam. My hand grazed the hem of his jacket.

When we reached the end of a row of headstones, he slowed. We bumped shoulders. I felt him watching me. "What color would you use?"

A grin spread across my face as I glanced at him.

My gaze swept the sky. "Titanium white. A white so pure you can—"

He stopped midstride and nudged me toward him. With a brush of his finger, he tilted my chin up. Only the span of a few inches hovered between us. Snow melted on my face. The wind didn't seem so cold anymore.

"Almost taste it?"

The gap closed between us and he pressed his lips against mine.

ACKNOWLEDGMENTS

My life has changed in so many crazy, amazing ways, and none of it would have been possible without the help of so many crazy-amazing people.

First, to my husband, JV, for never doubting me and for picking up the pieces when I failed again and again. Thanks for listening to my incessant rambling about abs, plot points, and perfect titles.

To my agent, Joanna Volpe, who is lightning-fast, who is always supportive, and who knows just what to say and when to say it. Without her, none of this would have been possible. I also suspect I would no longer be sane without her guidance and all-around kick-assery.

To my editor, Julie Scheina, who saw something in this book from the beginning and helped me make it tons better. Thank you for your wisdom, your kind words, and your unflinching support of hot guys.

Thank you to everyone else at Nancy Coffey Literary. Nancy, Sara, Kathleen, and Pouya. Thank you to the entire Little, Brown team, for being awesome in so many immeasurable ways, and for helping make this book shine.

To my beta readers: Holly Westlund, Robin Prehn, and Deena Lipomi. Especially to Deena, for her invaluable feedback and encouraging e-mails, and for being the best cheerleader EVER.

To my BFF, Stephanie Ruble, who has been with me from the beginning. We've traveled this road together. The adventure has only just begun.

Much love to Patricia Riley and Danielle Ellison, for knowing how and when to make me chuckle. Thanks for the revision cookies, the #hotboyswin tweets, and your unwavering friendship.

Thank you to my friends and family, for the love, encouragement, and support.

And a very special nod goes out to the WSB crew: Tracy, Diane, Jer,

Vicki, Karen, Josh, and Adam. You were the best coworkers a girl could have asked for.

Lastly, to the entire writing community, thank you for being awesome. Writing a book is sometimes a lonely endeavor, and no way would I have survived this journey alone.

AFTER FLEEING THE BRANCH WITH SAM, CAS,
AND NICK, ANNA IS TRYING TO MAKE SENSE OF THE
MEMORIES RESURFACING FROM HER OLD LIFE.

BUT ONE QUESTION STILL REMAINS: WHY WERE THOSE
MEMORIES ERASED IN THE FIRST PLACE?

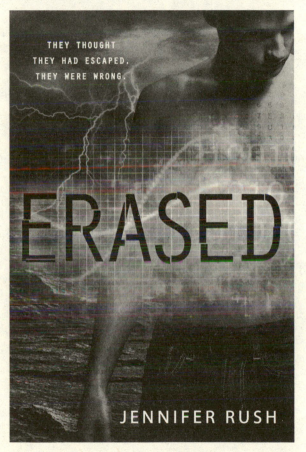

TURN THE PAGE FOR A GRIPPING SNEAK PEEK AT
ERASED, THE SECOND BOOK IN THE ALTERED SERIES.

AVAILABLE JANUARY 2014

1

LIKE CLOCKWORK, I WOKE AFTER MID-
night and immediately had the urge to see Sam.

There was a moment, before I was fully alert, when I wondered if
it was safe to sneak down to the lab.

And then I remembered: We weren't at the farmhouse anymore.
There was no lab.

In order to see Sam, all I had to do was roll over.

He lay on his stomach, hands tucked beneath the pillow. In the
murky darkness, I could just make out the black lines of his birch tree
tattoo spreading across his back, the branches twining down his arms.

With my eyes, I traced the dimples made by bones and muscle in
his shoulders. Imagined what pencil I would use to sketch him on
paper. In the months since Sam, Nick, and Cas had escaped the

Branch's lab, and I'd gone with them, I'd learned that nothing was permanent, not even my memories. Now I took every opportunity to savor what I had, just in case.

Waste nothing was my new mantra. And I wouldn't. Not when it came to the boys. They were my family, blood or not. Cas was like my brother. And in some ways, so was Nick, even if we didn't necessarily like each other.

And Sam...well, I loved him more than anything.

I reached out to touch him, to check that he was solid and warm and real, but thought better of it. We'd all been on edge lately, and I worried that if I startled him, he'd go for the gun tucked beneath the mattress. And then point it at me.

As quietly and lightly as I could, I slipped from the bed and made my way down the stairs of our rented cabin. I found Nick hunched over the coffee table, a fire burning in the hearth beside him, silhouetting him in orange-and-red light. A dozen paper cranes lay in a pile at his feet. There was another in his hands.

He'd started folding them out of nowhere a little over a week ago and had given no reasonable explanation for it. The cranes he'd already made sat in a box beneath my bed because I didn't have the heart to throw them away.

"Hey," I said as I sat down across from him in one of the ratty leather chairs. "What are you doing up?"

He didn't look at me as he answered, "Why does anyone get up in the middle of the night? Because they can't sleep."

"Right."

His eyes were dark and swollen with exhaustion. His black hair stood in raked waves and curled around his ears. A green flannel shirt hugged his biceps and hung open, exposing the hard plane of his stomach.

Like all the boys, Nick, even at his worst, was gorgeous. It drove me crazy. I didn't consider myself unattractive, but next to them, I was painfully average. They didn't know the meaning of a bad hair day.

I grabbed the origami crane closest to me. The folds were precise. The tail point was razor-sharp. Everything about it was perfect. Nick, like Cas and Sam, rarely failed at anything.

"Any idea why you're doing this?" I tried.

Nick formed the head on the crane in his hands. "I don't know. I..." He trailed off, like he'd caught himself about to say something more revealing than he liked. He turned to me. "Why don't you run back to bed with your boyfriend and leave me alone?"

I frowned. The old me would have scurried away, but in the last few months, we'd made some progress on our relationship, if you could call it that. It helped that I knew Nick better now, knew the reason behind his cutting attitude. He'd grown up with an abusive father. But he didn't know that, not yet. The Branch had stolen those memories from him.

I'd wanted to tell him for a while now. I just didn't have the words to explain it.

"Sam isn't my boyfriend," I said, because it was the only thing I could think to say. "I mean, not officially." I grabbed one of the pre-cut squares of paper and started to fold. "Besides, I'm not tired."

Nick grumbled. "Whatever."

Outside, the wind whistled through the trees and rattled the front door. Snow had fallen not long after dinner. It was now piling in the corners of the windowsills.

Nick finished his crane and tossed it aside. He looked over at me. Normally, his eyes were shockingly blue, electric, but in the firelight, they were leaden gray and guarded. "What's with that look on your face?"

"What look?"

"Like you have something to say."

In some weird way, not having a closer relationship with Nick made him that much better at reading me. His judgment, his gut instinct, wasn't clouded by petty emotions. It made it ridiculously hard to hide anything from him.

I swallowed. "I don't know what you're talking about."

He sighed, exasperated. "Don't play dumb."

I made another fold in the paper, thinking while I worked. Finally, I said, "There are some things about your past . . . that maybe you should know."

"What, and you do?"

"I don't know much."

"But you know enough."

I stopped folding. "It might help you understand—"

"I understand plenty." He cracked a knuckle, then another. He avoided looking me in the face, and realization crept in.

"You're having flashbacks? About your—" I stopped myself, just in case. "The flashbacks are more substantial, aren't they? More detailed?"

Sam was the first one to experience memory flashes. Cas and Nick had been having only minor ones since we'd left the farmhouse nearly three months ago. And me, well, I was having them, too—mostly about my older sister, Dani.

When I'd first left home with the boys, I'd thought I was a normal girl swept up in their extraordinary lives, only to find out much later that I'd been altered, too, like them. That the Branch had buried all the important memories from my past life, thereby wiping my sister from existence.

We'd found out she'd been killed by the Branch, and since then, I'd tried so hard to remember her. She came to me in fleeting images and ghost feelings that I later tried to sketch and make real. I hadn't been successful yet. And lately, the flashbacks had been giving me the worst kind of headaches. Enough to send me straight to bed. I hadn't told Sam that part yet. I didn't want him to worry or treat me differently.

"So what are they about?" I asked Nick. "Tell me."

He clenched his hand into a fist, knuckles rising and turning white. "I'm not telling you anything. So stop asking." He said it matter-of-factly, like no earthly force would pry the details from his head. With Nick, it was probably true. In some ways, he was more stubborn than Sam.

He swept out of the chair, breezed past me without another word, and disappeared upstairs, his bedroom door shutting a second later.

The fire in the hearth snapped.

I set aside my half-folded crane and took the last one Nick had made, suspended it between my fingers. That's how Sam found me a minute later, motionless, staring at that stupid crane.

He ran his hand up and down his arm as if to ward off the cold. "What happened?" he asked.

I let the crane fall to the table. "I pissed him off."

Sam sighed as he sat. He looked so tired, even though he'd been sleeping more than all of us lately. It was so unlike him. "What was it about this time?"

I hadn't told anyone else the details I knew about Nick's past. It should be up to him who he shared it with. So I just shrugged and said, "Who knows." A yawn made me pause, then, "I think I'm going to lie back down."

Sam nodded, and I knew that meant he wasn't coming.

"If I'm not up by dawn, will you wake me?"

"Sure."

I started for the stairs, but as I passed him, he reached out, snagging me at the wrist. He pulled me down onto his lap, wrapped a hand around the back of my neck, and put his lips to my forehead. I closed my eyes, breathed him in. He smelled like Ivory soap and fresh air. He smelled like home.

I love you, Anna. He didn't have to say it for me to know that he meant it.

I met his gaze. *I love you, too,* I thought as I pulled away and headed upstairs.

WHEN I WOKE A FEW HOURS LATER, I
could hear Cas singing a Celine Dion song in the shower down the
hall. "My Heart Will Go On," from the sound of it.

I threw on a baggy sweater over a tank top and black leggings and
headed downstairs. Sam sat at the small table tucked in the back corner
of the kitchen, and Nick stood at the stove, scrambling up some eggs.

"Is there enough for me?" I asked.

"Yes," Sam answered before Nick could comment.

After fixing myself a cup of coffee, I sat beside Sam. He was on
the laptop, presumably reading over the files we had procured from
the Branch. Many of them spanned our entire involvement, from the
time we entered the program to right before we left the farmhouse
lab. It was going to take us more than a few months to read every-

thing inside, but we were making good progress. Not that we'd found anything substantial yet. Sam's files were bigger than anyone else's. He'd been with the Branch the longest, sold into it by his mother. They started experimenting on genetic alterations with him and expanded from there.

"Anything new?" I asked, squashing the urge to read over his shoulder.

"Not really."

Nick sat across from me a minute later, his plate overflowing with eggs, two pieces of toasted bread beside the pile. He dug in without a word.

"I'll grab our plates," I said to Sam while shooting Nick a scowl. When I got to the stove, I found the pan nearly empty, so I divided what was left into three equal parts, leaving enough for Cas when he came down.

"We're out of eggs," Nick said. "Who's on grocery duty this week?"

"Me," I answered. "And you."

"Great."

I would have gone alone if Sam would have allowed it, but we'd agreed a long time ago that it was best if we traveled in pairs. Grocery shopping was always done with someone else, and we tried to stick to a constant rotation.

Sam downed the rest of his black coffee. "I'll go."

"No." I shook my head. "It's my turn. You and Cas went last

week." I took a bite of eggs, silently hoping he'd insist he go in my place.

But he didn't. I'd asked him to treat me like an equal. Apparently, I was now getting my wish.

"We'll go this afternoon," I said to Nick. "So don't disappear on me."

He tossed his empty plate in the sink and left.

My day was looking up already.

———

It'd been over two months since we'd escaped the Branch and encountered any of its agents, but that didn't mean we could lower our guard. Everything we did was calculated and thoroughly planned out. Like who went grocery shopping and when. Who checked the perimeter and when.

But it couldn't be *too* planned out, because then the Branch would be able to predict our movements.

Sometimes just taking a shower seemed like far too much work. At Sam's insistence, I always locked the bathroom door behind me, made sure the window was unlocked for a quick alternate exit should I need it. And my gun stayed loaded on the vanity.

Living a normal life didn't seem possible, not with the Branch still out there. It was why we were always on edge. We couldn't relax. Ever. And the longer we went without seeing a Branch agent, the more we felt like our time was running out.

After breakfast, Sam and I got dressed for a perimeter check. He wore a thick black coat with a flannel shirt underneath, jeans, and black leather boots. I had bought a heavier coat a few weeks ago when winter settled in. It was graded for below zero temps. With it, I wore cold-weather leggings tucked into boots.

In the woods, we made our way from one checkpoint to another. I ducked beneath a pine branch and squinted as the sun appeared, the blinding rays reflecting off the snow-covered ground. I had sunglasses on, but they didn't help much.

If an agent attacked me right now, I'd be caught off guard, unable to see. I often found myself thinking about little things like that. And about how many weapons I had on me. Whether or not they were loaded or easy to grab. Right now I had a gun on my back and a knife sheathed in my boot. I could remember a time when one gun seemed like one weapon too many. Now I wished I had more.

Sam trailed behind me by a foot, his steps quiet despite the ice that'd formed on the snow overnight. Every step I took made a loud and annoying crunch.

"I've been meaning to talk to you," Sam said as we rounded a mammoth oak tree. "I think it's time we move again."

I glanced over my shoulder, pausing for a second as he caught up. "Already?"

He stopped beside me. "It's been four weeks."

We'd moved twice since we'd escaped the Branch. I understood why, but I was tired of settling into new places.

I wanted to have the opportunity to rebuild the life that had been stolen from me, and I knew that started with piecing together my past and learning more about my family. I couldn't do that if we kept moving, especially when it seemed like we were heading farther and farther away from Port Cadia, the town where I'd grown up. It was the place where my life and Sam's had been altered completely when he and I lost my sister.

I wanted to know how Dani died and what had happened to her body. I wanted to know why the Branch had killed my parents. I knew the Branch had put me in the farmhouse lab, in the Altered program, because I'd already had a connection to the boys, especially Sam. They'd used that connection and twisted it into something scientific, something they could reproduce and later sell.

But I still wasn't sure if they'd killed my parents so that I wouldn't have a family searching for me, or if there was another reason. We already knew they had the ability to wipe people's memories. So why not spare my parents and alter their memories instead?

We didn't know the endings to any of the important mysteries, and I desperately wanted to.

I *needed* to.

"Anna?" Sam called out.

I stopped walking. I hadn't even realized I'd moved. "Yeah?"

"You're two steps away from hitting that bear trap." He gestured at a lump in the ground.

"Oh. Thanks."

"You okay?" he asked.

"Fine." I bent over to inspect the trap, looking for any clues that it'd been tampered with or set off. The cold bit through my leather gloves, numbing my fingers as I worked. "So, where are we going this time?" I asked.

"I was thinking Indiana."

"Maybe we should move north."

Even when I wasn't looking directly at Sam, I could still feel the full weight of his gaze. It lifted the hair at the base of my neck.

"No" was all he said.

I sighed and kept walking. I wasn't sure how I'd convince him that learning more about our past was a good idea, because when Sam set his mind on something, he generally didn't budge. His number one priority was to keep us away from the Branch and keep us safe. Obviously I valued my life, but it didn't feel like much of a life with so many of the pieces still missing.

And hadn't Sam been the one to finally break free of the lab, only to risk his safety and freedom again when it was his past he was trying to figure out?

Of course, there was one common denominator in all of this. The whole reason Sam had gone to so much trouble *before* the farmhouse, the whole reason he'd had clues to retrace in the first place.

Dani.

The sister who had been stolen from me.

Sam's old girlfriend.

Dani was a huge part of Sam's past. I knew he was curious to fill in the blanks surrounding her death, even if he wouldn't admit to it. And finding out more information about her would also give me more information about my family and *my* past.

It didn't escape me, though, that I was in love with my sister's old boyfriend, and that if she were alive, Sam and I probably wouldn't be together.

What if digging into our pasts reminded Sam of what he'd lost with Dani? What if it brought on the guilt that was already creeping into my thoughts?

And what would that mean for us?

I wasn't sure if I was willing to take that risk.

Page-turning suspense novels from Cat Patrick

THREE GIRLS. ONE LIFE.

THE ORIGINALS

cat patrick

REVIVED

cat patrick

FORGOTTEN

cat patrick